10,00

D1188453

Cock-a-doodle-doo

Cock-a-doodle-doo

Philip Weiss

FARRAR STRAUS GIROUX

New York

LIBRARY OF CONGRESS CATALOGING-IN-PUBLICATION DATA
Weiss, Philip.
Cock-a-doodle-doo / Philip Weiss.—1st ed.
p. cm.
1. Politicians—New York (N.Y.)—Family relationships—Fiction.
2. Man-woman relationships—New York (N.Y.)—Fiction. 3. Lawyers—
New York (N.Y.)—Fiction. I. Title.
PS3573.E4163C6 1995   813'.54—dc20   94-30187 CIP

For Cynthia Conrad Kling

Cock-a-doodle-doo

1

The third night of the Democratic convention I was supposed to work as a floor whip for Stony Walker. Being a whip sounds a lot more fun than it is. I always thought of wild animals frenzying one another into delight or exaltation, but it's nothing like that. Basically it's to organize your delegates on the floor, tell them how to vote, head off dissatisfaction, whip up allegedly spontaneous demonstrations.

During the primaries I had a big job in the Walker campaign, I headed issues. I was a lawyer. But on balloting night we needed almost everyone but Stony himself on the floor, and so at six o'clock three hundred of us crowded into a junior high school auditorium on Tenth Avenue for instructions. Everyone was shouting. There were young mothers with babies at their hips, and skinny gray-haired cadre-type guys with their only suit on, like a corduroy suit, with Adlai Stevenson buttons. It was a humble old public school with dark red doors and kids' art taped to the walls. And people were happy even though we all knew we were about to lose big. Their faces were glowing with excitement, they were calling out news to old friends. As usual things were starting late. Walker time. Finally Sam Treat,

3

who headed field, went to the microphone and the microphone was dead, so that was a whole other ordeal, figuring out the microphone.

"If you're a blue whip and we say Blue-Five, that means Stone to the Bone. We want that chant." Sam held up five fingers. "Just look at five on your list."

It doesn't matter what Sam was saying, my mind kept going away. I thought of this thing I sometimes thought about back then for no good reason.

A man is standing on a stage when you suddenly hoist him by the feet into the air. You have a rope around his ankles, a cable, and pull it up into the sky. Would his head hit the floor as he flew up? Probably it's a physics problem. Could the flipping-upside-down part happen fast enough so his head wouldn't slam into the floor, so he'd be O.K.? I drew a little picture of it on my pad. But I thought the faster you pull him, his head only swings around faster. He just hits harder.

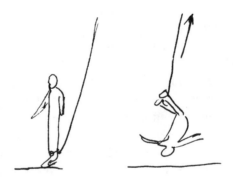

I wondered the same thing about a guy in a chair, like me. Could you pull him out of the chair fast enough so that one second he'd be in the chair, the next second in the sky without slamming his head? I drew a whole other picture about that.

But you couldn't say anything from the pictures. You'd probably have to rig the whole thing up.

Afterward everyone pushed out of the auditorium to go downstairs for the chow line. More Walker bedlam, and I snuck outside. I just wanted a breather, then when I got outside I decided to hit the hotel and put on a jacket for the balloting.

The Walker campaign had two floors at a place called the Powell. You've probably walked right by the Hotel Powell without noticing it, it's eighteen stories of lion-colored brick on West Fifty-eighth Street. We were proud about the Powell. All the other campaign organizations were in snotbag hotels to fulfill people's opulent fantasies about New York but the Powell was actually involved in the life of the city. It had a thick Lucite barrier over the front desk like a liquor store, and homeless people had used the front steps as a toilet. It was cheap. Abel Ritter actually said to me, I like being in a place where there aren't any brochures for soft porn on top of the TV.

But I got back to my room, and my room was a downer. The air shaft. The sad old magazine covers framed over the bed. The shower that leaked into the carpet and made the carpet smell. It was exactly the kind of hotel room my parents tell jokes about, Jewish-salesmen jokes. The salesman who doesn't have room for an elephant but when he gets a deal on two, etcetera. The salesman who dreams he's married to the Gimbels heiress. My mom tells those jokes and my dad laughs himself

5

red in the face. He's usually quite serious, my dad. He doesn't have a king-size sense of humor. If you want him to laugh it's got to be in his area.

I lay on the bed and turned on the television. Johnson and Kennedy were debating in black-and-white. That debate in a crowded hall at the Biltmore during the '60 convention. It bugged me. There were all these people making a racket stamping on the floor and Johnson and Kennedy giving their little speeches you couldn't hear. Everyone was behaving like fanatics. I put my head down for a second. There was a rough green bedspread, like burlap but made out of polyester, and when a fold of it went into my mouth I didn't mind. It had a good salty numbing cloth taste.

The knocking was heavy and I tried to work it into my dream then I couldn't and I sat up. The TV was going, and for a second I forgot where I was. I shut off the television and went to the door. Ralph Lopez came in dancing. He's a lawyer, too, he worked as my deputy in issues, but it's something he does. He'll dance when something's happened. He was grinding his hips and juking his shoulders.

"Onward," he said, making a fist.

"Hey, Ralph, what's the smut." That's Ralph's favorite expression, the smut.

But Ralph was gone, he was doing a whole bee dance, wagging his butt like a bee in the hive.

The air shaft was dead dark, and it came to me I'd slept through the balloting. I just hoped Abel Ritter wasn't a tattletale. Abel was assigned to work Michigan with me, and I started feeling guilty as hell, wondering if that was the smut, I'd crapped out.

"Talk to me, Ralph, what went down," I said.

"You'll never guess," he said.

"Right, I won't," I said.

It was my voice, it was my whole tone. He straightened up, "What's with you?"

I sat on the bed and thought about what I could say, then I started feeling emotional.

"Hey, fuck you, Jack, you're not the only one who lost," he said, "You need to process your personal shit man—"

I nodded.

"Am I right or wrong?"

"You're right."

Ralph stepped on my foot in this affectionate way. "Now let's shake it."

I reached my jacket off the chair and he waited at the door.

"What's our agenda?" I said.

"Victory party. Wake up, bro."

"I fell asleep."

"Yeah bullshit, you were having a wank—"

I got my tie, this new tie I'd bought for the convention, and we went down the hall in silence. I'd forgotten about the victory party. Stony Walker was having a victory party because he'd polled more votes at a nominating convention than any black presidential candidate before him. At least he was supposed to, before I fell asleep. The rattling aluminum elevator took us downstairs and Ralph held the heavy glass door for me. Outside, the wet heat clamped down on us, and I stopped and got out a cigarette.

"That's a foul habit," Ralph said.

"Now you tell me," I said.

He laughed. "I worry about you, man, you're like an addict."

"You mean you feel sorry for me."

"No. I worry about you."

Ralph had this way of looking at you like he loved you. He was very intense, women said that, he went to bed with a lot of women. He had long black hair almost like an Indian that he kept in a ponytail, and he always wore jeans and a tee-shirt, or overalls. He looked a little like a rock bassist.

7

"A good-looking guy like you smoking—Jack, what's it do to your teeth?"

"Probably fucks them up."

"Right, it fucks them up."

"I know, I ought to be horsewhipped," I said.

He laughed, he was grateful for that, and he began dipping again as we came onto Broadway. We went down Broadway and you could see the lights of Times Square, the neon, the bullshit, banging right up against the sky, lighting the sky. Because it was one of those low overcast New York nights getting ready to rain, and the sky, the smog, whatever, was like a gray umbrella right over us.

"O.K. Ralph, hip me, what's going on?" I said.

"Nada."

"You want me to hear lies?" I said. "If you don't tell me, bro, someone else is going to tell me lies."

He smiled, and you could see his crossed-over front teeth. The secret of his success in the sack, one crosses a tiny bit over the other.

"Who'd you sleep with?" I said. "I know, you slept with Keenah. I'm right, aren't I? You slept with Keenah Granger—"

He bit his lip, but the pride rose in his face, so I had him, and after that he had to tell me about it all the rest of the way to the Waldorf. How satiny Keenah's skin is, and her natural smell that is actually a fragrance. I was a little turned on at the same time as I was thinking, Ralph you're a bore. I really didn't want to hear about it at the same time as I was getting turned on, and I was wondering how that could be.

The victory party was in the Waldorf because of the strong feelings of arrival people had surrounding the end of the campaign. No one wanted a shitpile with aluminum elevators and WPA murals, they wanted the best. Just walking in you heard

8

the big music from the ballroom upstairs, and people were dressed and excited in the too-dark lobby. Ralph and I got on the elevator. Expensive dark wood surrounded us, and elongated women carved in metal. Art Deco, that whole sexless style.

The elevator took off with a mind of its own. Ralph punched Ballroom, but it didn't register, and then he turned and reached for my tie. I guess I'd been touching it too much, that was my crime. I pushed him away but the label came around, which I'm even embarrassed to say. I'd spent too much on that tie just to look pretty at the convention.

"My mom sent me a check for my birthday," I said. What a lie.

Ralph stepped back. "The man has been processing his personal shit."

"Salvador Allende wore thousand-dollar suits," I said.

"No he didn't, Jack." He laughed. "Man, you are such a bullshit artist."

The elevator had stopped in the twenties. A big guy got on. He was dressed up and touching his gleaming hair.

"Mr. Allende," Ralph said.

That startled him. He turned toward the door with his hands basketed at his crotch, that nut-protecting stance. He was completely put together. He wore an English suit with a wide white stripe in it and under that not even a vest but a waistcoat, a whole mini-jacket in green paisley. Everything was thought through, I mean the way it all fell and draped and broke, and his thin hair was cut in a sharp line across the back of his neck. This is his elevator, this is the kind of box that a swell like this comes in, I thought, and just then he turned to me and smiled with big curving teeth and I realized I knew him.

"Jack!" he said. "Jack Gould. You saved my ass!"

"Gold," Ralph said in a thin correcting voice.

But the guy ignored him, he grabbed my shoulder and shook me hard. "You did, you saved my unworthy white woolly ass."

9

"George," I said.

We were both grateful as hell I'd remembered his name, and he seized my hand. He was very good-looking in a traditional way. He had gray eyes that sparkled and those good curving rich-guy teeth. He was probably only forty, but everything about him was in an old style, the way he held himself on his feet, even the way he smiled.

"George Sides, Ralph Lopez," I said, "George edits *Larkspur*."

"I know," Ralph said.

But he was lying, and that only made George more nervous. His eyes raked the panel, and he punched Lobby a bunch of times and kept repeating that one thing.

"You saved this woolly mammoth's hide when he thought his hour was near, you came down on pulleys from the rafters," and all this other horseshit.

"It was a bogus case," I said.

"No, Jack. No. No. No. No. Not to me."

I turned to Ralph. "Some socialite put *Larkspur* in her divorce suit. They had run an item about her husband and another woman in a gossip column."

"Publishing column," George said. "Blackie Roberts."

"The writer William Roberts. His wife's lawyer came up with a crazy libel theory that her husband had used a newspaper to alienate her affections."

Ralph looked back dully. Because *Larkspur* was a hive of false values. It was a New York paper that prided itself on having a small circulation, it came out every other week, tabloid-size, but on greeny-gray-colored newsprint like a French right-wing newspaper. And the letters for *Larkspur* were hand-drawn at the top of the front page as flowers and flower stems with the roots dangling down. Everything in it was arch and many-layered. I couldn't read it. I mean, I could read it, I just couldn't understand it.

10

But that was all George and I had between us. He'd run out of things to say and kept peeking at the floor indicator.

"Jack. Jack. Jack," he said. "What are you doing tonight?"

"Victory party," Ralph said.

"Sifton Walker's victory party," I said.

George gave a big vaudeville nod. "Hallelujah," he said.

"Amen, brother," Ralph said.

George got bright spots of color in his cheeks, he smacked his hands. "Jackie, I know—Jordan River's deep and wide, but if you get any liberty later we're having an independent party. Ha!"

"This will run late," I said.

"O.K. O.K." The elevator slowed, and because he hadn't sounded genuine the first time he kept reinviting me. "There'll be some O.K. people there. Early Quinlan's suite. Sort of a generational doohickey—like, all right, Pedro, name that generation, are we lost or found or maybe just the lost and found?" He waved his arm around. "A sort of momma-told-me-not-to-come type situation."

He laughed helplessly and his cheeks shone. I laughed, too. He was funny. I mean, he wasn't a big pain in the ass. Just to look at him was entertaining.

Then the elevator opened and he pumped my hand, hard.

"Well Jack, swing low sweet chariot—"

The doors were closing and he jumped. His shiny black shoes sparkled, he was gone.

Ralph let out a cry. "You see that, Jack? How he jumped? Just like a fucking toad."

"He's harmless," I said.

"No he isn't Jack. He's probably got glands in his skin. And you touched him. Early Quinlan, Jesus, the forces of darkness."

We went back to the ballroom level, and Ralph just kept at it, saying my name too much. I shut my eyes. I hate it when people say my name too much, and I went over to George's

11

side. He was a red-faced wreck, but at least he didn't try to embarrass you in public.

"You heard what he called you. Jack Gould. Like you work for some white-shoe fucking firm."

The elevator stopped. I opened my eyes.

"Am I right or wrong?" Ralph said.

"You're right."

The doors throbbed with sound, and inside, the ballroom was jammed way past fire code. The music was so loud you could feel the dirty bass in your intestines, and people were doing a line dance. It coiled back and forth through the room, and there was nowhere for you to go. It pulled Ralph one way and me the other. So goodbye, Ralph, and fuck you.

I was grateful for the mob, to get lost in. A fat woman with cornrows had me in her strong sweaty hand and my back hand was in some blue-tweed professor guy's. So I went along and you didn't have to think about a thing, and the crowd was like a great serpent, like an organism. A loop would go up against the stage and squeeze people till they cried out with shock and merriment, and then another loop would surge over a table loaded with T-shirts and bumper stickers, sending everything to the floor with a triumphant howl.

And people were dressed well. There was good perfume right on top of the sweat.

The crowd roared at anything, and you didn't always know why. Once, it was because a bunch of kids with tall red canisters went up on the stage and danced with the band. The Stone Ponies. They were like the campaign mascot. Ever since Super Tuesday an army of kids had gone out collecting change for the campaign because we were always so broke. During the convention they were everywhere with those tall cans.

My mind went away. I thought about George Sides, I thought about *Larkspur*. It was a snotrag. It treated New York as a village made up of SoHo and Tribeca and the Upper East Side, a very hip, knowing village that even though I lived in I could never inhabit. Also, it had a reputation for being quietly vicious in a way that someone had to explain to you. I'd helped George a year back. I worked for a public-interest law center, the job I was going back to right after the convention, and when this weird divorce/libel suit had come up, we had taken it on. My boss didn't give a shit about William Roberts, he's intrigued by novel legal theories. I'd written a brief. The judge had quoted extensively from it in throwing out the case.

The crowd roared again, heavier now, and suddenly quit moving. Stony had come out. The noise was deafening, thrilling. Stony walked to the lip of the stage and danced a little, which he doesn't really do. I mean, he's awkward. He just bent his knees some, then people grabbed at him. They lapped over the stage and lifted him down. Stony's big, but people began handing him over the crowd in a throne position. They held his knees and his back and shoulders, pushing him up like he had won.

People had to touch him. They pulled at his hands and kissed his coat, they kissed his face. He came my way, and that was when I started having these subversive thoughts. What if he comes here and I don't hold him and he falls down because of me? That sort of thing.

Just like a dare he came closer, and people crushed toward him from behind, pushing me closer, to where I could hear the ones who were holding him up grunting to balance themselves, and feel the heat and sweat coming off them. Then there was Stony, dark and beautiful, with his big hands reaching out uncertainly. Because he was a beautiful man. His features were smooth and beautiful. I was maybe five feet behind him. I saw his scalp glistening through the thin hair at the back and the flattened Brazil-nut deal over his eye where the cops beat the shit out of him in Birmingham in 1963.

He was scared. You could see that. He was probably scareder

13

than me. His hands reached out to clasp at people's shoulders.

"Don't drop me brother."

"No we won't, Stony."

"Easy there, brother."

"Stony, I love you."

And his gentle voice, so stirring.

In the end I didn't have to hold him. He steered himself the other way, to the stage. He was wobbly getting to his feet. He shook his legs to shake out the creases in his good suit, and Amber, his wife, gave him a handkerchief he wiped around his neck. Because Stony didn't ever wipe his face. He liked his face being wet when he spoke. He'd told me that.

The band stopped, and Alvin Moorer, Stony's old friend, handed him the mike. His breath came husky, and he just nodded at the crowd.

"People. Family people." That low rasping voice. "You know what I say, people. Politics begins with the family."

Another roar, because that was Stony's big slogan. We had banners saying that. Then he held his right hand over us, fingers spread wide, sheltering.

"This is my family, yes, and when we set out on the road, sister. When we broke our axle, oh mama, when the horse's ribs stuck out like a washboard. Brother, I tell you—"

It was the way Stony talked in person, too, brother and sister with no plurals. We were *the* family, not *a* family, he said that, too. And people were already calling out Yes and Amen, the things they said when he spoke. More than anything Stony was a speaker. He didn't like the quiet wrangly political part of politics, and in a few minutes I was going to cry without thinking about it, I'd feel tears going down my cheeks.

I don't know what happened. The air was stuffy, like dust in my throat. I hadn't eaten all day, I'd missed the chow line. People were folding pieces of paper into fans and fanning themselves but there were too many of them in the room, and I

14

started feeling dizzy and hateful. We had lost and didn't know it. Cornrows didn't know it, blue tweed either.

I bargained first. Just count to sixty and you'll feel better, I said. But I counted to sixty and I felt lousier. O.K., a hundred. But I went right past a hundred and the feeling didn't stop. Because I couldn't even hear Stony, only muffled cottony sounds. I needed air or I was going to faint. Ralph says I'm a bullshit artist, I don't know. I felt like hell. If you're sick you could go. We need you so much that if you're sick, take care of yourself. Stony always said that. Lie down, eat something, then come back.

I had to squeeze past a million people. I smiled and made a face like I was faint, and they looked at me with understanding. Thank you. Thank you. Then I pushed through the white double doors and out into the hushed dark.

That was when I heard Stony's voice again. His muffled churchy voice went out through the doors into the whole back-lobby area. "At 6 a.m. on the streets of Los Angeles, they stand waiting near the parked BMWs. They take the morning bus . . ."

I knew that part, I could miss that bit. I went down the back stairs and out the lobby. I'd be fine in a minute. I walked past the sexless marble women and out onto Park Avenue, then I lit a cigarette and walked up a couple blocks. My mind was going like a squirrel, when a squirrel freaks out. It's put its nuts down and doesn't know where, and I didn't know where I should go. Yesterday I could make this whole moral argument for why we should pull together as a continuing political movement in American life, but today I'm sorry, I feel faint.

I had a second cigarette and walked around this display. They had a fake lagoon in front of a building on Park Avenue, some bullshit temporary display for the convention with fake little palm trees around it. You brushed right under those plastic palm trees and I thought about that guy in Vietnam who lit the

15

hut. My dad made me watch that on television, the soldier who lights up the villager's hut with his Zippo. I guess I was five or six, and my dad was pretty vehement.

So that was where my politics started, right there. That upset me. I was thinking, I bet I could light up that tree with my cigarette. I bet it's made out of plastic material that would just go up if I burned it.

No, probably not. The federal government regulates that. There's a retardant.

So I had that whole argument, and I walked around the lagoon ten times. Its bottom was painted turquoise, but there was pink stuff in the water, a chemical, I guess to keep it fresh, with a pink sheen on it even in the dark. I threw my cigarette in the water, and the hiss broke my mood. I walked back to the Waldorf. Who are George's friends? I said. I went up to the front desk and asked for Quinlan's suite, the running-dog former Secretary of State. Suddenly I didn't care.

They're not supposed to tell you that, to just give you that information. But this guy did. He thought about it for only a second then looked over his shoulder and penciled a number on a slip and pushed it across. It's my face. I have the kind of face people trust. People will say, You're honest, I can tell, after just a second of meeting me. Even if I lie to them they say that.

2

When I got to Quinlan's door on the twenty-first floor, a tall
guy was already there, hitting the door with the meaty side of
his fist. He had gotten it open with a key but someone inside
had chained it. "Open. The. Goddamn. Door," he said into
the gap. He glanced at me without any change in expression.
He was handsome in a rugged way, and the soft dark blue wool
of his jacket showed off his wide shoulders.

There was a clattering on the other side of the door before
George Sides swung it open. "James," he said, but the guy
brushed past him.

Then George saw me, and I was the last guy he expected.
He grinned and reached for my hand.

"Jack. Jack. Jack. Get on in here, Jackie."

Shaking his hand was like holding a giant helium balloon.
His eyes darted over my shoulder and he offered me a little
half-smile. "You lost the sidekick," he said.

"Ralph Lopez," I said.

"Ralph Lopez," he said in a teeth-clenched murmur. "Got
to remember never to keep an appointment with Ralph Lopez."

"Ralph's all right, he's just intense."

George's laugh was like a bark. "That what you call it. Well

17

I was just telling them—" He stopped himself, and his cheeks were bright red. "Listen, what can I get you to drink?"

I was already nervous, and the room was fancy. "A beer."

"A beer. Good, a beer." He smacked his hands and walked away, elegant and splay-foot, toward a baby refrigerator.

The generational party George had advertised wasn't happening. Besides him and the guy he'd called James, only two people were there. On the other side of a big Oriental rug from me, a pretty woman with long blondish hair was stretched out on her back on a couch. Her black halter top had pulled up off her stomach, and she had a drink balanced there. Her knees were in the air but tilted to one side so that she could watch television. Then on the far left of the room a little guy in a dark gray business suit was sitting on the floor. He was monkeying with a coat hanger.

I half-sat on the arm of an armchair pretending I belonged there. It wasn't an ordinary suite, more like a house. The furniture was big and plush with broad red stripes on it. There was a rolltop desk next to the fridge, and ship paintings in gold frames on the wall. It reminded me of those grainy black-and-white pictures you see of rich people's compounds where solid obedient dogs are looking out the window at the sea and some cool woman is having a fake-private moment reading a book with a drink beside her. The drink's in a glass just like that girl's glass, short and round with a heavy bottom. Or people are laughing effortlessly with horsy teeth. And I was right, because later George told me that Mrs. Buell, the governor's widow, had lent the suite to Secretary Quinlan for the convention.

James had gotten a bottle of Coke.

"Whose bright idea was it to chain the door?" he said. No one responded, and he sailed the bottle cap across the room at the guy with the coat hanger. It bounced past him, and the guy looked up.

"Blake's," he said.

"Thanks, ape," the girl said.

James turned to her. Then I recognized him. It was James Doyle, he was running Early Quinlan's campaign for governor. I'd met him once during the New York primary. He held his wide face at a slight backward tilt, and you couldn't really see his eyes. They were deep-set.

"What if I'd been the Secretary?"

"You open the door a crack and Negro children squirt in shaking UNICEF cans," she said.

"They work for Sifton Walker," he said.

George handed me a beer. "So does Jack," he said.

James looked at me. The girl tilted up on the couch on one elbow. Her gray eyes met mine for an instant.

"It wasn't him," she said.

All of them laughed, George too, and I could feel myself blushing. I didn't have to be there. I'd wait a minute and offer an excuse. I sat down in that armchair. I'd show them that I felt comfortable there then have a good excuse.

George squeezed my shoulder. He said, "Jack's a helluva lawyer. Jack saved my ass. He's smarter than Satan," etcetera. But no one gave a shit, and then he had to introduce me.

There was James. Blake was on the couch, and the guy making the coat hanger into a hook was Charles. No one shook hands. There wasn't a lot of shaking hands in that crowd. That was all right, I'd finish my beer and go sell them out to Ralph Lopez. Guess who I met, Early Quinlan's daughter.

I lit a cigarette. Quinlan had a daughter you read about, and that had to be her. She was beautiful in a hard way. The only time she moved was to lift that drink and sip. A normal person would choke trying to drink at that angle. Well, she was a crocodile. The word "Negro" is ten times as racist as "nigger." Like "Jewess," which Sartre said was the most racist word in the language. That is what happens if your father conducts foreign policy in a brutalized manner, it is going to have consequences at home. Your own kids will be fucked up.

19

I got a dish off the coffee table to use as an ashtray and snuck a closer look at her. Her little tits puffed down into the halter's armholes, and her stomach was brown, tanned.

"What is Charles doing?" James said.

"An abortion," she said.

"We don't joke about that."

Charles was on all fours, he had his face pressed into the floor so he could guide the hook under a door. His pants had traveled up and you saw he was wearing sock garters, then he gave a little grunt of achievement and sat back. He'd drawn out the hanger with a phone line in it.

"Burry's going to get us into the Better Earth benefit," George said.

"Look, she's probably meditating," James said.

"Oh lighten up, James," Blake said. "Burry was talking about this all week till you emotionally blackmailed her today."

"Because it's just what I don't need, Burry talking Swahili with a hundred reporters underfoot."

James walked to the door and stood over Charles. Charles looked up at him with round sincere eyes, he smiled and dropped the hanger.

"I'll handle her," he said.

"Sure, you wrote the book on it," George said.

Charles turned toward George, the smile vanished. "It wasn't a book," he said. "It was a pamphlet."

"But it was printed."

"That was the joke."

"What joke?" James said.

"How to spend a weekend at the Quinlans'," George said. "The ape wrote a whole book and mailed it around."

Charles flushed as if he'd been visited by a cruel injustice.

"I only mailed it to Early," he said. "It was a thank-you note. Early was the one who mailed it around. Early got a big kick out of it."

"Sorry," George said.

"No you're not," Charles said. "You can't be sorry because you knew that already."

He stood up and went to the table for a wineglass. I don't know why they called him the ape. He was short and agreeable-looking. His light brown hair fell across his forehead in almost a cowlick, and he had red lips.

"It was just a little brochure with made-up rules," he said, turning to James. "Like no shoptalk. You know how much Early hates shoptalk. No references to Tocqueville. No personal comments. That kind of thing."

They went on like that and I broke my vow, I got a second beer. I was just going to watch them.

Then Blake stood up, frisking her pants down, pale yellow pants in expensive thin-thin fabric, and crossing the room, yanked the cord. A phone smashed to the floor on the other side. Someone yelled.

Blake threw herself back onto the couch, and after that it was like a whole drawing-room comedy. George sat down on an arm of my chair, Charles sat on the couch at Blake's feet. Blake lifted a stack of pages from the table. She dropped them on that mean stomach and pretended to read.

The door lock rattled and a tall girl came out, about my age, maybe thirty. She had dark red hair that hung to her shoulders, and next to the hair her skin was fine, white. She was almost beautiful but she wasn't, my mom would say striking. Her eyes were big and tilted into the sides of her narrow face. She was trembling with mute anger, she looked around the room.

Blake flapped a page in the air. "Listen to what my editor wrote. 'More poke on the road.' "

"Charles, you dick," the tall girl said. "You broke the fucking phone."

"Blake did."

The girl turned to Blake, but Blake said, "That guy did," and waved the page at me.

The girl only looked at me for a second.

21

"James, who did it?"

James pointed with his bottle at Charles and Blake.

"I knew it," she said.

"You were on the phone an hour," Charles said.

George went over to the girl, he put his arm around her and squeezed her a lot.

"Burry, we missed you," he said. "We were jealous."

But she shook George off and went to the refrigerator. She wasn't dressed like the rest of them, she was barefoot and wore a black T-shirt and a long, faded flowered skirt. She looked like someone I might actually know, and you could see where the skirt was held by a safety pin and the white skin of her hip showed through. She got out a bottle of fancy water and glugged it. Water went down over her chin, then she gasped and turned to the room.

"You think it's the biggest joke, don't you?" she said. "Well, that was a violation of my constitutional rights—Blake, you knew I was talking to a healer."

Blake sat up. She put the manuscript and her drink on the coffee table and patted her stomach dry with a napkin.

"I thought it was John Ellen," she said.

"Who Ellen?" George said.

The tall girl dropped the bottle with another gasp. "John Ellen Rohr," she said.

George frowned.

"Dr. Rohr. Lenox Hill," Blake prompted him. "You did a funny article on him. Ear-nose-throat to the stars."

"Oh sure."

The girl moaned. "Blake, please don't be superior and jaded. John Ellen is very evolved. He practiced in Calcutta for years, he sits Zen. You're not even listening to me."

George went over, he put his arm around her again.

"Burry Burry Burry. Burry." He pushed the bright hair off her white forehead. "You're coming with us to the nature deal. The bitter Earthers nature thingy with halfwit celebrities."

"It'll be the same shallow awful people from yesterday," she said.

"No, more of them." She laughed, and he said, "See, we need you. We need your help if we're ever going to shift the paradigm on some of these spoiled celebrities."

"O.K.," she said, and she was back on board, just in that second.

She went to her room, I guess to set things right with the doctor, and everyone got ready. Blake stood, gathering up the manuscript. "Should I bring my book? Should I not bring my book?" she said, addressing no one. But in the end she left it.

I sat in the chair, I wasn't sure what I was doing, then the girl came back out with a pair of gold sandals and a notebook, she led the way out the door. There was a line of them, and George found me with his eyes. He gave me a big wink, he lifted his chin to say I should come. So that was that, I was going. I mean I wanted to, it was funny watching them.

James Doyle waited near the door. He nodded at me as I went by. When you were so close you saw where his skin was pitted.

"Hey, Jack," he said.

Then he came after me into the hall. He left the door open.

"You going over to Dummer?"

"Hell no," I said.

"It's going to be exciting."

"For someone else."

Dummer was the presidential nominee, he'd defeated Stony and was challenging Bagwell. Even before the convention there had been rumors that Walker people were going to work for him.

James kept at my side. He touched my arm. "Listen, you could be a pal. Burry sometimes blurs the line when there's media."

He had the faintest southern accent, a deracinated political professional's accent, and that's when I realized I had it wrong.

23

Blake wasn't Quinlan's daughter, Burry was. It stunned me to think that she could be that asshole's daughter. She seemed decent, the soles of her feet were black with dirt, etcetera.

"She doesn't watch what she says, and all these socialites encourage her," he said.

"I work in issues," I said.

"I know, but just to be a friend," he said.

But I walked away from him.

At the elevator Burry was pogoing on one foot to get her shoes on, she was using George's shoulder to balance. She wasn't wearing a bra and her tits moved in high round swings, and she had that notebook clamped in her mouth. James went right up to her, he put his hand on her shoulder and said things in her ear, just like a political hack. Then he walked away.

She got the sandal on and looked at me.

"Jack, you're a lawyer?" she said. "You saw that. That was a violation of my Fourth Amendment. When someone cuts off your phone call?"

"It wasn't very nice," I said.

"But isn't that a violation of my Bill of Rights?" she said. "When I'm talking to a healer—doesn't that invoke the whole religious-assembly question?"

George was grinning, Charles, too, the ape, but I liked how she said my Fourth Amendment, my phone call, my this and my that. Everything was personal to her, and I got that. Because it was always the spirit of laws I'd responded to. "Congress shall make no law . . ." It came to you like a song.

"It could," I said.

"Listen, do you do entertainment law?" she said.

George laughed, but she came right up to me. Her pretty hair was so coppery and shimmery, her eyes were dark but speckled with green.

"I'm a performance artist and writer, and people have been ripping me off," she said. "I need an entertainment lawyer for intellectual property things."

"Because you tell everyone your best material," Blake said.

"Blake, please, I give of myself is all. It's a human duty." Then the elevator came and she handed me that notebook. "Hold this—" and the edge that had been in her mouth was a warm wet semicircle.

3

Charles Tharp worked at *The New York Times* and he had a car. It was white with a red crushed-velvet interior, and George said it was a Puerto Rican limo, and Burry laughed her head off at that. What can you say, they were all racist and didn't give a shit if you heard them. Even Burry. She was all right, but that crowd was a bad influence. Plus her moral-bankrupt father, you couldn't blame her.

I sat on the more forward seat with George, and Burry was between us. We were facing in the wrong direction, and across from us in the other seat were Charles and Blake. Blake lay flat. She drank with her head tilted against the armrest of the door, she was an expert in drinking in that unnatural position, even in a car. She seemed bored. Once I caught her looking at me. I don't think she liked me being there. Well the feeling was mutual.

Still, I felt a lot more comfortable than in the hotel room, where people could see that my socks were too low. George poured vodka he got from a cabinet into square seaworthy goblets, and he and Burry had this whole relationship. He would tell a joke but just a part of it, usually the punch line, and she would fall apart laughing and then name the joke.

"Because they're meaner and hold more water," he said.

"The Gulf War," she said. "Dykes and camels."

"Right dykes and camels," he said. "All right, Burry, you can bargain with a terrorist."

"A woman with PMS."

"Wrong, a woman at that time of the month."

"That's what I said, George, a woman with PMS."

"PMF?"

"You don't know what PMS is?"

"Oh right, sorry, woman on PMS. Now. First spank. Then you screw—"

"That's the lightbulb one."

"No, the recipe one. How to make them."

I think they were mostly lesbian jokes, and I didn't get any of them. Burry kept squashing up against me when she laughed. The personal-space issue wasn't a big issue for her, and she had a smell I tried to figure out. It was part B.O. and maybe patchouli, or that alternative peppermint soap that comes in a tall plastic bottle with writing down the side for all your needs from deodorant to washing a dog. I know all about stuff like that. She probably went to Quaker high schools and an over-privileged college where all her hip friends said to use that soap instead of deodorant. Well I'm sorry, it doesn't work.

That's O.K. You smell fine. Then I thought of words that rhymed with Burry.

Jury. Hurry.

Worry and surrey. Flurry.

A fine rain fell, and the limo's long body made bucketing noises going over the sunken cobbles of streets downtown. You didn't know where we were, then we took a turn and the mist from the river came over us and we were in the meat district. The buildings have steel curving tracks that go out in the air to the street through rubber doors. They're to hang carcasses on. They hook the carcasses and glide them along those tracks. You smell the meat and the fat. Then the driver went left and we went farther downtown to an old industrial area, and the sidewalks were long and sloping and built as loading areas, with long corrugated iron roofs coming off the fronts of the buildings over the sidewalks and anchored to the second stories by long steel shafts.

I thought about Early Quinlan, the sellout Secretary. He made a big thing of his humble origins and his time with Bobby Kennedy, but mostly he had worked for Republican administrations. He'd signed off on indefensible policies in Vietnam and Africa, then there was a ten-month turn as Secretary of State when he was in his early forties. When the Democrats got in they forgot about all that and made him ambassador to England. He was good-looking and charming and loved attention and was basically an asshole. I always think about that thing he said after Kent State, about the body count going up today, that no one on the left will ever forget but everyone in the Democratic Party seemed to have forgotten now that he was running for governor.

Two more corners and there was the club. A couple hundred people were in the street, even in the rain, in good clothes. Women in high heels stilted over the cobblestones.

But no one was getting in. There was a purple velvet rope in front of the door, and three black guys in Nehru jackets stood with their hands resting on the rope. The small guy was the one you could talk to. I mean, he would look at you.

We pushed our way up to the raised sidewalk, and Burry talked to him. You heard her say "the Secretary" a couple times, and the bouncer looked away but Burry wore him down. He went inside for a second then he came out again and without saying anything lifted the rope for us. Enraged shouts went up from the crowd. Well fuck you. Everything is not a human-rights question.

Inside was packed and Burry disappeared. You heard her voice shriek-greeting people, and Blake and Charles went off, too, and George and I ended up at a table against the wall. I

28

got drinks, more vodka, and George kept spying people in the crowd.

He issued a running commentary all about the DaVilla family. Because the board of the nature group was lousy with DaVillas, and the DaVillas were pissed at George because of something in *Larkspur*. I didn't know who the DaVillas were, but the name sounded halfway familiar, and I nodded.

"See, the DaVillas don't go anywhere by themselves, Jack, they need an entourage," George said. "I suppose if I were a DaVilla I'd do the same thing, but the DaVillas are nothing like you and me."

"You and me are nothing like you and me," I said.

George laughed and smacked the table.

But after that he kept looking around for other people to sit down with us. He was nervous as hell being one-on-one, but silences were even worse, so a few seconds would go by and he'd start in again on his old favorite subject.

"See Jack, if the DaVillas are invited somewhere they've never been? They get the host to invite a bunch of their friends so they'll have a buffer. A wall of inoffensive flesh."

Charles sat down and George threw his arm around him. "Hello, young Charles. Charles, you're a thoroughly modern ape and great to have around."

"Can I see that—" Charles said, and took the pad from next to me.

He leafed through it, squinting at the notes, then Burry skidded up.

"Here you are! Write this, Charles. I just saw Martha Lightfoot. She says Father always comes backstage with an armful of calla lilies and now she's finally getting a chance to visit him backstage."

"You write it."

"My hands are sweaty."

"Burry, who are you covering this for?"

But she took the pad from him and wrote on it. She knelt at

the edge of the table between me and George, and her smell came up out of the neck of her T-shirt in a tease. Down the neckhole I could see the pale tops of her tits.

Then she was gone, and Charles said, "George, who is she covering this for?"

George gave a vaudeville shrug. "I don't know." Then he lunged his arm between people to grab someone. "Simi," he called out. "Simi Simi. Sit down."

"George—" Simi said.

She was a small woman with glossy, piled-up black hair and a hectic, pretty white face. She sat down next to me and across from Charles with her head held at an angle, looking at us but more at the room. You didn't know how old she was. Maybe thirty-five. She had that good heavy hair. But she wore lacquery lipstick and a lot of makeup around her bright little cat eyes. Her clothes were fine, her black jacket was held together with little wooden barrel-buttons, and nothing under it. When she moved you glimpsed white skin.

"Simi Simi Simi," George kept saying, as if talking to an animal.

"I thought you were non grata."

"No, I'm grata. You're gratatui. Ha. My grand delectable dame Simi."

Charles she knew, but George introduced her to me. She was Simi Winfrey and wrote for *Follies*, the magazine. Then she and George started talking about who was there, and some were famous, like Martha Lightfoot and Billie April, but most of them I didn't know. I didn't try to pretend to be in the conversation, I'd drunk too much to pull off a fraud like that, I'd stopped caring.

Burry came up, breathless.

"Hi, Burry," Simi said.

Burry ignored her. "Scoot over, Jack," she said, and I had to move my butt over to let her onto my seat. Her sweaty arm pressed against me.

"Billie April is here. She was in the Amazon doing a movie she likes for once, *Ovation*."

"*Oblation*," Simi said.

"Billie says the rain forest is ten times more glamorous than Hollywood, Hollywood has all the piranhas but just one Vine—"

She and George laughed hard at her joke.

"And Billie says she can't wait to appear at a speech with my dad, get their picture in the papers."

It was hard staying on the seat with her. I put my elbow on the table, then she hung her arm on my shoulder. The clovy tang of her B.O. went louder.

"Who else?" George said.

"Who cares?" I said.

Burry turned, bumping hard against me. "Jack!"

"I don't see how anyone can take these people seriously."

"We don't," she said. "That's why they're celebrities. We choose them. Then we put all our dark side onto them. This is what Robert Bly writes about. Everything society represses we put on to them."

"Do you believe that?" I said.

"Yes. What do you think?"

I thought of something my boss always said in consumer-fraud cases. "It's a snare and a delusion."

"Whoa!" said Charles.

"I thought you were nice," Burry said.

She had those great eyes, and under them the cheek-bones made her face look fine and strange. I was suddenly self-conscious, or maybe I was blushing. Probably I was drunk.

"There's Emmy Cline," she said, rushing off, and you heard her squeal. She was past redemption. She was decent and in-telligent, but growing up with that father, it had warped her. Like being a hostage. Hostages love their captors. And maybe someone would come along and rescue her, but it would be a

31

struggle. Both bodies would disappear beneath the raging surf, that whole stereotype.

"Clarification," Simi said. "Billie April hates Early Quinlan because he waffles on abortion, which she thinks is the same as liposuction."

"Simi!" George groaned. You could see he hated open warfare.

"She's weird about it, anything fetal she's weird about because she's a hermaphrodite."

"No she isn't."

"I know the guy who dressed her for *Simoom*."

"Aphrodite—"

"Hermaphrodite," Charles said. "You don't know what a hermaphrodite is."

"Of course I do," George said.

But he was uncomfortable. He got out a cigar and put it in his mouth and didn't light it.

Simi turned to me with her big smile. That close, her face was papery, it was white and lined prematurely.

"Is your name Jack or Jacob?"

"Jack—"

"No, your real name. It isn't John."

She laughed and I could tell she was Jewish. Jews always scratched one another to see how Jewish they were.

"Jacob," I said.

"Like Javits. Jack on the East Side, Jacob on the West Side."

"Well, I'm just Jack," I said.

But she threw me, and I could feel the color in my cheeks. I get these blotches of color. My mother calls it the Reshevsky color because it comes from her side. It gives me away.

I got to my feet. "Who wants a drink?"

I had another of those vodka tonics, which are too easy to drink, and I had to remind myself where I was. A club with frauds who think they are at the center of the universe. We thought we were at the center of the universe in the Walker campaign, but we'd spent a lot of time discussing how empty the lives of these very people were. Then you hung around them and realized that they'd never given one second's thought to what we said about them.

These people cared about themselves. They were ten times hipper than we were. If you were going to be hip, you didn't give a shit about anybody, only yourself. That was a startling revelation. Either that or it was stupid/obvious. Well, I was drunk.

People left and the club thinned out. Then you could see it. It was two large black rooms with exposed steel girders. Against the far wall was word art, red LEDs by a feminist artist that went up a screen against the wall, a whole installation.

IT TAKES A MILLION STARVING ETHIOPIANS ON PETER JENNINGS TO MAKE ONE GOOD TV DINNER . . .

THE AMAZON BASIN IS NOT IN MY BACK YARD . . .

VAMPED . . . DEFILED . . . RAPED . . . PHOTOGRAPHED . . .

NO WONDER THEY CALL HER MOTHER EARTH . . .

And on another wall were paintings on butcher paper of a fanciful rain forest. There were red monkeys making love to green monkeys, and pythons dropping from the trees and swallowing businessmen in three-piece suits with those gray fraud hats, fedoras. The guy had done the pictures right there, because you could see long drips of paint. Simi said that he was a famous illustrator, and they were for sale. Later people were rolling them up.

There was a cry and everyone turned.

"Oh God, Burry," Simi said.

At first I didn't see. Burry was dancing on a table, doing the swim. She'd gathered her skirt to her knees. She would share with anyone, wouldn't she. She was insincere.

"Now, that is Swahili," Charles said.

"Oh, lay off, the girl has talent," George said. He had the

cigar back in his mouth, rolling it around but not lighting it.

"Is she covering this for *Larkspur*?" Simi said.

"No."

"I never understood why you called it *Larkspur*."

George looked at her suspiciously from the corner of his eye. He removed the cigar and picked up his drink.

"Because"—he let the ice collapse against his teeth, then set the glass down—"it is the most beautiful word in the English language."

"The flower is ordinary," Simi said.

"The flower. The flower yes. I'm talking about the word. The word is exquisite."

We watched Burry. She did other sixties dances, and people made a circle around her. She kept flying her skirt up, she kicked her shoes off. Then Simi said, "Bye," and without another word got to her feet and glided away.

"Simi will get this in the papers," Charles said. "And Vacca will make Burry into the whore of Cairo."

"The whore of Cairo—" George slapped the table. "The great white whore of Cairo. The everlasting whore of Cairo."

He kept improving on the phrase, and Charles looked away with secret pride of authorship. He meant Joseph Vacca, Jr., the former New York attorney general. Vacca was running as a Republican for governor. He wasn't very likable, where Quinlan was. Everyone was saying Vacca was going to have to run a mean campaign.

George bumped hard against the table. "Why don't you stop criticizing her and marry her, ape?"

"Oh, bug off, she doesn't even return my calls."

"What's that got to do with it, I return your calls, that doesn't mean I want to marry you."

"But you don't. You don't return my calls!"

Charles sat up straight with more sense of injustice. But George wriggled out of it. He said he was grateful for Charles's calls. He liked the message slips lined up on his desk, pink, like petits fours after a nice lunch. He had that half-smile when he was nervous, but he could sell ice to Eskimos, he was that full of shit.

"See. Look," he said. "You're Charles Tharp. You're Charles Percival Edward Tharp, whatever the hell you are, now what are your options—" But Charles ignored him and he turned on me. "Better yet you're Jack Gold. How do you get ahead. You fuck your way up—"

"He's drunk," Charles said.

"So? That's the only time I make any sense. It's the only time I don't self-censor myself, which anyone will tell you is the worst form of censorship there is. Isn't that right, Jack?"

I looked away from him. "Some countries kill poets," I said.

"Oh, Jack, don't be a tub-thumper. I'm not talking about countries. Listen, your class ladder is to be gotten up by fucking. Fucking's the great equalizer."

"How many people will it help?" I said.

"Ah! See, this is why I failed as a pinko. They don't ever talk about individuals. That big economist knew what I'm saying, Don't ever talk about statistics. No one who's a statistic ever had anything interesting to say."

"I don't think it was an economist," Charles said.

"Yes it was," George said. "In the long run we are all individuals."

Then everything stopped. They turned off the word art and the music stopped. The rock music did. They put on Frank Sinatra go-home music, and the lights came on. I thought, I can leave right now and find the subway, I can have some integrity.

But I stayed there. Billie April walked by, and I smiled at her, and she smiled back. My mother would be shocked to find out I was at a party with Billie April. After that two guys went by pushing a steel food truck with a big sheet cake on it in the shape of a map of the earth, half-eaten.

Burry fell into the chair next to me. She leaned against me and I held out against the bullshit promises she made with her sweaty body. She laid her arm on the table and dropped her head on it. Red hair stuck to her cheeks in fine strings like that spice, that Spanish hair spice. I wanted to push the hairs back off her face.

Slurry curry dhurrie. I wanted to lick her skin, to taste the sweat. To taste the red wet hairs straying onto her thighs.

furry blurry

She pushed the pad at George. "Get this down. They used two hundred pounds of flour and ten pounds of macadamia nuts to make that cake, and it's all organic."

"Who are you covering this for?" he said.

But she gave more ingredients, and George wrote it down.

Charles got to his feet. "I'll be at the car—" Then he looked at George with his air of injury. "It's for *American Way*, the inflight magazine. That's how you get ahead. Have your father come out for airport expansion."

George clapped his hands. Any hint of scandal or corruption he loved.

"Brava, madame des avions," he said. "Brava. Brava, la madame de la bonne fusilage—"

He reached out for the crown of her head and rocked her.

"What was I just telling Jack Sprat? What is the only program for radical change, you fuck your way up. Look at my grandfather. He was just a fireman in Hell's Kitchen who married the commissioner's daughter."

Burry laughed, her mouth opened wetly. I pushed my chair away from the table.

"That's like telling a black kid to get a job in the NBA," I said.

"O.K. let's talk about the black kid," he said. "Who will fuck him, who will fuck Sifton Walker?"

I lit a cigarette. "Many many people."

36

Burry fell against me. She held my tie. "Stony Walker—" she stammered. "Stony Walker is so eloquent—"

"Oh don't be a tub-thumper, Burry," George said. "It's four o'clock in the goddamn morning."

"But he lost because he was never funny," she went on. "My father is the funniest man in the world and he can't lose."

George knocked wood on the table, and Burry had my tie balled in her fist, she pulled it to her.

"You should work for my father," she said.

"Look he's blushing," George said.

"No he isn't."

But that was a lie. She'd lied for me, and I was grateful.

George stood up. He was going to the car, he said, but he paused to push his hair back. He felt at his scalp with both hands, just the fingertips, like he was taking inventory of something precious and endangered. Then he set out on his journey.

"Burry, what is a tub-thumper?" I said.

But George heard me. "A bore," he said over his shoulder. "A political bore and sink of tedium."

Burry sent me to find her shoes. They were next to the table she'd danced on, someone had put them in a neat pile for her, and when I came out to the front of the club she was getting the leftover cake. A man held open a black plastic bag and she used a cookie sheet to shovel the cake in. They shouldn't throw away all that cake, she said. She was going to give it to the homeless, she knew a place that would take it.

The bag was heavy so I slung it over my back. Then when we were about to go Burry lifted a last hunk for herself from the tray.

The street was empty. The car idled at the corner. George had the back door open and sat on the seat with his feet resting on the wet cobbles. He'd finally lit that cigar. He was tasting it the way they do, holding it away from his face, and his jacket was off. I woke up a little in the cool air, and it came to me I was still there, I'd been with them all night. I really am a bullshit artist, I bullshitted myself.

Hold on, they're not all bad. Who do they hurt? Actually, a lot of people. I had that argument with myself, and a man came out from behind an iron pillar on the high sidewalk. He was odd-looking, with slitty eyes and stringy hair. He wore a rust-colored jacket. You didn't know if he meant harm.

"Morgan," Burry said.

Something came into her. She held her hands out with her elbows twisted up like a showgirl, the piece of cake lifted up. Her arms were so white. Well, she didn't spend time in the sun. People with no values sunbathed, Blake.

The guy got a camera from his jacket and took her picture. He backed away from her, the flash went off.

"I'm taking this to the homeless," Burry said. "On behalf of my father."

"O.K." He spoke in a low grindy voice.

Then she stepped into the street. She spun a little on the uneven stones, and it was true what George said, she had talent. Just the way she held her tits and her chin, not worrying what people thought.

George stood to let us in. Shiny black suspenders came up out of his halter job, the waistcoat, whatever it is.

"Ah, Swahili," he said.

"George, don't say that, it's racist," Burry said.

"Amen," I said.

George tasted the cigar again and flew it into the street. "Well, that's racist. Amen is racist."

The car slid a little turning on the wet stone and little clods of frosting fell from Burry's hands onto the red velvet. We got on the West Side Highway going fast, too fast. The driver was impatient for the night to be over. I was sure we would crash and my gut tightened, but we didn't, and after a couple minutes we still didn't. The speed of the car didn't scare anyone else. They acted as if everything was normal. Blake sat staring calmly out the window. So it was only me. I really was from a sheltered background.

"I should have brought my book," Blake said. "So many people asked about my book."

4

Something touched my neck and woke me up, a bug I thought, but when I opened my eyes it was a spear of sunlight coming across the Oriental rug. I had the rug, George Sides had gotten the couch. That had been the division of labor at 5 a.m. Then I saw I'd been using his shoes as a pillow. Fine, papery leather. Always look at the shoes. I pulled them back into shape and slid them under the coffee table. The manuscript was still there from the night before, with scribbles in the margins.

"March 19. Martha's Vineyard. Still no spring. Bleak, dead, everything gin-gray. Why don't they rename it Misery's Vintage."

And more bullshit like that. I crept out. I didn't want George to see me, I wanted him to forget I'd ever been there. Him more than anyone. More than me even.

I went down the shadow side of the street hoping no one I knew would see me. You could still smell everything on me from the night before, smoke, vodka, patchouli, and all of George's snob quotes, too, his words-to-live-by. When I got back to the Powell my room was dingier than ever and I was thankful for that. It was familiar. It was mine. I took a long

40

shower in the leaky shower stall and when I got out the carpet was spongier than ever.

Then I put on fresh clothes and set out down Ninth Avenue. In the sunlight the great swirled dome of the convention center was bright and alabaster, almost mosquelike. I was disillusioned. No, only hungover. I had that little symposium in my head then I got the papers at the corner and a cup of coffee, too, and sat down on the long escalator. I felt a wave of gratitude to *The New York Times* and *The Washington Post* for coming out this morning just like every morning before that. They were clean and flat, folded like sheets.

There were going to be meetings all day, hallelujah. First was a strategy session on voter registration in Conference Room C, and I was the first person at the Walker table. All the tools from the Dummer campaign were there, guys in their white shirts I'd met a while ago, and I only nodded at them and sat down. One of them was wheeling the blackboard over to their desk. First person grab the blackboard, a little rule of politics. Well, we had lost. Fuck the blackboard.

Keenah Granger came in in one of her outfits. She had on a fake leopard hat and a T-shirt with a giant photograph of people on it, a crowd of people. Keenah was sophisticated. She wrote about culture for *The Village Voice*. I would tell Keenah about where I'd gone last night, make a clean breast of it.

"Keenah," I said.

"Jack honey, where'd you get that coffee?"

"I'll get you some," I said.

"Just tell me where."

"I need more myself—"

"Hey, you too?"

"A long night."

"The longest night," she said. "That band?"

I moaned in my throat. "The band was great."

The long up-and-down escalators crossed in the middle from

a great ways off, and I saw Ralph Lopez coming up. He was transfixed by a shaft of light from the building's transparent ceiling. He was a fraud, he'd timed it so it didn't look as if he was with Keenah.

When he saw me he called out, "Say it loud—"

"Say it loud," I said back, but not so loud.

"We care—" He made a fist in the air and said it in a whole rhythm. "Say it loud—we care."

That was probably the tag line of Stony's speech. *Say it loud, we care.* Stony liked people to have something to take away with them from a speech. We called it the mission bite.

Ralph kept up the responsive chanting.

"Say it loud—"

"We care," I said.

So that was how we crossed, him staring at me with his fist in the air and no idea I hadn't been there.

At noon there was the weekly postmortem same as always, but I missed the beginning of it taking a nap and once I got there I wished I'd missed all of it. Everyone was sappy and still acting like Stony could win. Sam Treat read the poem he said he would have read at Stony's inauguration. Something about "voluptuous zeal." He actually wrote that, voluptuous zeal.

After that a lot of Walker people took the subway down to N.Y.U. in a loose band to check out a conference called Whither the Left sponsored by a magazine. It was a load of shit. People in the audience kept standing up to decry mistakes of the Walker organization, and Betty Roth who I once went out with talked the whole time three rows in front of me to a thin blonde with a strong nose and hung her elbow on the girl's shoulder. So she was a lesbian now, or wanted me to think so, wanted to torture me a little about that.

I left after fifteen minutes, I was getting good at blowing shit off, and Ralph came out after me. He slanted across Third

Street. So the gig was up, and I stood there, waiting for him.

"Jack, you heard the smut?"

"No."

"Listen, I'm hungry, are you hungry?" he said. That's something else great about Walker people, always answering a question with a question.

"What's the smut, Ralph?" I said.

"Let's grab a bite—"

We went to this pizza place on Sixth Avenue. He pushed the red pepper thing at me, the dusty plastic canister, and I was right back in my life with no interruption.

"Josh Speed went to Dummer," he said.

"Bullshit."

But I didn't mean it, I wasn't even surprised.

"Stony told me. He's going to be deputy assistant asshole press secretary for Dummer."

I had a bite of the pizza but I didn't taste it. "Well, Ralph, what else is he going to do?"

Ralph got this withering look.

"The guy worked for Alan Ahrens for four years," I said.

"I know who he worked for, jerkoff. That's not the point."

"What's the point?"

"The point is—you know you can be real fucking stupid sometimes. As Stony said, the point is his goddamn alacrity."

At 6:30 there was a whole other meeting at the Waldorf about the Palestinians. Eight Jewish congressmen who were big friends of Israel had been working for months on a statement about violations of the Palestinians' civil and human rights. I'd been involved because of my work at the law center, work I was going back to after the convention. It had been endless. Claude Roe, who works for David Binns of Ohio, had been faxing different language to us almost every day. Claude who changed his name from Rosenberg in law school. That's

43

Claude's big secret. There I go, turning into a gossip. Claude's a dynamite administrative aide even though he's a hermaphrodite.

On my way there I stopped for a minute in Rockefeller Center. There was a guy in the fountain who had on fishing waders, and I spaced out watching him. He pushed a long pool net around, catching papers and political literature. He would lift them and drop them flat on the slate edge of the fountain. The papers lay there, flattened and wrinkled, with the pictures of candidates or some group's agenda on them. He walked around the fountain lifting them out.

After that I went to a pay phone to call my machine. I was putting things off. I'd sublet my apartment for the campaign, but I kept my machine there, and I'd call in every day.

George's seal voice broke into my ear. "Jack—we can't read these notes. Listen, you remember what Burry said?"

I'm sorry, George, I've spent enough time with you to last me my whole life, so fuck you and your paisley halter.

"Listen, talk to Burry," he said to my machine.

"Jack—you're screening, aren't you?" Burry said. "Jack. I know you're screening, but help me, I can't read these notes." Then she said all the places she was going to be that day, *The Washington Post* office, Condé Nast, *Follies*.

I was late, and up in Claude's room they were all drinking tea. They'd ordered tea from room service. They were queening it up because it was the Waldorf. All these legislative assistants who dress the way they dress in Washington, and in the middle was a tray with lacquery pastries on it, little round tarts with strawberries. My father would say it was nouveau riche. My father can be derisive as hell. Meanwhile, they were passing around papers on human-rights abuses.

"The problem with the fifth protocol is we haven't maintained anything close to this standard in countless Latin countries," Claude said.

44

I was useless. I kept hearing Burry's voice in my head. Her voice tore through stuff and didn't give a shit. She'd gotten George to call me so she could get on the phone. She was different from the rest of them even in how she dressed. I remembered her falling against me, and I wondered if she had on underpants. Probably. Still that meant only four items of clothing counting her sandals.

"Well then, that brings in the special-relationship question," Miss China Oolong said.

"I think we want to avoid that language," Claude said.

They sat uncomfortably on the fancy chairs. They didn't feel right here. Well I do. I've been here, I slept here last night, in Secretary Quinlan's suite.

I flattened the protocols against my knee and made a list in the corner. *Burry 4.* Where George Sides the snob was wearing cuff links, suspenders, and everything else. I put a 12 next to his name, and the ape was wearing 6 just below his calves. Call it 15 in all. That was fucked. You could plot a curve, going from real people to frauds. Clothes per capita, a whole index.

"If we're going to say stones, if we're going to say rubber bullets, we have to deal with the hospital situation."

Everything about Burry started coming back and I was getting hard, so I excused myself to go to the bathroom. If I beat off I could get rid of that voice in my head. If you eliminate the desire, etcetera.

I was pale, I looked like hell. I opened my shirt and undid my pants and saw my fat curving cock, also my white belly, glossy and flat. My naked body reminded me of her naked body. That's just a fact about being naked, it turns you on. So she came right back at me, her high fat tit, her pealing laugh.

Why are you adoring yourself? Because secretly you are planning to run into her. That was no good, secrets are just lies, you could lie to yourself as easily as someone else, and without any fanfare I snuck out of there. I pulled the door quietly after, that way you can hold the handle so the metal doesn't even click, then softshoed down the hall.

The press was in the basement of the convention center. They were in a giant circular room the shape of a tuna can but big enough to fit the circus or railroad trains, which they had in there on other occasions. There was a teeming urban center of reporters there, which the reporters tried to make light of by calling it the village. Plus, they called their offices huts. As if it were the jungle. When in fact they had very modern techno-offices and the alleged huts were good-looking structures of painted chipboard with the logo on the outside in brass. And the more prestige the more tasteful. Some had dark blue almost-Sheetrock walls and actual molding around the door.

I went all over, I stopped twice at *Follies*. It had an actual tent, square and canvas with pink-brown stripes going down the sides and a door with ropes pulling aside the flaps like you could walk in and ask for a gin-and-tonic. Inside, there were just a few people sitting around trying to beat their hangovers. Burry was nowhere. She'd made a monkey of me getting me to even go down to the village, and then a tall girl almost fell on me walking past CBS. She pushed a newspaper at me.

"Jack, I'm in it," she said.

I didn't recognize Burry from the night before. She seemed bigger, or whiter. There was more of her. She crowded me, and for a second I didn't want her.

"That little bitch Simi sold me out—"

She hung against me as I took the paper. The *Post* gossip column had an item on the Better Earth benefit with a line about Burry, how she danced on the table. Burry said it was a column that Simi Winfrey piped, and it was a little mean. It described her dance and said she'd been trying to advance native cultures and her father's aspirations.

46

I read it twice before Burry pulled the paper away.

"I never thought she could be so vicious. They weren't high heels, and this is not a sarong it's a skirt—" She tugged at her skirt, the same one from the night before. That same patch of hip blinked through under the safety pin.

"She got it wrong," I said.

"No, she lied. Believe me, Simi knows from clothes. That's all they sell in Bendel's is sarongs. She was saying I'm a rich bitch. Which I wouldn't mind if it was only true, but I'm poor—"

She mushed against me in the lane. Her ripeness filled the back of my throat like smoke, and I stepped away.

"What's our agenda?" I said.

"You're not even listening, are you? I thought you cared about this kind of thing."

"If you dance on a table—" I began.

She stopped, and her lips were bright red, she was pretty. "If you dance on a table, what?"

"Nothing. It's perfectly fine. But it should also be legal for anyone to write anything."

But it was too late, I'd hurt her feelings, and we walked along in that silence.

Then she said, "Something doesn't have to be illegal to be wrong, Jack. The more behavior we put into a legal context the more we abdicate personal responsibility for."

Well, she'd plagiarized that. "I don't know," I said.

"Father says that. It's in his speech tonight. He's on the floor, I want you to meet him."

I didn't want to meet her father, but I took the escalators up with her. On the way she did a yoga thing to calm down, a whole position. Loosing her right sandal, she gathered her foot in her hands and rose slowly with it, bracing the sole flat against her left leg. Her knee stuck out of her skirt, and her sole was black as ever. They probably called it the Heron. She did deep breathing, too. All on the escalator.

47

Then she dropped the foot and exhaled. "Oh, I wish I could change my name."

"You can," I said.

"Are you always so literal?"

"You must not want to."

She made a low moan. For a second I thought she was going to cry.

"I'm paying for something, I know it," she said. "Someplace my soul has been."

We changed escalators and she did the same thing with the other foot, that yoga position. Her skirt fell like a curtain across her taut white thigh. I watched her. You were supposed to watch her.

"Burry, if everyone is reincarnated, how come there are more people on the earth today than in all of history before us?"

She dug her foot back in the sandal, she looked at me.

"There aren't enough past lives to go around," I said.

"You're being legalistic again and testing me."

"Why don't you say Jewish?"

Her face colored and she hit me in the chest with the side of her fist.

"Don't bullshit me, Jack. If you don't like me go away. Are you bullshitting me? You don't really like me, do you?"

I turned away. People farther down the escalator were looking at us. She made you feel naked.

"You're all right," I said, and I could feel myself blushing.

Then we got to the checkpoint, and she reached for my arm, she pulled me around.

"There's transmigration of animal souls. All the extinct and endangered species? We've colonized their souls. The dodo bird, the koala bear."

"The koala bear," I said.

"You know what I mean."

Then I had a pass and she didn't and they wouldn't let her use mine, but it was the same old story, she talked about her father and the guy folded in around three seconds. He pointed her to the New York delegation.

"I'm waiting here," I said.

It wasn't much for a convention hall. That's something I know about. I'd been going to political conventions since I was little. My dad used to bring me. My mom never went, but she has curled black-and-white photos of me as far back as '64 in some kind of academic-culture papoose deal my dad wore to carry me on his back through Atlantic City.

My dad's a government economist. Or he was. He's retired now. He worked in New York for the Labor Department, and even though he never got as far as he and his friends expected, he's still halfway famous on the left for some important theories about government spending he came up with and published while being a government analyst. Like when you read about how little long-term economic growth is generated by military spending, my dad was behind a lot of that. Meanwhile, he outlived McCarthy and Reagan and a hundred civil wars in the left, which is cause for celebration. He's odd-looking. He's tall like me but has a beaky nose and white hair that goes up on the top like feathers, a crest like Samuel Beckett's, and he cuts his hair himself. I've gotten a couple of jobs because of his reputation. Sometimes I hear people say, That's Jules Gold's son.

He took me to endless political deals. At Chicago in '68 he talked Yiddish to old union friends and he knew reconstructed Communists, too. They had a nervous shorthand. In '72 he was an adviser to McGovern on economic issues and so I went to Miami. Those places were giant black-and-white barns my dad could extol the hell out of, amphitheaters for the common hope. And so what if the common hope always got sold out. They were the best anyone had come up with.

Those halls are still glamorous to me. There were cigarettes

49

then, and men in narrow-shouldered suits, corn-palace halls that took an hour to walk through. Of course, in the old halls, even with twenty-five thousand people in them, you got bald patches on TV. But this convention hall was freaky, it was small and shaped like a cantaloupe slice so it would look crammed on television. It was more like a game-show set than a hall for the common hope.

Someone was standing too close to me, someone was in my zone. I stepped away and it came to me that it was Josh Speed—Josh Speed coming to pour out his black heart.

"Hey, Jack." And it wasn't Josh, it was James Doyle.

"Hey," I said, but my mouth was dry. He was so quiet, he was a crocodile. He kept his head tilted, and you saw his tongue, flicking around in there.

"She shouldn't wear that T-shirt on the floor," he said.

You could see Burry maybe two hundred feet away, standing in front of the old royal sack of horseshit himself. Quinlan sat on an aisle with his pretty-boy smile. Every once in a while he would bend his head back in a charming slow nod.

Then I hated her father. You never knew if he was being serious or mocking, and he has that look-at-me face, narrow and handsome, and that wavy black hair, and the famous scar that goes into his upper lip. Stony said Quinlan got it in the Merchant Marines. There was a whole story about how he got his name, too, and about him burning a novel when he was a Rhodes Scholar. He told the stories himself in those alleged diaries he published. He had been a playwright and a journalist before he found politics. After that his résumé was shameless. He loved hanging around the powerful.

Burry mugged for him. She was laughing, bending close.

Her mother was dead, I remembered that. And she had a little brother who was famously estranged, who had run for Congress in Vermont as a Republican.

"We got her a blue dress for the convention," James said. "It's simple and elegant."

50

"Why are you telling me?"

"Because"—he made a little fist and mock-hit me in the arm—"she likes you."

"Well, I think she should wear whatever she likes."

"O.K., then. Because you got her in the papers last night."

"She got herself in the papers," I said.

My voice went up, and he stepped away. He held his hands in the air. "Hey sorry, cowboy."

"You're like dogshit," I said. "Everywhere I go it's still on my shoe—"

He shot me a look of disbelief then walked away.

I tried to justify what I'd said to him. Because he was a croc is why, because his tongue moved like a crocodile's. Still, you didn't talk to someone like that. Then suddenly I was so ashamed I wanted to crawl under a rock.

Burry and I walked back to the Waldorf together. She wanted to get her blue dress and go over her notes. The streets were wet, it had rained, and her face shone. I was nervous. I wondered what James had told her about me, and should I tell her his line of shit. I thought not. She was high from seeing her dad, and it might bring her down.

"My father is so funny," she said. "I think that's the sign of true genius. When someone is doing something that's the most important thing in the world to them but they can still be funny. Don't you think, Jack?"

"I don't know that much about your father."

"Oh, you're so serious," she said.

We came into the spillway of the Waldorf. People pushed out past us in the pretty light. Burry stopped on the sidewalk, she touched my arm.

"Did I tell you his mustache joke?" she said.

"No."

51

"Never trust a white man with a mustache. Or a black man without one."

"Your father didn't say that," I said.

She was caught by a run of laughter and went away from me into the hotel. I went after her. Then I thought of course her father said it, Stony said Quinlan was a closet racist. Some of his statements about joblessness were perfect coded racisms.

I got to her near the elevator. She was laughing so hard her face was red. She was pretty, pretty like her father. She reached for my shoulder to hold herself up.

"Billie April told me that," she said. "But see, you believed me, you wanted to believe me."

I shut my eyes. "You baited me."

"Because it's so easy, Jack."

I walked into the elevator, and she came after me.

"Anyway, you know there's something true about it," she said. "Think of Hammer. Think of Clarence Thomas. Or Martin Luther King. We trust them."

"If there's anything true about it, it's because racism is such an overwhelming fact of black people's lives," I said. "Now, what's our agenda?"

I pushed the button for 21.

The elevator started and Burry's mood changed. She folded her arms. Her eyes gazed off, black and big.

"You know, you really hurt my feelings before," she said. "What you said about me changing my name."

"I just think you must get a lot out of it," I said.

"You act like I'm such a big insider."

"Burry, your father's on television every Sunday morning."

"Right. Father, not me. This is what Blake's book is about. Being written off because you're the daughter of someone well known. Jack, I've always been outside. Because of people like you that hate my father. Left-wingers in hip campaigns who take it out on me."

I thought about Blake, whoever her father was. She probably

had a successful-fraud father, too. A feeling rose in my throat, a sort of acid fury.

"The left has been on the outs for twenty years," I said. "We're almost completely marginalized."

"I'm not talking about the fucking left," she said. "I'm talking about tall privileged white men that want to get laid. They all have politics like you."

"Oh please."

"See, you're blushing. You believe that yourself. Where I'm just a writer and artist who has trouble getting her work out."

Then the doors opened and she shoved past me.

5

We drank wine and made out a lot and she ordered candles from room service but she wouldn't go to bed with me. She said we had to wait till we knew each other better. Meantime, she would do a show for me, which was better than sex, anybody else's idea of it. She melted the bottoms of the candles and stuck them in water glasses next to her bed, two and three per glass, and she had a boom box with sixties music, seventies, Cream and Jimi Hendrix. She went into the bathroom and I waited on the bed. She came back out wearing scarves, one like a sarong, another over her tits, and another turbaned on her head. Her skin was ivory white and she had a round stomach and long blady thighs. She danced around the bed to the music and played with my fingers, bent them and spread them and put them in her mouth. I danced with her, too, getting up on my knees on the bed.

I undressed. I got off my shirt and pants, and then it was just my black bikini underpants.

"Them, too, your man-panties," she said.

"First let me see your tits."

"No bargaining."

I grabbed at the scarf. But she sat back away from me, and I had this whole epiphany. Those are going to be the only tits I see for the rest of my life. So I didn't care, I slid the underpants off. Because the way she was, you couldn't be modest. And if you were going to feel naked around her, you might as well be naked.

She straddled me, she sat on my thighs, but not touching my cock.

"Do your johnny with your hand," she said.

"Let me come inside you."

"I need to see how you do your johnny."

"Don't call it a johnny."

"Oh, you're so fucking correct—"

She tilted over me and worked her mouth dripping spit on my cock. Then she flopped my hand down on my cock and wrapped the fingers round it, being careful the whole time not to touch me, and moving my wrist up and down. Everything about it turned me on, how clumsy she was, and the way her belly got, bent over, white and creased. It came to me that she wasn't going to get back in time for her father's speech and then I didn't care what she saw me do, I beat off.

She did more snake dances. She let the top scarf come off, first one side, then the other, and if they were the only tits I was going to see the rest of my life it didn't matter anyway because she'd put lipstick on the nipples. They were shiny and went wider than they really were in red-red circles. And she held her chest out like a shield for me, with her tits drooping off it. Her tits moved on their own, apart from her body.

Because that is what makes a tit beautiful, the droop. There's a theory about that an old girlfriend of mine has. Carmen Frankel, she can talk about that, a whole theory on the aesthetics of tits.

"Let me come on your tits," I said.

"No. I need to see your eyes when you come, Jack."

55

"I need to see you, too." I tugged at the scarf on her hips. "Play fair."

So she sat on my legs and wagged her knees from side to side like an old movie where girls do synchronized dancing, they smile and wag, and now and then she let the scarf ride up.

"I see you," I said.

"Peek-a-boo," she said. "Peekaboo Charlie Brown. Peekaboo Charlie Brown."

There was a hard honest sound in her throat even saying nonsense, and she squeezed my ankles to hold herself up straight. That did it. "Burry," I said. I was coming, a growl inside that turned into a rumble, a rubble, a slurry of words in my head.

Slurry. Purry furry   blackhat
mink blink
inkypink

She reached for my cock, she pointed me at her thighs. She held me and rubbed jizz into her thighs up under the scarf.

"Damn damn damn fuck it to hell—"

I woke up. She was moving through the television stations. It was all late-night programming, Argentinian soccer, black-and-white movies. In the wan light of the television her face was a way I hadn't seen it, chin and forehead corded.

"I knew we shouldn't have come back," she said.

I sat up. "I'm going."

"Oh, that isn't what I meant. Don't be touchy, baby."

She got all kissy. She said we should take a shower before I left. So we took it in the dark, and even then out of modesty she wore underpants, mine. She kept calling them man-panties and I was never going to wear them again.

We lay down in the tub. The water splashed down on us. It

drummed your skin hard and made it feel rubbery, and when I kissed her I couldn't really taste her mouth but only the water. So it was boring, which you're never supposed to say about sex.

It felt like fifteen minutes. What are the politics of a long shower where you're not even getting clean anymore?

So I got nervous. The personal is political, etcetera. Any action, even a shower, can be judged according to how it affects arrangements of power. In the waterfall I couldn't tell her leg from mine. Then I thought that was my big problem, the personal being political. Because where did it stop once you started thinking that. It didn't, it kept going till everyone was involved with everyone else's life. And in the long run we are all individuals. My dad would hate me if I said that.

All at once everything stopped. Burry cut the water and held her hand over my mouth.

Then I heard it, too, the dry kiss old feet make on tiles, and in the dark you could see a human form. The dawn of life, the Secretary. He'd come into the bathroom. Burry had antennae for him, and you saw his dark body and the cloudy shadow of boxers, but he didn't notice us.

He set a glass down on top of the toilet with a chink noise and stood there waiting. Everything was still. Then he hummed something, talking to himself, talking to his old pipes. We were all waiting. Finally he gave a little thankful murmur.

As soon as he left, Burry got up. She wrapped herself in a towel and scooched my man-panties down, stepping out of them.

"Jack, get the loo."

"The loo," I said.

"The loo," she said, going out.

Well, you can't be an outsider and say "the loo." I'm sorry, you can't.

First I peed. This is the Secretary's pee I'm peeing into, the royal sellout's pee. I said that to myself. Now I have lain down

57

by the waters of great men, and I foamed mine right in there crossing the Secretary's sword.

Outside it was still dark and no one was about. I had the street to myself and didn't worry if someone saw me. I felt calm for once, even carrying those wet underpants.

Back at the Powell I had a dream. In my dreams I'm always getting lost in the subway. I get a train and it's the wrong one and I'm in a different country, but trying to get back only gets me more lost. That took me to a stone chute of the sort dried beans must travel. Down down, twisting blindly. I came into an underground cathedral and a service was going. It was a large modern American cathedral like one some asshole builds out on the interstate, of metal shining in the sun, and the huge congregation was acting completely normal even though people were hanging from the ceiling. The unfortunates were maybe sixty feet in the air, six or ten of them in black clothes, and the Mass was going on the whole time. The ones on the ropes were grinning. I guess a noose makes you grin.

Someone banged or yelled in the dream.

They did it again, and I was thankful to learn it was outside the dream. The dream was a dream. The person kept knocking, and I rolled over.

"It's Salvador Allende."

"Fuck you, Ralph."

Ralph came in wearing just his overalls. He'll wear overalls without a shirt under, another of his tricks for getting laid. His hair was loose and he swung it around in another dance. He held a rolled-up newspaper he used to beat an invisible drum.

"Kay-kay-kay-kay-kay"—he shrilled, and jerked his shoulders to the rhythm.

You just had to watch him.

"Uh-kay. Uh-kay." Like a bird call now. "Uh-kay. Uh-kay. Uh-kay—kake!"

58

He came to the bed and threw the paper down, and he was grinning wickedly. It was *The Washington Post*, folded open to an inside page. They had a picture of Burry Quinlan with the cake. Of course—the guy hadn't taken her picture because he liked her. She held her arms over her head with that piece of cake. Her arms were white and her tits pushed out her T-shirt, which I guess is a rule of journalism: Anything with tits, publish. There was a caption. It described her plan for the homeless and quoted somebody from Quinlan's campaign who didn't know anything about it.

"Man with bag unidentified," the caption ended, and that was when I saw myself. My naked face had caught Morgan's flash. It was me, anyone could see that, bent a little under that bag.

"Man with bag. Man with bag"—Ralph had started a whole new chant and soul-train. "Unnn. I. Dentified."

For a second I didn't panic. In the picture I looked all right. I wasn't putting anything on. My eyes were wide open and my mouth was composed, a whole poets-in-their-youth expression you didn't have to be ashamed about. I was just trying to hang on to that good feeling for a second before the wave came.

6

The office of the Center for Creation of Law in the Public
Interest is on the second floor of a six-story building on Thirtieth
Street east of Third. I think it's a brick building, I completely
forget the outside. On the first floor is a travel agency operated
by the building's owner, Hector Albagorda. Hector is a Mexican
immigrant Communist former factory worker with smooth
brown skin, and he rents out the second floor for about seventy-
five cents a month. Victor's had his brainchild there for more
than twenty years. Victor Bandy, my old boss. From time to
time Victor changes the name to match his changing philosophy
of law, but he always keeps the word Center, and that's what
everyone calls it, the Center, even if it's a misnomer politically.
There's no sign out front. Victor says he gets enough cranks
just in the mail.

I'd been given six months off to work for Stony Walker while
Victor finished a book about coerced confessions and the death
penalty. Victor was a closet adviser to Stony, closet because
Victor is never openly partisan. Almost never, anyway. That's
part of his deal in life. We said six months because we knew
Stony wasn't going to win.

My first day back was in August, four days after the convention ended. That was the day a huge heat wave started, and when I got to the Center at 8:30 the fan was already on in the outer room, what we called the city room.

So Victor was there.

I hadn't been back in three months, I'd just talked to Victor on the phone, and the place looked different. It looked smaller, more cramped. I noticed shit I hadn't noticed before. For instance, the city room is kind of a warren. There aren't proper walls, just stacks of cardboard boxes containing the Center's publications, the boxes functioning like cinder blocks. I bet we had a hundred boxes of *Government: An Owner's Manual* waiting for people to order them, serving as walls. That's Victor's big book, and the one reason he's famous outside the left. I was co-author of the fourth edition.

I sat at my desk for a few minutes getting into the mood. There was a snowdrift of mail I tried organizing into three piles: actual letters, necessary bullshit, pure bullshit. The first pile was just a couple postcards and the second two piles got to be one pile, and then I noticed my baseball cards. I'd forgotten about them, my little collection of great street-smart players, Frank Robinson, Dick Allen, Curt Flood, Bob Gibson. They were hung on the shelf edge with yellowed tape. That was real adult of me.

None of them had a mustache. I could show Burry that. No, she was simply wrong. You couldn't do anything about that sort of thinking. More evidence would do nothing to convince her. Trying would be a giant waste of time. I'm guessing Burry realized our encounter was a mistake, too. She didn't call me, and anyway she'd said she was going to New Mexico. There was some kind of spiritual retreat she was going to near that place where all the artists lived, Taos.

So I left those cards right where they were, and I went over the things I was going to tell Victor about the convention for the tenth time in my head. Then finally I got up and went down the hall to his office. I did what I always did, touched the

61

water cooler and the fridge on the way and ran my finger along the top of the sill there, getting it black.

I'd been working for Victor for four years. A shadow generally lasted five. Shadow is what he called his deputies, and he had one shadow at a time. We did everything procedural for him, everything dealing with the real world, writing briefs, calling defendants in Walla Walla, research.

Victor's like a god on the left, and for a long time I was in love with him. He's completely eccentric, but everyone loves him. Everything about him, if they put it in a movie, people would say, He's adorable. Like his habits and his old-fashioned heroes. He would quote John D. Rockefeller the Antichrist a lot, and emulate John D. Rockefeller the Antichrist. For instance, he made his wife sew coins in the cuffs of his Brooks Brothers suits in case he ever got in a jam. He has a bunch of identical suits. Victor believes everything unimportant in life should be uniform.

The same with ties. Meals, too. I could talk about Victor all day and you'd love him.

In the third year stuff happened between us that's not worth going into. My old girlfriend Carmen Frankel, who met Victor a bunch of times, said that for complex psychological reasons he recapitulated the same crisis with all his shadows in the third year. Like a whole psychodrama. I don't know. Carmen's read too many books. First there was a case in federal court where I wrote a brief that used the Ninth Amendment in a way Victor didn't like, and it got in the papers. It's his favorite amendment, he says it's all about the mystery of democracy. Victor can cry over the Ninth Amendment.

Even though we won, he felt I'd misused it, and he held it against me. He's worse than Burry that way: my Ninth Amendment.

Then there was weird shit he did that I told myself I'd never repeat because he's such a god. Little things. Like he's a madman for price typos in ads. If a store got a price wrong, he would insist on getting the advertised price and make their life a living hell in the name of justice and the American way, which at other times he doesn't believe in. So he kind of fell off the pedestal.

For a year it had been more like work. Also Victor was on my case for little shit like swearing. Victor hates swearing.

The door was open and Victor was on the phone. He nodded his head at me like any morning and pointed to the chair in front of his desk. I sat down.

"No. Think of Walker in terms of Goldwater, '64," he was saying. "The party elders walk around saying he's poison, but he starts the movement by bringing in everyone who's going to matter for the future. It only took the Republicans sixteen years before they nominated Reagan."

Victor's favorite occupation: piping a column.

"No. No. No. We still don't understand Watergate. I don't. You don't. Tell me the real reason. See, you can't. It's like the Civil War."

He swung up in his wooden chair and grabbed a bagel. He tore it in half and held half out to me. Victor's always doing Old Testament deals like sharing his food. I took it and chewed at it, but I didn't feel hungry.

The chair springs squawked again and Victor hung up.

"Jacob. How are you, friend?"

He smiled. Victor's got white hair like a thistle and big milk-white teeth that are apart. His eyes are like doll eyes, baby-blue, transparent, almost like looking at the sky. For his age —he's fifty-eight—he's very young-looking.

"Good."

We shook hands.

"And the book?" I said.

"Excellent. We just got in a carton this big of transcripts from some schmo in Florida who they kept in the tank fifty-two hours without a lawyer on a capital offense. By the end he was confessing to the Kennedy assassination."

63

He laid his hands on the desk and looked at me in this sober way.

"So Jacob. What did we learn last week?"

I nodded a couple of times to get the engine going.

"It was a televised charade, that's obvious, and ultimately disappointing and ugly. The platform battles came down to sordid trades, just like I heard they would, and frankly, after the Central American thing we were demoralized."

"Huh," Victor said. "Huh."

He pressed his stomach against the desk and didn't lift his hands. He kept gazing at me. I looked away at the busted pillow Victor had tied to the back of his chair for a cushion. Dried-out brown foam pushed out the sides.

"You mean about the picture?" I said.

Victor nodded. "I think we need to talk about the picture."

"It was a mistake."

"That's good to hear."

I turned in the chair and exhaled. I looked at all the volumes of federal code. Victor read them while he was eating lunch at his desk.

"I was at a benefit for the environmental group Better Earth," I said. "They're very active in Brazil. A number of us went, and these people offered me a ride back. It was late. I accepted. She asked me to carry the bag."

"She," he said.

I laughed and shut my eyes. "I swear, Victor, I wish I could white-out the whole thing."

But that was probably worse. Victor had once told me he had never had any regrets.

He sat back with another groan from the chair. "I talked to Stony yesterday," he said.

"O.K."

"He wanted to know where you were. There was a staff meeting Saturday you missed."

"It was over," I said.

"That's not how Stony felt."

"The family's always last to give up hope."

That stopped him. His mouth twisted a little. "I hope you're not being cynical, Jacob. I hope it's anger, which I might understand in the circumstances."

"We'd lost and I was bored."

Another groan from the chair.

"I never understood that," Victor said. "When people say they were bored? I've never been bored."

I looked away. Out the window on Thirtieth some guy was opening his electronics store, a guy with a long black coat hanging over his shoulders, his coat worn to a dull sheen in the sun. He hoisted up the metal gate with that dull rattle sound. Orthodox. Hasidic. I wondered if that was why they called us sheeny. Well, that was just self-hatred. Do you hate yourself? Yes, I hate myself. But who could blame me.

Victor lifted something from his desk, a page, and flapped it around.

"Claude Roe faxed us minutes of the ad hoc Middle East session. I guess you went AWOL when they did the protocols."

"I missed the last half hour. Anyway it's not about that, Victor. You're stuck on that picture."

"Of course I am."

"They got it wrong."

"They always do."

"You pay a heavy price being somebody famous's daughter."

He looked up at me in shock. Sunlight touched his white eyeballs, lit them from the sides.

"Anything that happens to that man, as far as I'm concerned, he's got coming, Jacob. After his shilly-shallying on Vietnam? The things he's said about the inner city?"

"Guilt by association," I said.

"Don't be pious, Jacob. This is obvious. She's a party girl."

I felt a surprise wave of loyalty to Burry. She was too intelligent to be a party girl. She had ideas of her own. Well, Victor could be a fucking Visigoth.

"We shouldn't need to have this discussion," I said.

"I agree. It just makes me wonder where you are."

"Some of this is my private life."

He didn't even answer. I got out a cigarette and began tapping it.

"Could you postpone that, Jacob, do you mind, till we're done?"

"The prisoner always gets one last cigarette—"

"Jacob, please."

"Victor, if you're trying to fire me, just say so," I said.

"I don't fire people."

"You just reach a crossing in the road. People choose."

That was something he always said. He got this whole more-in-sorrow-than-anger expression staring at his hands on the desk, and it came to me that I ought to leave. Nothing was stopping me. I could just walk out. Why was I always deciding to leave and never leaving?

"You know, anyone can have values." Victor's voice was calm. "It's not hard to adopt a coherent set of concerns. Someone who makes a billion dollars a year has values. Someone who collects antiques, someone who goes to parties. The dishonest part is when they say, We have values, and hold them out as being worthy of honor."

"O.K.," I said.

"The choice we're given is to embrace a meaningful set. To love them and not desert them. That's the mind-over-matter part."

"Is that a choice, Victor?"

He frowned at his hands. They were small and white, a little puffy. Then he looked up.

"Tell me, what kind of name is that, Burry?"

"I assume it's a nickname."

"But what sort of person would choose that name?"

66

"I don't know, maybe she got cold once. People get nick-names for life when they're two years old. The goyim do."

"Why not Bunny?" he said. "Or Muffy? If you really want to announce to everyone, Don't take me seriously."

I felt dizzy. I got up and walked out the door.

"Where are you going, Jack?"

"I need air."

I was going to leave, but I got to the city room and my nerve went, I sat against a desk I felt so weak. Where was I going to go? Suddenly I was scared.

Victor's chair howled and he came after me. He made me sit in a chair he pulled around. He was almost sweet, he called me Jack a lot, which he knows I prefer. After that he got some juice from the fridge. It's one of Victor's little scams no one's supposed to say anything about. He never endorses anything, but the owners of this Vermont company that makes organic juice visited and then they began using a picture of their meeting with Victor in ads. Meanwhile, Victor reads the company's statements and faxes them back marked up, and they send us all the juice we want. He got two paper dunce-hat cups and we had some juice. It's actually very good juice.

You could see his mood ease, and he even rolled up his sleeves. So the two of us were sitting in office chairs being halfway normal, and I started thinking I could explain it all.

"Just because I go to bed with someone doesn't mean I've sworn an oath to them," I said.

"Jack, the things I want to say to you have nothing to do with her."

"Good."

He sipped from his cup. I guess it's not really that big a scam.

"Ideology always gets a bad name," he said. "But when someone believes in principles enough to organize all their thinking around them, boy"—he shook his head—"that's how you move the mountain."

67

I'd heard it before, and as he talked my eyes noticed stuff in the room. The black-and-white television we watched basketball games on. The old photographs of Victor's heroes. Chandra Something, the Indian socialist. Allard K. Lowenstein. Black and white and cracked, the way that old pictures actually chip away. Why did it feel like I was seeing them for the first time? Because it was the last time. No, that didn't seem right.

I stared at Victor. I saw his pale flesh-lips that went right into the skin of his face, his wispy invisible eyelashes. I felt achy. Then I was in love with him the way I'd always been.

"If you weren't so bloody-minded, Jacob, you would be the smartest kid who's ever worked for me."

He was doing a list: my doggedness, my anger, my intelligence. So it was like listening to your own obituary, and I started to cry. My throat got hot and my eyes filled and I rubbed my face to cover it. Because I wasn't going to let that dick see me, then I stood and crumpled my cup. I saw the door, the old familiar pebbled-glass door like from a Clifford Odets play.

I'd drop my cup in the trash and keep going on to the door. I had that little plan. It would have gone like clockwork, too, but then I missed the fucking can and instead of leaving it I bent to pick it up. Victor reached for my arm with one of his doughboy hands, then I was really crying.

"It's fine, Jack, it's fine. Jacob, it's fine, friend."

"No, it isn't fine, don't lie to me, Victor—"

"It's not a lie."

I caught a sob in my throat. Suddenly I didn't give a shit whether he saw me, the lie was so monstrous. "I know what a lie is, Victor. I've lied a lot in my life. That's a lie. I thought you had too much intellectual honesty to say something like that. Everything isn't fine!"

My screaming froze him there, then I pushed out through the door and went down the stairs. They were old iron stairs that made a good noise under your feet, a hollow inspiring rhythm as you went down that I knew in my bones.

"Jacob?! Jacob!" Victor screeching my name had a dire sound. "JACOB GOLD—"

I got to the bottom, but his voice only rose.

"NO ONE I LOVE LEAVES THIS OFFICE WITHOUT A HAND-SHAKE—" His voice was broken and scratching, and I turned. He stood at the top of the stairs, his face was red. Light through the Clifford Odets door lit up his burning hair. He was holding his paper juice cup, too, he still had it in his hand. Like he was saying a prayer. When people cross over, when people leave. I mean, there are prayers for all those occasions.

"Now Jacob."

He came down a couple steps, but I pushed open the door onto Thirtieth. Then I was really flooding and wiping my face and I said, Just get to Broadway. On Broadway there are a million people. You can walk down Broadway and be a complete fuckup. You can have anything you feel on your face and no one will start telling you about yourself, they'll let you go your way.

7

The heat wave took hold, the same funky pad of air lay on the city for days. It only made me feel more useless, so I tried to get some routines going.

I started taking walks to Strawberry Fields. That's the place if you're feeling down, just like the song says. The trees go around and make it like a room. It's really something. I mean, it's a real sign that civilization is making progress, something good being added to the world for what's been taken away. The only problem is, everyone else who's feeling down goes there, too, so it's halfway to a halfway house. You walk in there and there are all these other sensitive upset people wearing white socks and sandals or housedresses, people who don't even have their shit together to get dressed, no belt, maybe they're not allowed to have belts, sitting there on the benches right next to one another. And you can see where some of them are thinking, Only John Lennon of all the people in the universe was sensitive enough to understand me.

Also, after you came back a few times it was the same old faces and they'd look up when you came, like, Who's here today? So I tried to go in the morning when no one was there.

I tried to be normal and read a book. I wanted to hang there but I didn't want to be anyone's kindred spirit.

For another thing, I bought another Alger Hiss book and the new Nixon biography. Political biographies are my favorite books. I mean the big American tragedies. I have a whole set of L.B.J. books, also Nixon and Roy Cohn. I can always read Nixon's Alger Hiss chapters again, or Roy Cohn persecuting the Jewish scientists at Monmouth, or the escalation of the war.

When you read a biography, you identify with the bad guy, you can't help it. I do anyway. My father once said to me, You have to respect pure evil. Because even if they say it's for Mom and apple pie, they have to know they're fucking up other people's lives. They have to know that about themselves. I wonder what it's like to know you're evil, that you're doing evil things.

I read the Hiss book out on the fire escape to escape my place. My place bugged me, it was such an old hole.

My building was on West Ninety-seventh Street, and not the great Upper West Side either. They put my building up in the sixties, cheaply, of yellow brick. There must have been some bricks left over from a school or hospital. There wasn't a doorman, just a wall of security glass across the front. It's so you can go down and see who's there and not let them in. A lot of the interior was left over from whatever it had been before, a tenement building. I mean the wooden stairs and the floors. They had old smells, and the staircase tilted a little going up the five flights to my room.

I tried to fake myself out by giving my place a make-over. I rolled up the wall-sized painting and put it in the closet. It's from this time when Carmen Frankel did feminist art. She'd use household things in her art like women were supposed to use in life, Handi Wipes and rubber gloves. Now it was falling apart and no one ever knew what it was. Also, I bought a new coffee table made from melamine. They make everything from

71

melamine today, it's a miracle laminate. I liked how clean it was, and even. Melamine, you can't even cut it with a knife, they say, but you can.

Taking down the painting left a giant square on the wall I tried to ignore, but I couldn't, so I had to paint that wall.

I was halfway done when the phone rang. It was my mom calling from Phoenix. My parents moved there from Yonkers four years ago for my dad's health and to be near my older brother.

"Jack." Just in her voice I could tell she knew everything. "We heard about the heat. How are you dealing with the heat?"

"I'm O.K.," I said.

"Well, I want you to be careful. They say it's very unhealthy. The ozone readings are at record lows. Or highs. It's supposed to be very bad."

So we had that whole Potemkin village conversation, then my mother said, "Jack, why didn't you call?"

"I've been busy."

"We had to hear from Victor."

"It's been really hot up here, and I'm kind of focused on my place. I'm cleaning up my place."

"We wish you would let us know about such an important decision."

"What decision? I got fired."

"Jack honey, don't say that. You quit."

"Victor's lying."

"Oh Jack."

"I got fired for being bored. It's an occupational hazard of working on the left."

"Jack don't be that way."

Then I didn't say anything, I stared at the brush with paint drying on it, and she said, "Well, your father and I were talking about it, and we both feel it's a good thing," just like your mother. She wanted me to go out there for a few days.

"Things are kind of crazy here right now," I said.

"O.K. All right."

My mom gives in so easy, it's like she's guilty. Like she's covering up something terrible she can't bring herself to tell me but she thinks any minute I'm going to find out and go bughouse.

"I'm going to send you a check for the flight," she said.

Then she put my dad on and he did his best not to sound like he'd picked up the wrong kid from the hospital.

We talked about Stony's campaign, stuff we'd talked about before. Blah blah blah California. Also, my dad was frosted about this speech Stony had given at the University of Chicago. Finally he goes, "Well. What are you thinking?"

"I'm not, I'm painting my apartment."

"That sounds good," he said.

"I better finish up before the fumes kill me."

But I didn't. I put the brush in water and walked over to Strawberry Fields. This time they were all there, though, so I kept going over to the Ramble and walked through there, trying not to cry. My dad sounded so nice on the phone you could tell he was freaked out underneath.

When I got back there was a message on the machine from Burry Quinlan. She'd called me from New Mexico, and her voice was high, it had all this air in it, excitement. She swam right up at me. I thought about her round high breasts painted with lipstick, and I didn't look back, I went into my bedroom to beat off.

Then I thought I should make a little ceremony. Because I liked her. She was smart, you could hear that in her voice. She wasn't just some girl I got fixated on in the library when I wasn't able to read. I mean, you shouldn't beat off with your shoes on. That's degraded. You should honor it a little. They could put that in the international beat-off treaty.

I got my clothes off and pulled down the shades. I put on a blues CD, Joe Turner, and closed the door so you could only hear it muffled. I lay on the bed and said her name a lot and pretended she was crawling on me. You can do that with a pillow. You can press the pillow down on top of your chest and stomach, use a sheet to bind it a little. It's a trick to fool yourself the other person is there. Someday I'll write a whole goddamn manual.

Burry called me back later from a place called Mitchell, or Michael, I'm not sure. She said it was in the woods, a little town, and along with her Zen retreat there was a conference of people learning how to marry rich. There were these gurus of how to meet rich men and marry them, rich women too, in the next campground. The people in Burry's camp were called pilgrims. They were in little cottages and not supposed to use phones or makeup or spend any money, but a lot of people broke the rules and crept out to pay phones between sessions. Zen teaching allows you to lie, she said. Or it accepts that you lie.

So it was just like old times, she could be a flake and serious all at once.

Then she said, "Jack, I want to see you when I come back."

"O.K.," I said.

"Just O.K.?"

"The feeling's mutual."

"Say, me too," she said.

"Me too."

"That's better. Now, I'm flying into Kennedy on Friday—"

She gave me her flight number and wanted me to pick her up. Immediately I started thinking about the cab and dinner. It's a long ride from Kennedy. Victor had never paid me very much, thirty-two-five, and now I was spending down the three thousand dollars I'd managed to save. Plus the check my mother would send me for the flight. Call it $329. My mom would look up the fare and send me the exact amount, with perfect penmanship.

"Jack, there's something else," Burry said. "We're doing

74

deep work here, and my unconscious is supposed to be clear like a cloud."

"Your unconscious," I said.

"My unconscious. Jack, don't be a New York primitive. Like a thin white cloud against the sky, and all I can think about is those pictures he took, Morgan."

"Fuck him," I said.

"I know," she said. "I can't. I can't put it out of my head. What if he sells them to the papers. You know how hostile people are to Father."

"Burry, who's Blake's father?"

"Blake's father"—she stopped as though I were some kind of moron—"Blackie. Blackie Roberts. He's one of our oldest friends. The writer."

"William Roberts?"

"Everyone calls him Blackie. Now Jack, can you just do me this favor."

She wanted me to get the rest of the pictures from Morgan, the actual negatives. She had talked to James Doyle, he said that was the wisest course.

"Why doesn't James pick them up?" I said.

"Jack, you've worked in politics, you know about this kind of thing."

"It would look awful if it got out."

"Right."

It seemed almost funny till the next day when James sent over the money. The buzzer rang and this guy in turquoise bike shorts came up holding the front wheel of his bicycle, a black guy with little round filmmaker glasses, his hair in buckwheat twists. At the Center we never used messengers, we used interns. My dad can give you the whole theory behind it. If the rich could only arrange it, my dad says, they'd have other people shit for them. But there I go, quoting my dad. Fuck my dad.

When he left I ripped the envelope and a hard stack of twenties fell out with a fax twisted around it like a diaper. The fax was from George Sides to James, or maybe the other way round, and had Morgan's phone number on it. It's twelve hundred dollars for negatives, the fax said. Sixty twenties. You can't look at that much money without feeling like a complete sellout.

I met Morgan at 6:00 on Friday on my way to the airport. He told me to come to the federal courthouse. There was a jury out and he was in on the press stakeout.

It reached 100 that day, and people avoided the streets. Water ran hot from the tap, I mean even the cold water, and you saw pigeons hunched in the shadows looking half-cooked. Their red eyes were stary, and the garbage stink from the night before hung in the air outside the Tex-Mex restaurants on Amsterdam.

At the courthouse all these photographers and reporters were gathered in a swarm at the top of the steps. It was an insider-trading case, Bertram Corso. They were just waiting around, and a lot of them were unshaved. I'm not very romantic about the press. You saw the magnificent courthouse and then this pack of mercenaries lounging around on the marble, sprawled on the steps, peeling ice cream sandwiches and setting their cans of diet Pepsi by the columns. I remembered the way Stony used to look out the bus window and say, What a pack of hyenas, or, What a pack of carrion dogs.

I stood on the sidewalk looking at the reporters draped around the columns like broken desperadoes with their self-invented romance, and then Morgan separated himself and came down.

"Hey," he said. He didn't shake hands, just nodded. I'm never sure when you're not supposed to shake hands. In the Walker campaign we often hugged each other.

He walked over to the granite block by the side of the stairs and began feeling in his coat pocket. It was the same rust-colored coat he had on the other night, despite the temperature, and the lining was busted. You could see his hand moving through the side of the coat. Under that he wore a white T-shirt, and black jeans. He was very pale, and his unshaven cheeks were dark, spotty, his long hair was lank and unwashed. You could see little lagoonlike places his beard didn't grow, but you couldn't see his eyes. His skin there was dark and creasy.

All at once Morgan got up and lifted his camera from his neck. A homeless guy was walking by, bent over, with a big plastic bag of cans on his shoulder. The man had been sleeping in the dirt. His body was reddish and wormlike, his clothes were like a worm skin.

"Don't move," Morgan said to me.

He was up to his old tricks, trying to put me in the picture. Fuck you, I said to myself, and sat on the steps.

Then Morgan sat down, too.

"Fucking homeless," he said.

"Do you ever think about it and then decide, No thanks, I'm going to respect that person's privacy?" I said.

He dug in the jacket and peered at me. "We're in Foley Square, man."

He'd gotten out an envelope. He held a strip of negatives by its edge close to his face. His eye moved from one image to the other an inch away. The sun was in his eyes, it was going down between the buildings across from us, and he made a face, squinting, an ugly frown, even as he slipped the negatives back into the envelope. It hit me that he didn't like this any more than I did, and I got out a cigarette.

He dropped the envelope on the step.

"You got twelve hundred?"

I gave him the money. "Thanks," he said, but he didn't even count it, just tilted back on the step so he could squeeze it down into his jeans. Then I felt his eyes on me, looking hard at my cigarette.

I held out the pack.

"No thanks. I'm off tobacco," he said. But in the same moment he reached for one. I lit it and he inhaled deep, lung breathing you're not supposed to do. I mean, you're not supposed to smoke, but especially not like that.

It changed his mood. He rested his cigarette hand on his knee. He didn't seem as strange.

"You working for the Secretary?" he said.

"Are you nuts?" I said.

"No offense."

"He's got shitty karma," I said. "People forget the things he said. The way he made excuses for Cambodia."

Morgan took another hit off the cigarette, then in a convulsion withdrew it and flicked it into the street, less than half finished.

"Believe me, that's one guy I could Twelfth Step," he said. "But Burry's all right. Burry's great. If there's anything wrong with her, it's because of him."

I pushed the envelope into my jacket and got to my feet.

"Is that why you follow her?" I said.

He looked up at me. His eyes opened for a second, they were gray and wet.

"I've always taken Burry's picture," he said. "She likes it. In the clubs. At Performance in the Park."

"O.K.," I said, and I felt like an idiot.

"Something bugging you?"

I shook my head. For the first time he seemed halfway sympathetic, but I wasn't going to say anything. Then I felt the envelope in my jacket.

"This picture cost me my job," I said.

"No way—"

I nodded. "Just about. I worked for a public-interest firm. They take that kind of thing seriously, the homeless."

I felt self-conscious. I sat back down and looked at the square for a minute, I tried to sort everything out.

"No one else would understand this, but everything is like a statement of purpose to them," I said. "Even little things like where you buy your clothes. What kind of tie you wear. It's everyone's business. After that picture, I don't know, it wasn't just the picture, I'd reached a crossing in the road. So I quit, or I got fired. The picture didn't help."

"Sorry." His voice croaked like a rusted bolt giving way.

"It doesn't matter now," I said. "Actually, if you really want to know, I probably quit a minute before they were going to fire me."

For some reason I felt a lot better saying all that. I hadn't told anyone the story and I felt a little swoony, or that I might start to cry. I lit another cigarette. Morgan had another, too, and we sat there smoking in silence.

"Well listen, Jack," he said. "Quinlan hires left-wing smart guys."

"They're all sells," I said.

He laughed in his croaking way then he did the same violent thing with his unfinished cigarette. He watched it roll along the street. He was quiet for a second, then he turned to me. He had a queasy expression.

"Tell me something, you go to parties on Fifth Avenue?"

"No."

"Because if you ever do, I'd really like to go inside. Just to chronicle. Look, here's my card—"

"I don't go to those places," I said.

"But if you ever do—"

"But I don't."

I got to my feet again. He rose, too, and stood there with a creased white card sticking out. Finally I took it. Morgan was the only name on it, in fancy bullshit letters, like a fashion photographer's. I guess in that business people go by one name, Kalinka, Dede, pidgin names like that, I mean it's not a real verbal culture. And under Morgan was a phone number in red ink, applied with a rubber stamp.

"Just to say something honestly for once," he said.

"O.K."

But what is honest, who is honest? Who doesn't say they're honest? I didn't say any of that, I went away. We still didn't shake hands, and he went up the steps two at a time. His jeans were too long, they made heavy folds around his black sneakers, and then he disappeared into the crowd.

At Kennedy I almost didn't recognize Burry. You'd think after her retreat she'd be spiritual, but in fact she had on a black miniskirt and a black low-cut jacket and a lot of dark eye makeup. Her hair hung down in that hard red fringe. She looked a little like Elvis in henna.

When she saw me she ran up and it was like a naked dream, you're naked at Kennedy Airport. People were looking at us. I tried to shake her hand, but she threw herself onto me and kissed me. "Jack, I have a secret," she said.

"What?"

"You have to wait."

It was nine o'clock but so hot we had all the cab windows open, and air swirled around us like water. A blind spirit fell on me. The whole way we weren't talking, just making out in darkness. She was hungry against my face, making me dizzy. I tasted her tongue and her lips, and she undid me, darting into my mouth like a crazy fish that knows where to find its food. Her spit was sweet.

We came to the toll and I held her head with both hands, I lifted her away from me. Her mascara was smeared and her lips were fat from my biting them.

"Now tell me," I said.

"Then it won't be a secret."

"Burry, I just did you a giant favor." I put the negatives in her lap. "This was blood."

"Wait till we're in the city."

The tires howled on the open steel grids of the bridge and

the car sailed a little from side to side. She sat back in the corner, she got perfect posture and tugged her feet into her lap in a whole position like Allen Ginsberg, and that is how we arrived in Manhattan.

"How would you feel to know I'm pregnant?" she said.

"Burry," I said.

She was gazing at me. "I've got life inside me."

"But we didn't—"

Her eyes swelled with hurt, and I stopped.

"We did a lot," she said.

"But we didn't what you wouldn't do."

"We mingled, Jack."

"Not fluids."

"Oh, you're awful—"

"Have you done tests?"

"I know my body. It only takes one. I smushed them around. They know where to go. She knew."

"She."

"That's something else I'm feeling."

"Burry you're shitting me," I said. "That's nuts. Biologically. Emotionally."

She collapsed a little, she dropped her feet to the floor.

"You were shitting me, weren't you?" I said.

But she didn't answer, she turned and reached for her bag. The cab glided down Lexington through the Eighties then took a right. There were trees up and down the block, it was one of those secret Manhattan blocks, hideaway blocks. The cab stopped in front of a small building, and a doorman appeared in the window of the brass door, a guy with white gloves on and a blue jacket, but not dark blue, robin's-egg, powdery blue. It felt completely secret, like a fairy tale.

She got the car door open and lingered a second, fixing her bruised mouth with makeup.

"Burry, where did you get your name?" I said.

"I'm not talking to you."

She got out, and the doorman held the door for her. Just like that she was gone.

"Second stop?"

I looked up. The cabbie was African, and very black. The cab was so clean. It smelled good, as if he sprayed it with something. He wore a short-sleeved white shirt and his thick bluish-black forearms were nicely shaped.

"No," I said.

The meter said $33. I balanced two twenties on the front seat. He lifted them off one by one.

"Where are you from?" I said.

"Ghana."

"Abidjan."

"You thinking about Ivory Coast. Abidjan is Ivory Coast. I'm from Accra."

"Oh Accra. Right. I forget. Accra is the capital of Ghana."

"How you know about Accra, man—" He found my eyes in the rearview mirror. "Huh? What you know about Accra?"

"I know. I know where it is."

He laughed and held the change up over the seat, but I waved it off.

Epaulets, that's what the doorman had on his jacket. What are the politics of epaulets? He was giving Burry her mail and her dry cleaning, piling her arms. She turned and wordlessly handed the clothes to me.

The lobby was Deco. There were inlaid mahogany panels that had mermaids in goggles riding seahorses, and between the panels were strips of dull silvery nickel. Everything was understated and secret. The rich are great at keeping secrets. My dad talks about that. He's almost bitter about it. Only the powerful are good at keeping secrets, he says. It's the reason men don't gossip and women do, the power issue, and the reason the Irish are good writers, because they're an occupied country. Also, it's the genius of the First Amendment: establishing an independent reward path blah blah blah. There I go, being a tub-thumper.

The elevator was more of the same, mahogany and nickel. Burry pushed 14 and a letter fell from her hand.

"Berenice Quinlan," I said, picking it up.

She pulled it back.

"Are we fighting?" I said.

"You fight everything."

"Burry you were testing me."

"If I was, you failed."

The elevator stopped and you came out into an old rich apartment building with worn Oriental runners on the floors and prints on the wall, birds, Audubon, Grebe and Loon and Pileated this, those gentleman-type birds from the secret private America.

"Have you ever let yourself have a fantasy with someone?" she said. "Romance is a shared fantasy, that's all it is."

"But what if it's not my fantasy?"

"You're so literal. You know that, baby? It's like a prison you're in. If you're going to love me you have to break out."

Well, that was the first time anyone had said anything about love.

"O.K.," I said.

She had stopped at the last door on the hall. She got out her keys and opened the door, then paused with her hand on the knob as if deciding whether she was going to let me in. Finally she shouldered it with a little sigh.

"Father uses this apartment as his legal residence. He keeps an office here."

Father. She swung the door all the way and hit the light.

You came into a little anteroom and after that a small rugless hallway with photographs, maybe forty photographs in all, hung on both walls, in frames, etcetera, and every one of them of the Secretary. Burry stood watching me, and I went down one wall and up the other, like a museum, which it was. There was history in the pictures, famous politicians. Antoine Amos, the Harlem congressman, was in one picture, and Pat "Kicker" Carlson. Big liberals, I mean. And in all the pictures the Secretary had this act, with his eyebrows and mouth, like, Hit the loo, where you wouldn't have known he was from Schenectady.

For instance, he was dressed in tails and balanced on one foot as he poked a long black umbrella toward the sky over a castle. The umbrella was open, as if he might fly away.

"The royal wedding," Burry said. "Father was ambassador."

Burry was in a few pictures, but there wasn't really room for her. The Secretary had this image that worked, a myth or a belief about himself that he seemed to carry with him even in the most private moments. Even when Robert Kennedy was killed, he was the Secretary. In that picture, Quinlan sat at a table, slumping away, with a bruised expression almost like someone had beaten him up. His thick black hair rose in spikes, and there were newspapers with black headlines and a glass, too, a little heavy glass. You could see the famous scar across his lip.

The next picture over, the Secretary and two other guys sat on horses. The Secretary held a Panama hat against his horse's neck, and they were on a hill in the tropics somewhere with tropical trees and big raggedy leaves hanging down and in the background a bay.

Fidel was on the next horse. Fidel held himself up by grabbing a long hank of the horse's mane. He was wearing his hat. I guess he's got a myth going, too, even bigger. The third guy was built wide, with a big mustache and a familiar face.

"Márquez," Burry said.

The rest of the apartment was halfway normal. I mean, it was almost poor. The living room had all this Danish modern furniture, but dinged up, like it had come from someone's

84

house. A door led off it to the Secretary's office, and at the far end of the room, down three steps like a swimming pool, was Burry's room.

I felt comfortable there. The walls were painted cream-of-tomato and all this misspent-youth shit lay around that you could relate to, a frayed Navajo rug on the floor and a low sofa coming apart with a paisley throw over it. The only new things were a clock by the bed and a large black television set, and the top of the TV was peopled with darkened metal African figures. I mean, I know global-pillage girls like that, with politically correct clutter. I sat down on the bed.

Burry left the room, and I tried to get the Secretary out of my mind. It bugged me that so many liberals were friends of his. They didn't seem to hold it against him that he was a political hack with shifting beliefs. Nothing succeeds like success. My dad always says that, with a ton of irony.

She came back with a bottle of wine, and we drank from the same glass and she lit incense in a clay pot, also candles. The fight was done. She showed me a prayer position she'd learned in New Mexico and put on a tape of spiritual music, I want to say Egyptian, because there was that thudding one-stringed instrument you hear in jazz sometimes. An oud. I think it's an oud.

A dull chant began, then a high, high voice. We made out a lot and Burry did another show on the bed. She stripped to black underwear and dripped oil on herself and rubbed it in in slow circles, not worrying about it going on the bed or on her bra. Where a lot of girls would worry about spilling oil on the bed. In their head they'd already be throwing those sheets in the hamper. A candle flame reflected perfectly on her thigh as if it were burning inside, and the voice on the tape was high and faraway, almost not like a person.

Burry did other dances and dipped over me. I did like always, I beat off, and she made shit up. She pushed her hands down

85

her hips so the underpants twisted into a hard bumpy cord across her long white thighs, except the middle, the stretched square she kept as a screen over her pussy.

The tease made me hungry and hollow, and angry. Why should I be the monkey?

I pulled at her crouched ankles till she lost her balance and sank on my face. The stretchy middle of the underpants gigged on my nose with all of her inside it, like the diary of her body. It flattened across my mouth and nose, but I licked right through it till she unsnagged it. She stretched it out of my way, snapping the binding back over my head like a backwards doctor's mask, and there she was.

I was there, too, walled by her thighs. Walls, shaggy vine, flower, salt, all that upside-down familiar world. I mean a familiar place instead of that goddamn hallway.

The door slammed and I woke up. Morning. Burry was asleep. The Secretary had come back. I thought of how I'd introduce myself and did you call him Secretary or Ambassador?

There was a knock on Burry's door, and before I could say anything James Doyle came in. "Hello, lovebirds," he said.

He had all his shit with him, papers and a cup of coffee, and he lifted the armchair with one hand and turned it away from the bed to give us quote-unquote privacy. He was just going about his business. He put his coffee on top of the TV, he ripped open an overnight envelope and sat down.

"What are you, some geek?" I said.

He slid a videotape from the envelope. "I'm dogshit, remember?"

"Hi James," Burry said.

"Morning dollface."

"He walked right in," I said.

"I knocked," he said.

Burry sat up. "James gets to use the office."

I got my jeans on and went past him to the bathroom. You could smell aftershave on him, and he had on Saturday gear, khaki pants and a white dress shirt with the collar not buttoned.

"Jack, I'm sorry," he said. "But this is the Secretary's television." He put on this whole explainy voice. "And I get mail here."

It was 8:30 and hot already. I put my head under the faucet and ran cold water through my hair. I brushed using Burry's toothbrush. When I came out, the TV was going and they were both watching. Burry sat on the bed. She had a fierce focused expression I'd never seen.

It was an ad for Joseph Vacca, Jr., and it was cheap. He didn't have a whole lot of money. The screen filled with a still, black-and-white image of Vacca that the camera went closer and closer on while this woman's voice told you all about everything he'd done, his achievements busting up the mob and violent criminals and drug traffic. "Joseph Vacca, Jr., was there for you," she'd say after each achievement, and then the camera closed in further on his big soulful eyes and long melancholy face. As if he really were there, right in the room.

I'd followed Joseph Vacca at the Center when he was attorney general. We'd done press releases about him every time he ran roughshod over someone's civil liberties. Burry said I was primitive, Vacca was straight out of El Greco, an itchy righteous man who was always talking about how he almost entered the seminary in Buffalo.

The camera went all the way in on Vacca's wet eyes.

"When high-flying real-estate developers bribed state highway officials at a four-star New York steak house, Joseph Vacca, Jr., was there for you."

"Four-star New York steak house!" Burry laughed.

Then the screen went black, and the voice said, "Good old Early Quinlan. When was he ever there for you?"

"Oh boy, I'm so afraid," Burry said.

James held up his hand. It wasn't over. You heard a crackling noise, then the spooling of metal on glass before the pouring came, ice shifting in a glass, etcetera. So just like that it turned into an attack ad about drinking.

"Oh God, please," Burry said. "James, turn that off."

James shut off the television. He bent to free the tape. Burry tightened the sheet over her tits and moved around the room, the sheet trailing behind her like a Greek play.

"They can't say that. Can they, James? That's illegal. It's a slander."

She was really upset. James turned the chair back toward the room then bent and flicked a speck of something off his shoe. He dusted his pants, too, with the side of his hand and frowned at Burry's furniture. Finally he looked up.

"They won't air it. They just want some useful idiot to write about it. Put the issue in play."

"But it's a lie, James. A bloody lie."

"I know."

She looked at me. "Jack, they can't say that."

"I don't know, he's a public figure," I said.

Burry wailed. She pushed her free hand through her hair, and I saw where her armpits weren't shaved. The hair there was dark red, pretty. Just wait till James got a hold of them.

I walked out of the room.

"See, this is why we have to keep a clean nose," James said.

"I am." But her voice ran up defensively.

To get to the kitchen I had to go back through the Father gallery, the whole reeducation center. Then the kitchen was big and prewar, with yellow wooden cabinets and red Formica countertops. I made coffee and stood next to a window with a truncated view of the park. On the wall were framed official photographs of the five Presidents under whom Quinlan had served. I looked from one to the other, reading their dates, and my mind went in a circle.

Am I a sell for being almost in love with her? How did everything start for the Secretary? When did he start believing

88

that bullshit myth about himself, was there a moment when he got to choose, and did Fidel and the Royal Wedding all come from that one choice?

James was talking Burry down. They came out of the bedroom having the same discussion and then he stuck his head in the kitchen. He hugged the doorjamb a second.

"Hey, listen, Jack, thank you—" He held up the envelope with the negatives.

"Those were for Burry."

"It's O.K., it's all family."

He smacked the wall and went out.

"I just worry what he'll try next," Burry was saying.

"Don't. This guy's a human sacrifice. He's praying for 44 percent so they make him attorney general. More likely he hits 35 and he's ambassador to Zambeziland."

"Has Father seen it?"

"No."

"Well please don't show it to him. It will upset him. Character assassination upsets him." Then the door shut.

8

On Monday there was this thing at the New School called Lessons of the Walker Campaign that Ralph Lopez said Stony wasn't happy about. He didn't like the setup or the panel so he wasn't going, still he wanted some forceful advocates on hand. Victor Bandy might be there, but I didn't give a shit, I went downtown. As it turned out Victor didn't show.

The panelists were mostly writers. Stony always used to say, Be careful when you bring in a writer. A writer is for himself in his words, words are his only way of getting laid. They're not that good-looking so it's in what they say that they try and stand out. The two younger writers wore their shirts open, and they got tied up over the decision we'd made in California to distance ourselves from Gayza Pekhrun, the immigrant activist who'd made this speech decrying white patriarchal culture. I'd been in on the decision, which was an obvious one, but I didn't say anything. Ralph stood up next to me and regretfully explained it. I knew what he was going to say already, I just zoned out.

There was one good speaker, former U.S. Attorney General Del McLean. He didn't say much. He has a dry white round head that sits on his unmoving shoulders like a stone on top of a wall. He writes books about New York history, and he knows my dad from the McGovern campaign. Every once in a while the moderator would lean over and say, "Del—" Then McLean would make a little stammering noise and say something.

"There will always be the problem of self-interest," he said in a dry voice. "The lesson is not to pretend it isn't there but to honor it and give it its proper place. That's the goddamn trick."

Then the rest of them would just get going again about the tide of history going our way, i.e., which of us is going to get laid . . .

Afterward I went up to Del and reintroduced myself. He was nice. He started going about how smart my dad is, and I made a lunch date with him. I needed to find a job, and he's completely upright and inspiring and also has a shitload of contacts. He said the day after tomorrow at this coffee shop he said he always goes to.

When I got back to my place there was an invitation to a cocktail party Friday night at Simi Winfrey's. It was fancy. A stiff cream-colored card where you can feel the printing from the back. And at the bottom it had French. *"Tenue de Canotier,"* whatever that means. I'd ask Burry. Then over in the left-hand corner it said "RSVP Edward," and gave a number at *Follies*.

Edward. Not Edward Jones, or Edward Arlington Robinson, just Edward. Well, that was a dick in the ass for Edward.

Upstairs there was a message from Burry. Her voice was scratchy, panicky. "Jack? Jack? Jack, I'm headed out of town for a week or so. It's the best thing. I'll call you later."

You could almost hear her walking around her apartment shoveling things into a bag in her last free hour like Ingrid Bergman or something. I called back but there was just her machine, and on the machine she said, "I'll be out of the country till the twenty-fifth."

91

Was it out of the country or out of town? A week or eleven days? Those were real discrepancies. I called Quinlan headquarters and asked for James Doyle. But they put me on hold for a year, then the same one got back on and said, "We'll have to return." I.e., kiss my ass.

I tried James three more times that afternoon. Because he was at the bottom of it, you just knew. But each time he was busy, and the last time I just hung up.

It got dark with no one calling me back, and I went to dinner at this Hunan place I go to on Broadway. I'm like royalty there. They call me Mr. Jack and they try and give me a table on the street, they're always giving me free food, sesame noodles or a drink. I'd just sat down when I had a whole epiphany. The situation came to me a different way. Burry wasn't going under her own power, and meanwhile here I was sitting and waiting for the phone to ring. But take a human-rights case. You'd never do that. You're pro-active, you develop information, contacts, etcetera.

I walked out and flagged a cab, and the whole way to her place I was rehearsing how to talk to the doorman. The doorman would know where she was.

It was the same guy from before, in epaulets and that powder-blue costume. He was dapper and held himself up straight like a Polish movie actor. He was very handsome, only his neck was too skinny in the shirt collar. It came out like a stick, with a giant Communist-bloc-type Adam's apple.

"Excuse me, sir." I shook his hand. "I am friends with Miss Quinlan."

"Barry?"

"Miss Quinlan and I are very good friends."

"Barry went away."

"I know. She told me. Now, it's very important for me to get in touch with her."

"Barry is not here." He kept pronouncing it Barry.

"I'm sorry but I have to get the number, please—she said she left a number."

The color rose in his cheeks. "I am sorry, my friend."

I probably leaned too close. "Tell me where she is—"

He squeezed his little white gloves in the air at his chest, little beseeching fists, then he opened them, the fingers spread and helpless.

"Indonesia?" he said.

I walked back to my place through Central Park. My shirt was sweated through, and I realized I'd got it all wrong. It wasn't like we were equals in his mind, so I'd only managed to scare the guy. Where are your social skills, Jack? Don't you have any social skills? I had that whole conversation with myself, running myself down.

Burry still didn't call and the next day I met Del McLean at the diner he goes to every day right off Washington Square. He was all flirty with the waitress, but he didn't say much to me, mostly listened. He squinted at me and nodded. He's from North Carolina so his manner is slower, not so talky.

I told Del everything. I told him about the work I'd done for Stony and the truth about the Gayza Pekhrun affair, which he agreed with, then I told him about the photographer Morgan and the cake and Victor's reaction. The whole time he didn't ever change expression, just nodded now and then. I told him about George Sides and about all the pictures in Burry's place, and how Early Quinlan acted like such a huge success even if he never stood for anything that mattered.

Finally Del sat back. "All right, Jack. What's next?"

"Well, I need to get a job," I said.

"Good. Why not work as a waiter," he said. "Do an honest job at something you can feel good and true about."

"It doesn't pay," I said.

93

"What's important?" he said.

"In all honesty I'd like to be free at night," I said. Immediately I felt shitty about saying "in all honesty." Liars say that. The same with anyone who says "frankly."

Del made a sound in his throat. "Jack this is the truest thing I can do for you." He licked his thumb and tore a sheet out of the back of his little date book. He set it down on the table and wrote something out on it with his trembly hand.

I kept thinking it was going to be someone's phone number. But it was a poem, a really short one by Emily Dickinson. I guess all her poems are short. I read it a couple of times, I nodded the way you do after you read a poem. Then I folded it twice and later I couldn't find it. All I remembered was it was written to a lad in Athens and the last line was about perjury. Del probably picked it up in a book of poems for lawyers.

"Thanks," I said.

"That's gold, Jack," he said. "Gold from the gods."

"I thought you might know someone who was hiring," I said.

He pushed his plate to the edge of the table, impatient and arthritic. "I really can't say where you should take a law job right now, Jack. Not the way you feel about law."

We hadn't even talked about law.

"The law's a screwy profession," he said. "It's a lot easier to do bad work than good. It's very easy to do work you end up wishing you hadn't."

I felt like hell, and we stood up in that silence. He got the check, he slapped his hand down and wouldn't let me pay, and he left three quarters on the table for the waitress. I put another dollar down. You have to do that with these old skinflint leftists who talk about values all the time.

Outside he was chipper as hell, and in the sun I saw where he had a little scarf of hair on his neck. He'd probably missed it shaving a whole week in a row for it to get that long.

"What a day," he said, squinting up at the sky. "Goddamn, what a day."

Clapping his hands, sighing. I thought he was going to get going about God next, so I said goodbye and thanks. He gave me a long firm handshake.

As soon as I walked away I thought of all these things I should have told Del. I wanted to tell him that on the left people always said anybody successful was actually a giant failure. I could argue that about anybody. I could tell you why Leonard Bernstein was a fraud, or why William Roberts is a giant failure. Even Sandy Koufax. Sandy Koufax is completely overrated. Blah blah blah. And was that right?

James Doyle called me that afternoon.

"Hey, Jack," he said.

"I have to talk to Burry."

"Burry's left town. The papers have it out for her. It couldn't be a more sensitive time. Everyone thought it was best. Myself, the Secretary, Burry herself." It was like he was reading a statement.

"Where is she?"

"Jack—I think this is a need-to-know situation."

"She's in Indonesia."

He laughed a little, then he eased up. He said he might have something for me tomorrow. After that he had to get a dig in. "Frankly, you know you're not much of a team player."

But when I talked to him the next day he said to wait till Simi Winfrey's party. He knew I was going. He was going, too.

As for Burry herself, she'd forgotten about me. I argued that in my mind. I'd line up all the evidence against it, all the things she'd said to me and stuff we'd done in bed, and try to tell myself she was sincere. You can't ever do that. Emotional stuff never adds up. It might have been one little thing you did or said that made them say, I'm never seeing him again. It could be a facial expression. It could be missing a belt loop with your belt. Still, I didn't hear from her.

My mom knows French so I called her about Simi's invitation. I told her I'd met Billie April at a party, and my mom couldn't believe it. You can bullshit your mom. Anyone can do that. My mom gets this whole hushed attitude about New York parties.

She told me to hold on while she looked up that expression, and it meant Clothes of the Boatman. I.e., Dress for sailing. We discussed my outfit. I had some linen shorts I could wear and tennis shoes, I'd put on a white T-shirt but I wouldn't wear a belt. I'd wear a rope, like a French sailor.

Friday afternoon I went downtown and got a blues CD and a new T-shirt for the party. Coming back I sat in the subway reading the *Voice*. It was cool in the subway. The stone was like the wall of an aqueduct. I watched this guy cleaning out the station. He had on rubber boots and carried a long red hose with a brass nozzle, he liked his job. He used the high pressure on rat holes in the wall and hit the platform with soap. He had some sort of lather with lemon ammonia zing to it that cut right through my mood. He cleaned shit out of the corners and had to get down on his knees in places. I guess that's what Del McLean was telling me to do, get a job like that guy in the subway, cleaning the great concourses of the common man.

At Columbus Circle I left the subway and walked home through the park. There was finally some wind. The trees were heavy and fragrant, the leaves, and the branches made groaning sounds in the breeze. I stretched the walk out by going up to the bandshell.

A little crowd was gathered there, and in the bandshell itself guys in uniforms stood in rows with glinting metal. You might have thought it was a band with brass instruments, but when

I came through the trees I saw it was cops, police chiefs, three rows of them with their buckles and guns catching the sunlight. They had a red association banner behind them and out front Joseph Vacca, Jr., was shaking hands with the chief of chiefs. Two photographers were there, and Vacca was holding the shake for them. His fake smile was drying on his teeth in the sun. I guess he'd gotten the cops' endorsement. I stopped by a tree to watch.

The whole thing was pathetic. Vacca had droopy posture and a boneless handshake. I thought of Del McLean's handshake, what a good handshake he had. I tried to feel how good my own was by shaking my own hand. There's this trick. You grip your own left hand, but not the palm, the back of it. You try and make it bony and hard.

After that Vacca gave a speech from index cards. The guy was stiff, and the speech was amplified too loud. It echoed off the bandshell and really lit up the park. It was like a mass rally where they expected a million people in the streets of Munich, but it was just forty hard-core supporters with Vacca buttons and some passersby. I sat down on a flat rock there, I tried to be a team player for once and look at the speech from the Quinlan point of view.

"But if everyone has permission, it follows absolutely that no one has freedom," Vacca said, reading those cards. "Gangster rap and insider trading represent outbreaks of the same pathology. Heedless self-interest is a virus out of control in the blood of a free society. Every part of the body experiences the toxin and suffers."

Before long he'd get going about liver and blockages. That's what paranoids do, use health metaphors when they're talking about social conditions. My dad says that. He's smart about shit like that. It's how paranoids convince themselves that change or dissent is an assault on their person. It's why John Dean said to Nixon, There's a cancer on the presidency. He used the only language a paranoid could understand.

97

"The moral values of Aquinas, of Teilhard de Chardin, of George Washington, they summon conservatives today. They urge us to preserve. They urge us to cleanse. They urge us to hold—"

Vacca thrust his big hands out and mimed the actions. When it came to "hold" he clenched his fingers into fists.

After that there were gifts. A little redheaded aide brought Vacca a brown paper bag from which he lifted a hanging cheese, a fat cheese with rope around it that Vacca gave to the chief of chiefs.

The chiefs had a chief hat for Vacca. A cop in boots from some motorcycle unit presented it and Vacca put it right on. Then Boots saluted Vacca crisply. He snapped his heels together, and Vacca the same, and erect posture for once, like, all right, here are some lessons we can draw from the Nazi experience.

"Fuck this," I said, and got up to go.

I think this fat guy heard me. This fat guy in a coat and tie twisted around, and his face was dark with disapproval. His dark mouth opened as he stared at me. His undershirt rode up past the knot in his tie.

"The man's a fascist," I said.

The guy took his hands from his pockets. "Excuse me?" he said in a loud voice.

"No, excuse me—" I started walking away.

The guy lost it. "This one," he shouted. "This one—watch him."

That set off a whole commotion at the mike. I kept moving, and that guy was going haywire.

"He called Joe a fascist," he said.

He was probably Vacca's father or something, and then Vacca had the microphone and was shading his eyes with his hand to try and see me. "Come forward . . . Come forward." His voice shrieked out over the park.

I went back through the trees and the dappled tree shadow.

There was a path where thick tree roots struggled out onto the ground and went back under. For some weird reason I thought about that dream I'd had during the convention, the one in the cathedral with the people hanging down from the ceiling with their strange grins. Then after a little I came to the grass in the woods. The grass was thick and ample. There was a slope and the grass was long and flattened against the ground like thick hair. Just walking down on that smooth thick grass and through the dappled forest calmed me, and the sweat came. With the forest to myself, maybe not a forest but a stand of trees, I began sweating to beat the band.

9

Simi Winfrey lived in a great marble pile on West End Avenue. It's a historic building, I believe they put it in a movie once, in the seventies. It's white and it has an iron gate almost like a castle. Then you go into the courtyard and there's a circular driveway with uneven cobbles and grass coming up in the dirt between the cobbles. You don't usually get cobbles so uneven here. They have that in France, or Rome, a whole different style. But in America usually the cobbles are even. I know. My grandfather used to sell goods like that, flagstones, and that glazed peanut-brittle stuff people use in their driveway.

I got in a brass birdcage elevator with a gate that made a thrashing sound as it closed. The motor had a well-oiled hum and near the top you could see the skylight in the roof, an old-timey skylight with glass that had wire imbedded in it. You could see right through the elevator ceiling to the wire in the reinforced glass twisted into hexagons, and here and there a little crack and some rust.

As soon as I walked into Simi's I saw that most of the people had completely ignored the Canotier thing, and the ones that had gone with it didn't look anything like me but like they were in an Impressionist painting. They had on nubbly off-white linen trousers and woven leather open-toed shoes. Or they'd have on a fancy loose-knit boating sweater. No one wore shorts, except me. No one looked like they were ready to get into a boat.

Everyone knew each other, and a lot of them were journalists. Not carrion dogs, either, not the ones who lie out on the steps of the courthouse, but fancy ones. The place was crowded, and I tried to stay anonymous till I found some other loser who'd actually want to talk to me without constantly looking over my shoulder. There was a bar with a stiff white tablecloth and a guy in a white jacket, and I got a beer and then went over to the window, looking north. I looked at all the water towers on the horizon, the wooden deals, I tried to count them. Then I moved on to fire escapes.

But then you get into a whole definition thing. What is a fire-escape? What is an outdoor stairway?

Finally I drank enough to where I could walk around. Simi's apartment was big and decoratorish. It had high white walls with a lot of molding at the top and bare wooden floors. Now and then along the walls there were dramatic art objects that were a little useless. For instance, a tall white spike that someone said was a narwhal tusk.

I wandered down the back corridor, and Charles Tharp was standing in a doorway. I recognized his cowlick and those big glossy eyes.

"Charles," I said.

He smiled widely and held out his hand. "Mike," he said.

"No, Jack."

"Oh, Jack, of course. Jack. Burry did that cake thing with you, right."

For the first time it seemed like something I should be proud of.

"Now, why did I forget your name?" he said.

101

"I don't know," I said.

"I don't usually forget people's names. I'm sorry. I'm terrible on faces, but usually I don't forget names."

Then a second later he'd start up all over again. "You don't even look like a Mike, you look like a Jack."

He had his shoulder turned so you couldn't really get past him, and inside someone had on a television. I tried to see what was going on, but Charles stiffened.

"It's just Peter," he said. "He wanted some privacy."

But I heard what was on, that same Vacca ad, and I walked right past him.

Inside, two guys were watching the television. One guy was young and half-sat on the arm of a blue velvet love seat. He looked up amiably as I came in. He was blondish, he wore old jeans and a T-shirt, but fancy shoes. All in all he was dressed as badly as I was, and I felt a wave of gratitude toward him.

The other guy stood right in front of the television. Maybe he was nearsighted. He was sixtyish, his hair went off his large head in a short white bristle all around. He wore the jacket from a dark blue pinstripe suit over new jeans. His hands were shoved sloppily into the back pockets of the jeans. The gnarly palms faced out, and his thumbs hung out, too.

The ad finished, and he made a strangled sound in his throat. "They're going to kill us all," he said.

Charles came in all nervous.

"This is Jack," he said.

The blond guy tilted his head as if trying to place me. "Hello Jack," he said.

The old guy walked right by me, and his leathery old face seemed halfway familiar. Hooded eyes, Indian cheekbones, smoker's wrinkles everywhere. I knew I'd seen him. But he didn't look at anyone, he was frowning and sour.

"If the man had any integrity he'd go to the top of the Chrysler Building with a Mannlicher carbine," he said.

"Exactly," Charles said.

"I don't know if I'd call that integrity," the blond said.

"In a certain way you would," Charles said. "Integrity to his anger."

"But in a certain way I wouldn't," the blond guy said.

The older man had found the makeshift bar on Simi's desk. There were bottles and glasses, and a hammered silver ice bucket, and off to the side was Simi's girl-reporter gear, three fat fountain pens and an old-fashioned black telephone.

He made an absent clumsy effort sorting out bottles and then Simi walked in, followed by a dog with a red ribbon around its neck.

She'd completely ignored her own dress code. She wore a glamorous outfit, a tunic and pants of dark brown silk with a rich silent pattern in it and big dark brown buttons. It was cut like sexy pajamas.

"Jack—" She hugged me. Her face was white and powdery. "Now, what are you wearing?"

"Tenue."

Simi and Charles laughed.

"The invitation said Tenue," I said.

"But what's this?" Simi said.

"Sailors wear ropes," the blond guy said.

"That's pirates," Simi said.

"I'd agree with my hostess," Charles said, the oily bunny.

The blond guy squinted at me. "Do I know you?" he said.

"This is Jack," Simi said. "He works for Stony Walker."

"Worked," Charles said.

"Jack, this is Peter Sisley," she said. "You already know Charles. And did you meet William? This is William Roberts."

The old guy nodded and I did the same back. So just like that I'd met William Roberts. But even if you wanted to practice your handshake with him you couldn't, he stood there with his drink.

Peter slid off the couch arm and went to the VCR for the tape. He was tall and handsome with good ruddy skin.

103

"What have you been watching?" Simi said.

He glanced at the tape. "Gorgeous models drop their undies for you."

"I know, you've been watching that ad," she said.

"Hell I thought nobody knew about this," Roberts said.

"Generally speaking they don't," Peter said.

"Well Miss Winfrey is notoriously indiscreet."

Simi jerked as if a spear had hit her.

"Blackie!" she said.

Charles took a step toward Roberts. "It's widely known," he said.

"It's better that way"—Peter waved his hand, improvising—"You take out the competitive part. You make it an honor-among-thieves game theory situation so no one writes anything."

He had an even, chipper voice, and William Roberts stared at him trying to figure out whether he was bullshitting. But you couldn't tell and Roberts turned away. He stood there with his drink at his side. The dog snuffled his crotch, but he didn't notice. I think he was plowed, or well on his way.

The dog began nosing the drink.

"No, Rodrigo," Simi said.

Roberts looked down and pushed the dog's head away. It was a pretty dog. Its head was dark brown but its fur was gray and sheeplike, with darkish spots.

"Rodrigo wants some vodka," Peter said.

"This isn't vodka," Roberts said, lifting the drink. "We call this a silver loudmouth. I wager you've never heard of a silver loudmouth."

"No," Peter said.

"It's a martini. I wager you couldn't mix a martini."

"I stick to what I know. Vodka and Valium."

I liked Peter. Everything he said was making fun without Roberts fully comprehending it, and meanwhile everyone else was kissing the guy's ass. After that Peter went to the bar and dumped the nuts out of a nut bowl onto Simi's desk and mixed a Bloody Mary in the bowl. Simi cried out a lot but she didn't do anything. He made it complete with two bread sticks and put it down in the middle of the room.

Roberts watched balefully, then he looked up at Simi. "Do you intend to hunt with this dog?"

"Blackie, hush," she said.

"Well, I bought him for his lines and you're getting off on the wrong foot if you expect him to track quail," etcetera.

The dog nosed the drink then, glancing at Roberts, withdrew a bread stick and dropped it on the floor. You know when a dog knows he's being watched. He's on his best behavior, he doesn't wolf his food, he looks at you from the corner of his eye. He made a little helpless sound then broke the bread stick up and ate it. Everyone was curious what he'd do. Same as in movies: just put a dog in it and everyone watches it. Then he nuzzled the drink, began lapping lightly at its surface.

William Roberts made another strangly noise in his throat and walked out. Simi went after him. The dog left, too. Charles picked up the bowl. He frowned and dropped it on the bar.

"You sure know how to kill a party," he said accusingly.

Peter sighed and sat back down. "That old wreck bugs me. Our families had summer houses in the same WASP ghetto so he always acts like we have writer's block together."

"Listen, whose dog is that?"

"Blackie gave it to her. It's supposed to be a giant secret."

"Of course." Charles nodded solemnly. "I guess they met when she did that thing about American heroes for *Follies*."

"I guess."

James Doyle came to the door. He just stood there. He wore a dark suit, and he held his head back, you couldn't see his eyes.

"Hello, James," Peter said.

James stared at him. "What's that shit on your teeth?"

Peter touched his mouth.

"You've got shit on your teeth," James said.

Peter flushed. "Oh go away," he said.

"You're drunk," James said.

"You know the government could use someone with your talents," Peter said. "Can you smell pot through Samsonite? I can get you a job at Kennedy."

Charles laughed, but James brushed by him and fooled among the bottles. He opened a fresh liter bottle of Coke. He ignored the already opened Coke that was there. Just like Lyndon Johnson. In one of the memoirs he's always opening a fresh bottle of seltzer even after he opened one for the last drink.

"How many people know about this ad?" he said quietly.

"James, I just fed the press a better story," Peter said. "I gave them that Vacca item they're going wild for."

James walked over and took the videotape. He tucked it inside his jacket.

"Look no one will go near this," Peter went on. "They all like Early too much. The *Times* won't touch it."

Charles stood up straight. He folded his arms. "There will be times when someone's private behavior reflects on their fitness for office," he said.

"See. Charles won't touch this with a ten-foot pole."

Charles coughed. "It's not clear that in this instance we've actually crossed the line."

But James had moved on. He stared at my outfit, then he turned to Peter. "Look, don't be a jerk and push our luck," he said. "I have enough to worry about. I have to worry about this joker getting Burry in the papers—"

He reached for my arm, but I stepped away.

"Get off my cloud," I said.

Peter yelped and smacked the couch. "Now I know where I saw you. You were in the park. You called Vacca a fascist and he flipped."

"Was that you?" James said.

I shook my head.

106

"I'm sure it was you—you were under a tree," Peter said, hugging his knee. "Oh this is good, this is priceless."

"Jack, was that you?" Charles said. "I think you should come forward. We're mentioning Vacca's obscene gesture in the paper tomorrow."

They were all looking at me, and I went to the bar and poured a vodka.

"Peter, where's Burry?" I said. "Do you know where she is?"

He looked at me then at James. "I think she's at Rennie's," he said. "Isn't that where she is. James, where's Burry?"

James only sipped from his Coke.

Peter waved at him. "See, he doesn't drink, he's proud of that. But he's drunk on power."

It was the first time I'd seen James embarrassed. The muscles tightened in his jaw, they bunched under the skin.

"I'm about to give him her number," he said.

But Peter was right, James was sadistic, and I walked out of the room. I was going to leave but then I got mixed up on hallways and instead of going out I ended up in the bedroom. William Roberts was there. He was staring at a picture and feeling blindly at his jacket pockets. He didn't notice me.

That was the first time I thought about his books. People said he was washed up, but you could never take that first novel away from him, the sharecroppers one, *Blood's Tale*, what it had done for civil rights. My mom bought two copies, which she never did, bought new books, and I carried one around for weeks. I don't think I read it, just cried a lot through the red clay and lynching sagas. Years later I learned about the controversy over Roberts's work, the freedom he took with facts and other people's material. But so what, he'd helped move a nation.

"Blackie"—

I was just trying out that name. The creased face turned. "Here—" I held out my cigarettes.

"Oh thanks."

Then lighting a match for him, etcetera.

"Mother well?" he said.

"My mother," I said.

He tapped the glass with his thick thumb. "Motherwell."

"Oh." I went up to it. A yellow map, Uruguay maybe, with red crayoning on it. "I think so," I said.

Blackie shook his head. "All the praise and money a body could want, but what a deeply lonely man," he said.

"So I've heard."

It got to be 9:30 and no one had left the party, myself included. Simi held court in the living room. She lay across the couch with three or four guys around her and her white belly showing through the loose tunic. One guy basted her forehead with an ice cube. The water melted her makeup so the lines showed and she seemed brittle, but she had a hectic sway over men. Because later another guy massaged her foot.

I had another vodka and rehearsed what I'd do if James came up.

Hey pal, I have nothing to say, and walk away.

Me and you have nothing to . . .

James, if I wanted a go-between, believe me I'd find someone decent. Then the same, walk away.

The door buzzed and a guy in soggy kitchen whites came in carrying a carton filled with cups of coffee. He was from the Greek place on Broadway, Simi had ordered what she called room service. That's what Del McLean said I should do, serve people honest food instead of lying about knowing Robert Motherwell and sucking up to burnt-out writers.

I decided to sober up, I took a cup of coffee. I went to the kitchen for milk, and when I closed the fridge James was there.

"James, give me the number," I said.

He stood back. "Someone didn't go to charm school."

"Fuck charm school," I said. "Charming's lying."

"Calm down. I have her number for you."

Then he leaned against the counter, watching me, and I felt dizzy. I'd drunk too much. I drank down half the coffee then went to the sink and washed my face. I pushed my hair back wet.

"Listen, Jack, you and me have to talk," he said. "Was that you in the park? With Vacca?"

"Forget it."

He felt in his jacket and got out a slim fountain pen then patted his pockets for a piece of paper.

"Jack, talk to me," he said. "Listen, you and me have already broken our plates with each other."

He looked at me, and for the first time he seemed halfway genuine even if you did see his tongue when he talked. It touched his lips, it moved around.

"I was just walking by," I said.

"O.K. Good."

"I didn't plan it, and I didn't see any obscene gesture."

"He did this"—James frisked his fingers against his throat. "Now Peter says Vacca didn't see you."

"I don't know. The sun was in his eyes."

"How far away were you?"

"Fuck you, give me the number."

He went to the refrigerator for something to write on and reached around on top. There were bottles of good olive oil that he pushed around then his hand came back down with a Polaroid. He showed it to me. Blackie Roberts and George Sides were sitting on some patio. They were holding an issue of *Larkspur*, they were tugging at it from opposite directions. James flipped the picture over on the counter and wrote *Burry*. Then he stopped and put the pen down.

"Listen, Jack, you could do me an enormous service. I mean you could really help Burry and her dad—"

"That's O.K.," I said.

109

"I need someone ballsy to sit in the Valery-Michael when Vacca spends the night in Manhattan. See who he's with."

"No thank you."

"Just sit in a fancy hotel room? Keep your eyes open."

I thought about the Valery-Michael. It was right off Fifth Avenue, I'd been to a wedding there once, a friend from high school. Afterward we'd all gone up to the best man's suite. It was quiet and luxurious with lots of free things. The towels had raised V-M crests on them, and we had drinks from room service at midnight. You could do shit with the phone, mess with the lights and the air conditioner.

James was watching me. I pointed at the picture.

"I don't know why I'm doing this," he said. "This is a giant leap of faith."

He wrote the number. He put the pen away and stared at it. "Listen, Jack, don't be an asshole, O.K.? I don't know what anyone has led you to understand. During the campaign the Secretary's family is my business. I make all the calls."

Then he edged the picture across the counter toward me. "Somehow I don't feel you appreciate that," he said.

"O.K.," I said.

For a second we were both holding the picture before he let go. The number began, 518.

"Where is this?"

"Adirondacks. The only town anywhere near it is something called Guy Park. West of Saratoga Springs. Don't give that number to anyone, O.K.? It's Rennie Barce's country place."

"Rennie Barce," I said, nodding.

It took a second before I realized who he meant, Rene Rutledge Barce, the painter who does those anatomical paintings. I always thought it was pronounced Re-NAY. Carmen Frankel had taken me to a show of his. All the paintings were called *Inner Body Dilemma* and had numbers not individual titles. And Carmen said that Barce was deeply fucked up, almost evil.

110

There was this whole story that he had shot one of his wives accidentally on purpose and nothing had come of it.

"Burry knows Rene Barce?" I said.

"Sure. Rene and Early and Blackie are old asshole buddies," he said. "We're using his farm as a staging area upstate."

James tore off a bunch of paper towels and wiped down the counter. Then he hoisted himself up and sat there with his hands holding the edge, white-knuckled. He wasn't what you would call a comfortable person but he talked about the farm for a while and actually relaxed. It was a couple thousand acres of wooded hills and farmland. Barce leased the arable land; a neighbor ran sheep through it. He had reconstructed old buildings on the land almost like a sculpture park.

"Burry has the run of the place, she uses Barce's studio."

Etcetera, and I just nodded as if it were the most familiar thing in the world to me, two thousand acres and getting to paint in Rene Rutledge Barce's studio. Of course Burry wasn't going to call me, not if she had friends like that to hang with.

Then James pushed himself off the counter with his hands and touched my back.

"Listen Jack I don't want you to pay any attention to Peter Sisley," he said. "He's just an out-of-control faggot press person who can't hold a job to save his life and whose father bankrolled Gerry Ford."

He followed me into the hallway.

"He's rich, he doesn't believe in anything. Not like you and me."

"Tell me what you believe in, James."

"Oh come on, Jack, you know what I'm saying—my dad ran a foundry in West Virginia, all right? Who was your dad. Some pisher, right?"

He stopped. He was frowning at me, and I was suddenly proud of my dad, so proud I wasn't going to say a word about him.

111

"Peter Sisley's a dollar-a-year guy," he said. "You and me, we're both hungry."

"Right," I said.

So we were friends, and a few minutes later when I left, James followed me out. It was after eleven o'clock, and the party was supposed to stop at 8:30. Because everything these people did was in code, and the code was, Losers leave at 8:30, hip people stick around. James said he'd just wait for the elevator with me, but he was nervous and didn't say anything, and when the elevator came he got on it with me and stared at the floor.

"Jack, I meant what I said. I need someone who's smart as they come but also a little motivated," he said.

He meant that Valery-Michael thing. "Not me," I said.

"Just keep tabs on the characters he comes with. I like you because I think you know all the political characters. You'd stay in a beautiful room."

The elevator opened on the lobby, and I told James I could do other stuff. I could look up all Vacca's filings and his writings. I'd graduated from N.Y.U. Law School ten years after Vacca, I knew how to find everything he'd written there.

He just nodded. "I'd love to see that," he said. "But this is a live option. Talk to Burry about it."

Instead of going back up he walked out with me. We went across the uneven cobblestones in silence. He held his head down like a regular person for once. But he didn't say anything. Then we came out through the archway to the street and he stopped.

"Good night, Jack," he said.

We shook hands and he had almost started back in when he turned and sighed.

"Jack. You don't know this," he said. "No one knows this. But between us?"

"What?"

"The Secretary's been praying for Burry to meet someone like you."

I didn't say anything.

"Someone he can relate to. Someone thoughtful and serious who can maybe bring her a little to earth"—then he touched me on the arm and he was gone.

10

The phone line to Rene Barce's house made a rural bleat when it rang, and Burry broke on as though from another continent. "Jack—" she said, and just the way her voice flooded over me I knew we were still together.

Why hadn't she called? Because she was scared. People had scared her. I guess that meant James, but I left it at that. She'd written me four letters. She'd written a ten-page letter the first day and three shorter letters since. Well, I hadn't gotten any. No, she hadn't mailed them. It was a half-hour drive just about to a post office. Also she didn't know my address. There was nothing you could say.

I talked to her an hour that morning and another hour that night, and the night after that we did phone sex and I beat off. She did a virgin story, pretending to be discovering things about herself with her fingers and holding a mirror. Then her girl friend came in the room and discovered it, too, and she held the tips of her fingers to the phone and tasted them. She made her tongue go over the holes in the phone, fat and wet, and she said her friend's fingers tasted like olives. Etcetera. She could make you feel naïve.

I was all set to go up there but Burry said no. Rene Barce

was in Morocco and she couldn't take liberties. I'd have to wait till Labor Day. Father was going to give a big speech in the county seat one county over, it was the ceremonial kickoff for his campaign. Father. So Labor Day I could take a bus to Guy Park and stay the weekend at Barce's mountain.

Plus she was coming back the twenty-sixth, she said, for the Aesop gala.

"The writers' group," I said.

"Father's speaking this year, and Blackie will be talking about politics. Guess who I'm taking?"

"I don't know."

"You. I'm taking you you you you you baby you."

A person is always different from how you remember them. She was isolated so she was a little whacked out. She said things like when I got up there we'd sit like Krishna by the chattering stream, and when we made love the sheep and the owls would see us, her grandfather, too, because her grandfather had come back as an owl. Sometimes she could be a flake. I wasn't totally in love with her, I could hold myself back.

But she was intelligent, you couldn't forget that. For some reason in her psychological upbringing—I'm thinking about her father being such a sell, her mother's Betty Crocker programming—she hadn't been encouraged to take herself seriously. She didn't have confidence that way. Still, it was in her, I just had to draw it out.

We talked about that hotel idea, the Valery-Michael. Joseph Vacca lived in Buffalo, but he stayed at the Valery-Michael whenever he was in New York City, which was often.

"James told me," she said. "Jack, the only thing that matters is you. You should listen to your heart. Only do it if this is something that will help you be more yourself."

"It's not my politics," I said.

"I know," she said.

"I wouldn't be comfortable there, it's a ridiculous hotel."

"Well I'm only going to say one other thing. So much of life

115

is uncomfortable. They said that in New Mexico. Our path will bring us to mountains and rock slides and raging streams. Great discomforts. Even things that look easy can be bad. Inherited wealth is like a swamp."

"Burry do you know Robert Motherwell?"

"He was a friend of Father's. Why?"

"Blackie and I were talking about him," I said.

"Him and Rene used to visit us at the Hay-Adams and stay up all night. I love the Hay-Adams, it's almost as nice as the Valery-Michael. Jack I'm only saying if you do do it you should take care of yourself. Order room service. Make James pay you well."

"I don't think I'm going to do it," I said.

"Fine. That's fine."

The next night Burry told me that her father had been sick. He had a cold, and it made her worry about the whole campaign.

"See for me Jack, this has nothing to do with politics, it's about my family," she said. "It's about Father, what I don't think he should do . . ." Her voice died off.

"What do you mean?" I said.

"If I tell you this I don't want you ever to tell anyone."

"O.K."

"Jack, I'm serious."

"Promise," I said.

"I really don't know whether my father should be governor. I don't know if that's the fullest use of his talents. I think he should be on the Supreme Court, or they could make him the head of Du Pont."

"Burry," I said.

"He could, Jack. Don't be legalistic. He's hugely creative, he could run a big company. He was on the Du Pont board. But he loves New York and this is what he's chosen. So I'm going to honor that. I'll support him with every fiber of my

116

being. But the awful thing is I've had to watch his heart get broken again and again when old friends betray him. People who haven't been there for him. Or they've even given money to Vacca."

"Republicans," I said.

"Republicans, Democrats. See, Jack, to me this isn't about politics, it's about relationship. It's about what someone wants who I love."

In the end I had to move her to a different subject. She told me about this mink farm over the hill she wanted to liberate. You smelled the anguish of the minks in the air, in the waste-product smell of animals in cramped conditions, and all we had to do was get a wire cutter for the chicken-wire cages. When someone's a flake, they talk about animals instead of people. Still I kept thinking about what she said about relationships being more important than politics. Stony Walker said that, too: If there's no love in your commitment, no devotion, then your action is a dry and worthless thing. Don't work for anyone you can't love, he said.

"If I did it I would just stop in at the hotel in the morning and at night," I said.

She was quiet.

Then she said, "That would really help me. It would help my family."

"I wouldn't actually stay at the Valery-Michael."

"O.K. but Jack, I want you to be good to yourself for a change. You should buy yourself new clothes. If you're coming to the Aesop gala with me, you can't wear a rope."

She laughed. James was such a fucking cop.

"It was on the invitation."

"I know, Jack. It's the cutest thing I've ever heard."

When I actually did it, it didn't feel uncomfortable. The lobby and the dining room of the Valery-Michael are public places.

117

I thought about something Victor used to say: if he could do only one thing to clean up government he'd pass a law requiring politicians to make public their dining schedules, who they went to breakfast and lunch with. People always quote Victor saying that. I said it, too. I mean, my name's on the latest edition of *Government: An Owner's Manual* and it's in there.

I'd go to the lobby at night and try to blend in. I'd have the *Financial Times* in my lap and look up to see who came through. Generally Vacca came in with his redheaded aide or sometimes a college friend, Harry Marks, who owned a chain of electronics stores.

In the morning I'd get there by 7:00 for breakfast. Vacca'd come a little later. He held court at the same table. He met money. I'd make a duck blind with *The New York Times* and if I didn't recognize the people, I'd find out, usually by tipping the maître d'. The maître d' was halfway decent once you got to know him. I.e., once you gave him a five.

Vacca broke bread with a lot of major-league assholes. Michael Orlando of real estate fame and Aram "Bidder" Lefkowitz the big Jew. A. T. Robinette the banking guy, Pinky Kiatowski the onetime slugger and all-around nut, Paul Speake the former Senator. And I guess Speake had been a friend of Burry's dad. All that in three days.

During the day I did other stuff. I went to N.Y.U. and looked up things Vacca wrote as a student and said in court. He had a paper trail going back to when he was a Bobby Kennedy liberal in law school. He supported busing and a broad reading of Title IX's equality clauses. Legalese will bore anyone to death, but every once in a while he'd get off some line about oppression or disenfranchisement. He'd talk the talk. I'd photocopy that and send it to James along with a memo on the case and what it said about Vacca's thinking, his evolution. Basically stuff I'd been training to do for the last three hundred

118

years. And then I'd put in the names of everyone I'd seen with him that day.

James told me I was coming on as a consultant and I held out for double what I made working for Stony Walker, $1,250 a week. I was pretty cleaned out.

It was going to take a couple weeks to get checks cut, so James sent me to the campaign's deputy treasurer or associate something. He had a real estate office in the Empire State Building. I loved going in there, it was cool and dark and classy. The guards wore their storybook uniforms and your feet grazed the metal spines on the lobby floor that ran between the tablets of worn-down marble, I guess the marble wears down faster than the metal. The treasurer was on the eightieth floor. Gold, feathered arrows on the wall pointed you to your destination, and his old secretary sat behind glass. She had stiff gray curls, the whole trip, and she wordlessly handed me a manila envelope that I carried out to the hall before looking inside. It had a string closure, where you wind the string round and round the red cardboard button, and inside was a second envelope, sealed, with twelve hundred-dollar bills in it.

I don't care what anyone says, a hundred-dollar bill will make you feel like a class criminal, so I spent most of it in a hurry. Burry was right, I needed clothes. I didn't have anything to wear sitting in the Valery-Michael. Plus there was that Aesop thing, the gala with Father.

Burry sent me to this store on Madison Avenue I won't even say the name. The clerks are all like former dictators, deposed or exiled. They have accents and big teeth and this aristocratic protocol just walking up to you. This bald one measured me a lot and then he studied me, tilted his head over and didn't say anything, like he was noticing shit, and not something good either. It turned out my left shoulder was lower than my right shoulder and that's why my jacket didn't fit me right.

I bought a dark suit I could wear to the Aesop deal and

119

another jacket, both altered for the shoulder, and the dough was gone. Of course after that none of my old stuff fit me anymore so when I got home I put a lot out on Broadway, two suits I had, two-for-$299, that I used to wear all the time to court or public hearings. Dacron. You could sweat right through one of those suits running around to federal agencies all day in Washington then hang it in the shower overnight and wear it the next day. They wear like iron. They look like iron, too.

Also my Bob Dylan jacket, which I bought because of Bob Dylan. It's a long story that I'm embarrassed to say. Bob Dylan had been in this store just ahead of me.

I put them all out on Broadway in a shopping bag, and everything was gone when I went out for dinner an hour later. Some other guy was already wearing my work pants. He was putting my suit on and looking in the mirror and feeling like he'd made out. So both of us were happy. That's the trickle-down theory in a nutshell. My dad would kill me if he heard me say that.

On Friday no one showed up at Vacca's table and he just read the papers.

He had an active relationship with the paper. He frowned at stuff he read, and just turning from one page to another he'd snap the paper out flat in the air like the paper was to blame. Or he'd make notes to himself even while he was reading. They brought him the giant politician breakfast, and he ate without looking at his food. You're supposed to look at your food. Both aesthetically and physiologically. But Vacca was all nerves. Once he put his coffee cup down absently and it hit his orange juice glass hard on the rim with a bell-like sound that made everyone in the place jump.

Then at 7:45 he got to his feet. I sort of followed him

into the lobby. The redheaded guy was standing next to the car on Fifty-fifth Street. I think his name is Blanchard.

Back in the dining room all Vacca's papers were still spread out, hot from his eyeballs. I grabbed the *Post* and then I saw where Vacca had scribbled doodles on the back of the *Times*. There was a full-page ad with a lot of white space Vacca had done cartoons on. He'd drawn Sam Knowings, the Tigers centerfielder and villain of last night's game. Vacca was an O.K. drawer, and you could tell it was Knowings because of his number, 32.

I went into the subway but I kept thinking about that picture. Vacca had made Sam Knowings look like an outlaw, with his Afro boiling off his head like smoke. Plus there was some weird attachment on his leg, a harness or a rag.

The train came and the doors opened when I realized I should have taken it. I stood there and people mashed by me. What are the politics of taking that picture?

Then I turned and ran out through the turnstile, still arguing with myself.

The papers were gone. They don't leave shit lying around at the Valery-Michael. If they did, it wouldn't be the Valery-Michael. I found the maître d', I told him I'd left my papers. Another lie.

"Talk to the busboy. Jimmy."

He wasn't a busboy, he was pushing seventy. Don't let anybody call you Jimmy when you're seventy, with big watery blue eyes and that yellowy white hair where it goes in feathery clumps down the back of your head. I guess it's a royal pain to wash it, or more to the point, if you're Jimmy nothing comes to you from washing it. He said he always put the papers in the kitchen for the cook. He took me back, slow-foot, and I almost ran up his back.

Jimmy. Jim. I was saying to myself, Call the guy Jim. How many people have been good to Jim? And why?

121

So I felt like hell for Jim, which didn't help him any. Don't cry for the common man. My dad would always say that with this dry expression. But fuck him, my dad doesn't ever cry, period.

The papers were on the butcher block. I found the cartoon, and there was a chain around Sam Knowings's ankle, almost a shackle. It was tied to something, you didn't see what. I messengered it to James that afternoon.

11

It's a summer night I'm thinking about, late August, and I'm walking through Central Park. The western sky is pink like the inside of a clamshell but the east is already darkening blue, and I'm feeling light, I'm feeling completely drained. The breeze pulls at my new jacket, which doesn't have a vent, blows it like a sail, and I go with it.

The night before I'd spent with Burry and all that morning, too, seeing how many times I could come. She looked different after her time in the country. A diet of nuts and vegetables made her skinny, bony, and she smelled different. Her bones looked too long for her skin. Her legbones poked up at her hips like tentpoles. Also, she'd cut her own hair again. Everything about her excited me, the paprika tang of her B.O., the shock of her metal-red hair against the white of her scalp, her pussy hair like fire when you saw it from the side, fringing off into nothing in the candlelight.

I'd left her place at 11:30 in the morning. I had a surprised feeling coming out and seeing the midday sun after hours of not being sure if it was day or night. She had wrapped the windows in her Indonesian batiks, blocking out the light, the same as when they wrote the Constitution.

Then I was grateful for the day apart. I'd been with her so much, inside her, on her, squished by her bones, I got almost nauseated by the richness. Tasting her too much, smelling my dried jizz in her hair from getting off on her tits, and licking her so much you could taste the iron in the blood. It was that same quandary, you're not allowed to say you're bored by sex, even if you are.

I spent all day in the library, then that night was the Aesop thing at the Pierre, and she said to meet her at the East Seventy-second Street entrance to Central Park.

She was early for once, and she had on a black dress with thin straps over the shoulders. Her high heels kept sinking into the grass. Then she held me and she'd bathed. I could smell the soap. "Jack, you are a great man," she said in a husky whisper.

"Right," I said. Because she'd been complimenting me like hell the night before, too.

We walked to Fifth Avenue with our arms around each other. I liked the solemn shifting bulk of her against my hip, and she kept saying, "You are great, Jack, I saw what you did."

It turned out she'd been to her father's headquarters. James had shown her Vacca's drawing.

"It's all about repressed rage," she said.

"I don't know."

"No, I'm serious, baby, listen to me." She stopped and held my jacket. "It's about race and rage. I'm an artist, I know how to look at these things."

It was full twilight now and the sky was that bluey-lav color, the gay color but charred a little, and the dark came right down over our shoulders like a cape and gave us privacy, which I liked with her. Because she talked too loud, people looked.

"Baby, you have a great future in politics," she said.

"That's what they told the Rosenbergs."

"Jack!" She hit me in the chest hard with the side of her

fist. "I don't like it when you put yourself down, that joke was full of Jewishy self-hatred."

"Well, I don't like politics."

"I know, but be here with me. Don't be somewhere else. Are you feeling insecure?"

"No."

We crossed Fifth at a devil-may-care angle, and a block from the Pierre she bent to a car mirror to fix her makeup.

"Oy, so this is how the girl shows up in society," she said in one of her accents, a Borscht-belt accent.

"Burry what is society?"

"Not a what. A who."

"They say society but they don't really mean society. Like saying humanity if all you mean is rich white people."

She stood up and snapped that deal, her compact, and dropped it in a silver bag.

"Oh Jack, you're being obtuse. And we're late."

She took my hand and we crossed the street. There were other people going in, in all their fucked-up regalia. I guess I was nervous, I pulled her hand.

"Burry, tell me what you mean by society."

She stopped but didn't look at me. "Society is three things," she said quietly. "People with talent. People with families. The beautiful. Now Jack we're going in, baby, so you have to chill." And tilting up, she kissed me on the nose.

Because she'd published monologues in a performance-art magazine, Aesop had inducted Burry as an adjunct member. It was the same for Blake Roberts. Her first novel wasn't going to be published till next February, but it was under contract. And of course, both their fathers were speaking that night.

The Pierre's big ballroom was dark and cool as a cathedral. All you heard was the endless heavy rumble of voices with now

125

and then a bright shot of laughter. Everyone was drinking. I stood off to the side and watched, I was scared to walk around. Even the tables had a musty swank. For centerpieces there were piles of old leather books with quills and peacock feathers and cobwebs sticking up from an inkwell, and real Spanish moss falling from the arms of candelabra. You almost expected all the big-dick writers to come in in a procession, swinging pots of smoke.

Victor Bandy used to rage about this gala. He got Aesop's filings from the New York secretary of state's office and leaked the figures to the press. Aesop puts out beautiful reports showing how the money they raised forever altered the trajectory of a dozen oppressed writers' lives. But it bothered Victor that they had an office on Fifth Avenue with modern sculpture in the reception area. And how much of the half-million-dollar budget actually went to writers?

Well fuck Victor, he'd never been here, and I had. I found our table, right up at the stage on the left, and there was a party favor at my seat, a datebook with marbled covers and a quote a week from a tortured or imprisoned writer.

Each table also had a more-or-less famous writer sitting at it. Ours was Din Mallinckrodt. He didn't smile like he does in all his pictures. "He's nervous because his archrivals are here," Burry whispered to me. Every once in a while one of the archrivals would come over and say hello, and Din would spring up to demonstrate his health. He'd slap the other guy a lot on the arm and nod. Then he'd hold his forehead and look at the floor.

"I have to tell you. Your book. Wonderful. Deeply comic and passing strange. Passing strange . . ." and other shit like that.

Blake was there, she was nice to me for once. She wore a black shirt with buttons all the way up to the neck and see-through sleeves on it, and her wrists coming out of the cuffs were so delicate. The actual shirt wasn't really see-through, but

I could see her black bra through it, the scalloped edge of the cups.

You can't not be nice to a beautiful girl. You just can't. Either that or mean, and when they were clearing the main course, I leaned over to congratulate her on her book.

"Why thank you," she said.

"What's it about?"

She picked at her silverware, and I realized I'd said the absolute wrong thing.

"Gosh. You know, I just—I don't talk about it. I don't talk about material I'm still dealing with."

"Right," I said.

"I'm sorry, but you know the saying, Don't make the gods jealous."

"Sure." I was nodding and dying at once, and grateful when the waiter came for my plate.

Then Blake's father walked onto the stage with a drink in his hand just like he was walking onto the back porch. People clapped like hell. He had on a black velvet tuxedo jacket like the Stones might wear and his big face was lynx-eyed, charming.

The huge rumble of voices stopped. At the podium Blackie turned a stiff piece of paper in his hands, considering it. Then he folded it and shoved it into his side pocket, the hell with this, and looked up frankly at the crowd.

"Television has all but destroyed the adverb. It is moving in on the adjective," he said. "So much I have suffered in silence. But now journalism bears down on our politics, and I for one can't hold my peace."

Gusts of excitement went through the crowd. Blackie had everyone eating out of his hand, and he knew it, too. He stopped right there and got out a cigarette.

The first part of his speech was all about journalism. Journalism has turned to the dark depths of people's lives, their unspoken feelings and heart of hearts. But journalism is neither

127

wise nor loving enough for that undertaking. Moreover, it comes with only the crudest of tools, factual reporting, and the recent introduction of the anonymous source and the public figure, which Blackie said with a ton of sarcasm. And he held that cigarette between his thumb and forefinger but didn't light it, just held it as he talked, which I guess was his beat-smoking system.

But let us not forget, personal revelations that serve to explain a fictional character's motivation are, in the press, only the barbed shrapnel of gossip.

So picture him, the public novelist (which he contrasted to the private novelist) going out into the woods to collect his armful of twigs . . . Yet journalism encroaches as surely as the Sahara cuts into the forests of Africa. There is less and less for the public novelist to gather . . .

"His arms are light," and other swoony bullshit like that.

But people listened. All you heard was the soft clinking of coffee cups and now and then a fork being set down. Next to me Burry's back was arched in a religious posture of attentiveness.

"Now a critical function of literature is to instruct a people in its manners. So a society without literature has a politics without grace," he said.

Then Blackie stopped and let the mood change. The cigarette trickled down through his fingers, and he caught it again, a whole magic trick he saved for right then.

"The friend I introduce will speak about Robert Frost. It is left to me to tell you about his political fortunes."

Blackie coughed. Burry reached for my hand under the table.

"Brother Quinlan's likely opponent in the governor's race, his name escapes me, does not have what we used to describe as manners."

"Vacca!" a man shouted from the back.

Blackie pointed his cigarette in the guy's direction. "Thank

128

you. Mr. Vacca is steeped in the graceless politics of television. He likes his politics personal—"

"Amen," the same guy shouted.

People groaned, they shifted around to try and see the heckler. He'd stood up. All you could see was his head held stiffly and his black jacket, a red or orange shirt underneath. He said something else you couldn't hear, and then a door opened near me and a security guy came in. He began wading through the crowd. People pointed the way, and I thought about my dream again, my dream about the cathedral with the hanging people.

Blackie finally lit his cigarette. He reached for the microphone with his cigarette hand.

"Mr. His-name-escapes-me seems to think it matters that he still has a wife while Early lost Gloria three years ago. Or it matters whether and how Early chooses to take the edge off the day."

"How?" the guy shouted.

People heckled him back, and then Blackie's voice banged against the sound system.

"None of your damn business—"

The crowd broke into savage applause. Burry put her fingers in her mouth and whistled, and Blake stood, clapping. The heckler was leaving. You saw him squeezing between chairs. People tilted out of his way. Get out, I said to him in my head. Get out. Get out. He got to the doors then turned.

"Quinlan's a war criminal," he shouted.

Burry twisted as if she'd touched a bare wire. People booed. "A coward's lie!" Blackie cried.

But he was rattled. His face was flushed. He came out from behind the podium to the lip of the stage. He walked along the edge as if he were laying for the guy. When he got near our table he lifted his glass.

"Heart. Heart—get me some ice babe."

Blake got up and took the glass from him.

129

Blackie walked back to the mike. He stubbed the cigarette out on the side of the rostrum and absently let it fall to the floor. He rubbed his eyes and smiled as Blake came back through the tables. "When Blake's book comes out, you're going to forget my name," he said. "It's called *Bottle's Daughter*. It's about the love that knows no rival on the green face of the earth, the love between father and daughter."

People cheered like wild, and Blake handed him the drink and he bent and kissed her. But something had changed in him. He was stiffer and paler and dry, like something you found on the beach. He sighed a couple of times, getting back into his speech, and his face twitched with feeling. He buttoned his jacket.

"Early Quinlan and I share a grand misfortune. Both born in dirt. But introduced to politics by someone who knew the difference between public and private. Between his sin and his service. I am speaking of course about Jack Kennedy. Though the same may be said of Brother Martin. Or the man on whom I based the senator in *The Pattern American*, Brother Robert—"

After that he lost it. And not only him. A woman at the next table was choking up and right next to me Burry cried softly.

Blackie blotted his face on his jacket and did the end of his speech away from the microphone, something you couldn't hear about The great lights of my age, and Our gods walked among us. He was like an actor, declaiming, and he gave a little bow and turned away. At first he couldn't find the break in the curtain, then Early Quinlan pulled it open three feet from where he was looking. Blackie threw his arms around him, and disappeared.

The applause came like rain. A lot of people yelled Bravo, and finally Blackie came back out and kissed his hands and bent slowly. His charm was back, his smile.

Then the noise went down and it was the Secretary's turn. I

studied him. He was big-chested, with thin legs, and his face was almost as pretty as Burry's. He got his half-glasses from one pocket and his folded speech from another.

Not looking at anyone, he said, "Nearly a hundred and fifty years ago, crossing Brooklyn ferry, Walt Whitman lifted his gaze on a mackerel sky—"

Big pause, like he was in his study. But how did he know what the sky was like a hundred and fifty years ago? He didn't. He was a bullshit artist, he was worse than me.

Afterward, in the lobby and on the sidewalk, Burry introduced me to her friends. I met about fifty. She could have a whole intense conversation in a minute and then in the next few seconds as we walked away tell you everything about the person.

There was Harry Heffernan, a descendant of the Boston Adamses who'd burned down his former girlfriend's summer house but never been charged even though the police found the siphon he used on his Range Rover. After that, Ann Laddie Regis, the daughter of Daphne Regis and an actress herself. She had designed the centerpieces. Also Kizzie Elmendorf, a skinny blonde with a hook nose but kind of beautiful who was Burry's roommate at Bard and whose grandmother was Maddie Lister, the artist and giant lesbian, which Burry said proved it was genetic because Kizzie was bi. Kizzie was a brilliant writer. And she'd had her tits done, Burry had seen the scars at the gym.

She transmitted all that adoring and outrageous information in the same tone without transition, and I could only nod. I felt like a hick.

Then I met Lisette Wolf, who writes literary profiles and ten years ago was the other woman in the Fox-Fischer cadet scandal at West Point but whose name never got in the papers thanks to Father. And Burry was cool to her because her husband had

131

given money to both her father and Vacca. Then Jigger Janes, who looked just like his father, Roamer Janes, but didn't have the stomach to get work in Hollywood.

But Jigger was happier making wrought-iron candlesticks and other crafts, decoupage . . .

It tired me out, and I went to the side. I was thinking about who my friends were. I wasn't seeing my old friends, and did Burry think these were going to be my new ones? That was a dick in the ass. I stood at the edge of the sidewalk with just my toes on the curb, rocking. I was on a precipice. At any second I was going to be cast down into a molten sea of triviality.

But if you thought about it that was unfair. Burry knew how to deal with these people. She sold them out to me in a whisper. She was like a court painter. A court painter ventured into society then went back to his studio to paint portraits that told people the truth about the powerful. Burry had that in her, that honesty. You couldn't forget that.

A car stopped a few feet from me, a silver Lincoln with a hatted driver, and James Doyle got out of the passenger side.

"Hello, James," I said.

He made a little nod but didn't look at me.

"Nice ride," I said.

"Jack, let's sit inside."

So we got into the car. The driver looked straight ahead. He wore a putty-colored uniform with a dark blue stripe around the cuffs and the hat was the same putty.

"The Secretary spoke at the U.N. today. That's why we have the car."

"O.K."

He kept looking out the window and making a face. "I hate these fucking phonies. If a bomb took them all out the human race would only be the better for it."

"They're Burry's best friends," I said.

"Exactly."

132

He laughed. He touched me on the knee respectfully, and I didn't mind him. We were almost friendly.

"Did Burry tell you about the girlfriend?"

"What girlfriend?"

"We hear Vacca has a girlfriend. She comes to see him at the Valery-Michael."

"He doesn't have a girlfriend," I said.

Then Burry came over laughing and got in, so I was in the middle, and the driver pulled away. She lowered her window and let her head lean against the window frame. The wind blew her hair across her eyes and just when I felt completely distant she reached for my hand. She pulled it under her dress and held it against her inner thigh. The skin there was sweaty, you could feel the volunteer hairs high on her thighs.

"James says you have something to tell me," I said.

She squeezed my hand harder. "I was going to tell you."

"Well, I don't think it's true, and b, he's not running for pope," I said.

"I know, Jack. But it makes me heartsick. The way he uses his kid in the ads." She sat up in the seat and held my hand on her knees. "His ads have his little girl in them. Throwing her in the air. It's cynical and using that kid for political purposes she won't understand for years and years till the damage is done."

"It's what you do when you run against a sixty-eight-year-old," James said.

She leaned hard across me to address him.

"I don't care. I know what politics does to children, James, it eats them. You see evangelists going down the street with their five-year-old in a suit preaching? That child didn't get to make a choice. It's completely unfair. Father and Mother always did their best to protect me. Sometimes they succeeded and sometimes they didn't."

"They did fine," he said.

133

She sat back. "They wanted me to have my own life. Father always worried about my life being overwhelmed."

She never said my mother or my father, always Mother and Father, as though we all had the same father and mother. I wondered what she'd think if she ever met my parents. She'd say they were odd. I stirred with a loyalty to my parents like a kind of nostalgia.

The car turned north on Park Avenue. James shifted sideways, he put his arm on the driver's seat. I saw his fingernails glowing pale in the streetlights, square and neatly pared.

"Jack, it's a rumor. I'd like to know if it's true."

"Where's the line? Is there a line with you?"

He sighed. "I'm not going to do anything with this, Jack, I'm not going to out anybody. The guy just happens to be Mr. Righteous P. Asshole. He's into everyone else's life."

"Blackie Roberts just gave a speech about this," I said.

"I know."

"You weren't there."

"Jack I talked it over with him. Why Jack—do you agree with him?"

I let my head fall back against the seat. "He's a weepy wreck," I said.

Burry gave a cry. "How can you say that, Jack. He's one of my closest friends."

"Well I do," James said. "I agree with Blackie."

"Bullshit," I said.

"I like campaigns clean. I hate them getting personal. Which is why I need to know this."

The car glided down Burry's street and stopped. It was windy. The trees swayed so the yellow dapply patterns of light from the streetlamps swung back and forth on the sidewalk and over the asphalt. They moved, and even if you wanted to you couldn't have stayed in the yellow part, you would have to jump whenever the wind came. A game like that started in my head as I watched the shadows.

134

James opened the door. He started to get out then stopped. "Listen Jack. If it was up to me the Secretary wouldn't drink so much."

"Oh God, James," Burry said. "Not you, too."

"Burry, this is hypothetical. I'm talking about his image."

She leaned over me to look at him. "Father has a drink at the end of the day. Maybe two. People don't understand. But it's generational." Her voice was sharp and groany, older-sounding. "It's called cocktails."

She laughed hard and James laughed too.

We all got out, Burry last. She flattened the crinkled black dress down against her legs almost properly. Then the doorman drifted up to the door with his robin's-egg getup on. He didn't come out, he stood there, looking the other way down the street, with his hand held up at the glass with the white glove that stopped at his wrist.

James leaned against the back fender. "I've got to make sure Vacca doesn't even think of bringing that stuff up again, Jack."

"I get it, blackmail."

"We call it deterrence, Jack. It worked with the Russians."

It bugged me how many times he said my name.

"A lot of politicians have girlfriends," I said. "It's a big reason they go into politics, to get laid."

"Not Father," Burry said.

"Why do you say Father?"

"Because Father doesn't have affairs."

"But why don't you say 'My father?' I mean, he's not my father, he's not James's father."

"Jack, that's hostile, you're acting out on me."

"I'm sorry, but a lot of them have affairs."

"We're not talking about Stony Walker."

"Oh come on, Burry."

"You know he does. Everyone knows. But Stony Walker's allowed. Blacks have permission."

"And white guys who remember Kennedy have permission to drink."

Her face colored, and she stepped away from me to the door. James didn't move against the fender. They were both quiet, and I was there by myself on the sidewalk.

"Jack, if I could leave you with one thought that doesn't go anywhere?" he said. "The race is getting very tight."

"I thought he's a human sacrifice."

"He makes us fight for our own base. Jews. Working-class Catholics. Everywhere Early is weak he's strong. If he wasn't so stupid he'd be deadly."

He went on like that, the things you hear windbags saying on TV, the ethnics, the upstate vote, the suburbs, crime and family values, with numbers thrown in. Then he pushed himself off the car and walked over to me.

"Jack this is easy. This is a lay-up."

"James don't," Burry said.

I looked at her. "Don't what?"

"Oh, Jack, I don't know. I love you, I just don't know whether you want this."

"You can think about it," James said.

He was holding out his hand, and I reached without thinking. A small heavy thing fell into my hand in a glove-leather case. You knew at once it was a camera, with a bulge on one side. James moved back to the car. I bent and dropped the camera on the curb.

"Just think about it," he said.

Then blah blah blah, and other shit he said in a blur. And after that the door closed and the car went away.

So it was just me and Burry, and I kicked the camera into the street, and she went to get it. I yelled at her that she was in on it, and she started crying. We went inside, the doorman held the door not looking at us, and on the elevator Burry said stuff to calm me. "Jack, we should be happy," she said. "We have each other."

136

Back in her room she held my cheeks.

"Look at you, you're red. You have so much anger in you, Jack, you scare me sometimes."

I touched my cheeks, and she was right, they were hot.

12

My dad used to talk about how many workers the Labor Department had saved. He would actually get out a pencil and count lives. But did he care about the people that were saved? No. When he was around actual people he was totally uncomfortable. At a table he would lean over and pick up a place card when he had to say the person's name, rude shit like that. He would forget what you told him, important information. People always say he's a survivor, that he survived the Red scare and Reagan. I guess I don't know what that means. He's so mistrustful. He's not nice to anyone except poor people. Actually he's bitter. He'll have a fifteen-minute conversation about pricing structure with a shoeshine guy he'll never see again but a double standard for anyone who has a leg up in life, myself for instance.

You could come in the room crying and he'd want to talk about what Kissinger did to Cambodia. That happened once.

I thought a lot about my old job, too, working at the Center, fighting wrongs under fluorescent lights that drain your skin of anything alive, with walls of boxes filled with *Government: An Owner's Manual*. And Victor would leaf through one of his bibles, a book of federal regulations, and tell you how many hundreds of thousands of people had been saved by a certain automobile safety regulation, 63,000 this, 27,000 that, and their "fisc and family" preserved. And meanwhile he didn't give a shit what was happening to your life, being a little gray soldier of human progress.

The same with politics. You were supposed to think in masses, groups, the suburban middle class. From which arose noble concepts like the common man. The little man. Not even concepts—at least a concept you could think about. Slogans.

Well then what happened if the group was saved and the individual got lost? I mean, being completely personal about it, what if I didn't feel good soldiering my life away?

I don't know why, I hated my old life. Sitting under fluorescent lights and worrying about other people in other continents. And Victor Bandy's same old suit day after day with the tie blackened at the neck by sweat, and here, Jack, for you a few gritty fifties-type left-wing highlights to get your rocks off, like the time Carmen Frankel and I fucked in Central Park by the reservoir. Just lying down on my coat. I spread my coat out first under the bushes. It was 8:30 on a summer night, still light, and my prick got stiff just from my walking in the park alongside her because of the thin blue dress she was wearing, the way her ass moved under the dress.

It had been me that pulled us into the bushes. That was all right, that was great. But then I'd gone and ruined it by a few days later telling Victor about it. Like it was any of his business.

I had those arguments in my head. Walking down the street, riding the subway, in the shower. I wore myself out. And in the end when I told James I'd stay at the Valery-Michael, I looked on the positive side. To stay there, to treat myself. I wasn't going to take anybody's picture. But I'd get a nice room there, I'd keep my eyes open. I'd tell James what I saw.

What are the politics of sitting in the Valery-Michael spying on a jerk-breath politician? I don't care. Because I am doing it out of something true, my love of a real person, and not

139

because of some bullshit slogan, love of mankind, love of a vast group whose members I wouldn't even necessarily like. That is what I told myself. I was doing it for personal reasons, I was changing my life.

Burry left for Barce's place again and I got a room in the Valery-Michael, on the same floor as Joseph Vacca, Jr.

I had a whole personality to explain what I was doing there. Loads of movie people stayed at the Valery-Michael, so that's what I'd be. I got sunglasses and an L.A. Dodgers cap, and I wore a T-shirt under my jacket, with jeans. And James said screenwriters make so much dough they read *The Wall Street Journal*. So I did that, too. Every day I carried the *Journal* out to the elevator.

The main thing was to watch Vacca's door. Just sitting in the lobby, I saw when he came in, and then when he went upstairs I'd mark his door. You used a broom straw. You leaned the straw up against the door and checked it during the night, and if it fell down that meant he had company. So in the morning you could keep a lookout.

There's something about being up when other people aren't up, you have freedom. You could shine your shoes with towels, you could order anything you wanted from room service. You could get a pizza or cold antipasto salad, you could order lobster and no one guilted you about it, they treated you like fucking royalty. That's the kind of people they hire at the Valery-Michael. Hit the loo. They don't even arch an eyebrow. You could get a VCR, which I got, and order in movies from this we-deliver joint on Madison Avenue. One porn, one legit, that's how I did it, where the only time I'd gotten porn before was with friends and it was a giant goof. You were supposed to say, How fucked up, how boring. But what if it didn't bore you.

So I would order a serious one my mom might have taken me to in the Yonkers library film series when I was in high school, *Rashomon* or *Aguirre: The Wrath of God, The Discreet Charm of the Bourgeoisie,* then in the same sentence throw in *Dripping Wet Oriental Number Three.* And the person writing it down wouldn't think I was some sleaze but a well-rounded person that was exploring the full range of human experience.

At midnight I watched the De Sica movies and that Spanish guy who's pretty filthy himself, then if it dragged I might take a break and look at *Amateur Lesbians. Amateur Lesbians: Chrystie, Amateur Lesbians: Hester.* American girls with broad flat American accents who were lesbians or being paid to be lesbians, which Victor would say is a meaningful distinction, in bullshit all-American situations. Swimming-party snafu. The wrong babysitter. I'm sorry, ma'am, we're here to repossess the couch. And all with that how-to-mix-cement background music that makes you feel like a moron.

It got me off my rhythm when they faked the sound track. They'd have someone moaning after the fact in the studio, where the moans didn't line up with the actor's mouth, or both people were moaning when one's mouth was filled with the other. Also it threw me when they took their clothes off right away.

I wanted it to be real, I wanted it to be halfway honest. One time this girl said, I guess to the director, I don't like doing that, meaning eating the other one, she just murmured it but you heard. Then she didn't really lick her, just pretended to, and touched her a bunch. Well, that was honest, that turned me on. Or sometimes you would see them get wet really, without fake magic tricks. When one girl licked another's wide flat-dish nipples they twirled up stiff. You can't lie about that. And her pussy opened like in a nature show, the hairs spittling into sticky curled spears that poked at her round butt and thighs.

I even liked the greeny-yellow skin tones, because that was true. They were shooting in shitty locations. Motels I bet, or tract homes, in Imitation Oak Panel, Colorado.

The Valery-Michael was just like Burry promised. They gave

141

you all this stuff to make your body happy. Soaps that were shaped like pieces of fruit in little yellow boxes with an etching of the fruit on the cover. Plus they had fragrant skin butters, dewberry and pear and mango, in soft foil packages. I guess you're supposed to massage your spouse. You come to New York and stay at the Valery-Michael, and after the theater you massage your wife. Or in the afternoon. You know, sex with the sunlight waning. But my wife was gone and I used them on me. I could tear the foil open with my teeth while I was beating off and not go out of the rhythm.

Then dinner would come from room service. At 2:15 they'd knock and I'd wash my hands and throw on a giant robe with V-M embroidered in burgundy red, like royalty, and tie the knot right in front to make my hard-on behave. I got the same thing every night, the next day's papers and a double order of shrimps with cocktail sauce, a bottle of Guinness, baby greens salad, and melon with that thin drapy ham around it. The waiters had little tags with just their first names, Javier, I remember, and Witold. And no last names, no country of origin either.

Afterward, I liked playing with the camera James had given me. I'd take pictures of myself in the mirror in my robe, or things on the TV. I'd freeze myself with the flash.

The fourth day or so I stopped at my place to check my mail and my credit-card bill was up to $2,700, most of it from the Walker campaign. I called Ralph about it but he wasn't home, so then I called Alvin Moorer, the former chief of staff. Alvin said they wanted people to forgive personal expenses and take it as a deduction. Stony was still in debt, so if you wanted actual cash you were probably going to get forty-three cents on the dollar, if that. I agreed to forgive half.

Well, James Doyle will pay that off for me, I thought to myself. James will make this contribution to the Walker campaign.

Then Ralph called back and we met for a drink at this place we always used to go on Seventy-ninth Street, a holdover from the old Upper West Side. Beller's. You go down steps from the street and it's black-and-white mosaic tiles with a long crack going through them and sawdust, and the red booths are sticky from beer. Someone's always trying to fix it up to appeal to a better clientele, but they never manage to do it, the waitresses are still mean and the same ugly one-eyed cats are always there. I mean real cats, winding around the legs of the booths.

I felt nostalgic as hell just walking in there, even the old graffiti was familiar. Then Ralph slid in across from me and gave me a soul-shake. He had on overalls and a white T-shirt.

"Hey blood, what it is?" he said. "You look like hell."

"No sleep," I said.

"You been slipping it to that daughter one."

"She's all right."

"Burry," he said. "Where is she?"

"She's out of town."

"You embarrassed to bring her along?"

I'd forgotten stuff about Ralph. His eyes goggled a little when he got worked up about something, he didn't listen well.

"She'll make you work for her father," he said.

"I am. I'm doing negative research on Vacca." I'd rehearsed telling him that.

"That's O.K. Just so long as you don't go to Albany to work for that asshole. Remember how he ran cover for all the hawk intellectuals at State. Jewish right-wingers, he was their shabbas goy."

Ralph had a brand-new bag. He was working at a think tank in the Village that was funded by the eccentric left-wing millionaire John Jesus Terrill. The Foundation for Fair Uses. Actually the Foundation for Fair Uses (of Power). They'd given Ralph a little office where he was doing computer studies of campaign financing in every congressional district in the country. He had an idea, he wanted me and the rest of the old

143

Walker people to regroup in the next cycle around local races.

You couldn't disagree with him, but when I went to the bathroom, the stinky pisser there with a long porcelain trough and dreary rust stains that went down from the top where the water drizzled over it, I felt depressed. I remembered Ralph as gleaming, focused. But he wasn't gleaming, he seemed battered. He reached into his mouth with his finger to get at food caught in his back teeth while you were talking. He'd done that before, too, I remembered. Only then I hadn't given a shit.

When I got back to the Valery-Michael I was drunk, and that night the straw fell. Actually Thursday morning, I discovered it at 1:30. After that I couldn't sleep. Finally I got out of bed and went downstairs for the papers and a quart of orange juice. It was 5:30, and I was hungover. I sat on the ashtray at the seventeenth-floor elevator.

I read the *Daily News* sports and moved on to *The Wall Street Journal*. Then a little before 7:00 Vacca came out. You could hear his morning noises, rude sounds he made with his throat, but he was alone. I looked at his tasseled loafers, and from the corner of my eye I saw the fringe of his wet hair grazing his shirt collar. He'd shaved too fast, his neck was speckled red.

"This your paper?"

I didn't answer before he lifted my *Times* off the ashtray. He hummed reading the front page, grunted a couple times in disapproval, flapped it around to the sports.

"Shame about the Yankees," I said.

"Don't get me started."

The elevator didn't come and Vacca was restless. That close he had a bullish presence, his big head, his hands.

"May I ask you a question," he said. "How do you read wearing sunglasses?"

My armpits prickled. "I'm a screenwriter."

"So. I'm a lawyer. What's that got to do with it?"

"I took the red-eye from L.A. It's too early for me. My eyes haven't woken up yet."

144

He nodded as if he actually believed that, so then I felt shitty about lying.

"Plus a hangover," I said.

The elevator sounded. He rapped the paper with his knuckles and his eyes were wide open. His eyebrows went up in a way that reminded me of exclamation marks, naïve.

"I'll tell you two reasons I don't like reading this before I've had coffee."

"All right."

"First it's dirty, it gets on your fingers. They keep saying they've licked it but they haven't. There's a chemical they could get, I know because a friend of mine is in the business."

The doors opened and he motioned for me to get on. So I wasn't going to see the girlfriend. I'd blown it. She'd probably slipped out at 5:00.

"It's a French chemical that costs just half a cent a paper, but that's too much," he said.

"Now I know what you're going to say," I said.

His face was chalky and dark at the same time, it looked straight ahead. "What?"

"Jews run it."

"That's not funny. I bet you're Jewish."

I nodded.

"Of course they run it. So what. Jews are good at that—" He stopped. "I mean, they like doing that. Media. News-papers—" He was completely tongue-tied. "Look, I'm Italian. Do I complain about who runs the pizza parlors?"

"What's the other reason?" I said.

"They never print anybody's birthday."

"Like Phil Donahue is sixty today?"

"For instance, I would like to know, instead of Pete Smith, forty-three years old, what's his actual date? They don't give you the year even. Sixty years of age. I'd like it if they gave you the year, 1950, '51."

"What about obituaries?"

"Everyone says that. Obituaries you get the birthday. Well, I would like to see that policy extended to the living."

We were both waiting for the elevator to stop. He touched his hair, flattened it across his wide head, getting ready for the world. He was nervous. The closer we got to the lobby, the more I relaxed. He took a deep breath.

"For instance, what is your birthday?" he said.

"My birthday?"

"Sure. I like numbers."

His eyes were black, enveloping. He was a nut. I wasn't going to tell him my birthday.

"August 6, 1959," I said. That's my mom, August 6.

He hummed with his lower teeth holding his lip. "Five-six-eight-nine. Rearrange it and you're almost a straight. See that? You can think about this for a while."

The doors opened, but he hung there an extra second.

"I'm June 9, '48. I'm a slight variation of your series—" He got a grim smile. "Four-six-eight-nine. People always say it's just random, but who's kidding who? It's all chance? No way, my friend."

He smacked the paper against his hand, and just like that he walked away, through the lobby and out to the street. I saw the redheaded guy waiting for him, Blanchard, and where Vacca had been there was just a warm vibrating space. He was such a restless case. Plus he'd taken my paper. The dick had walked off with it.

The sweat came and I walked around the lobby a few minutes, nervouser than ever. I got a fresh *New York Times* and more juice. When I got back upstairs, my shirt was soaked. A door down the hall cracked just as I opened mine. Vacca's. I walked back, and a woman was leaving the room, a tall black-haired woman moving toward the elevator.

There was this way I'd practiced taking pictures, holding the

146

camera at my side and coughing so you wouldn't hear the shutter. I got her picture by the elevator then a second time going down while pretending to read the paper. She had a broad forehead and face powder, she was almost plain, and I couldn't help thinking Vacca might have done a lot better. I smiled at her to get a look at her, but she was thinking about her day, looking ahead. She carried a cheap green fake-crocodile bag, and on her feet were yellow flats, flats because she was so tall.

The dress she wore was yellow, too, but with flowers. I got another shot in the lobby and two more in the street before I went back upstairs and collapsed on my bed.

Not my bed, the bed. Whatever, I was wasted.

13

The Labor Day weekend came and I went to the country, to Rene Rutledge Barce's farm.

I got a 7:00 a.m. bus from the Port Authority that took six hours going up the Hudson and through the woods, through the forgotten hippie towns with rainbows and crystals in the windows and cafés that only play Van Morrison. I changed buses someplace near Phoenicia. After that it got rural and hilly and the driver waved to people he knew and the bus skidded a little stopping on a stone bridge before the guy turned and motioned to me. So this was the famous Guy Park. Not even a town but an old river crossing was where I got off. The air was thin and clean, and underneath was the Antiochus River.

Burry was waiting on a dirt road that went into the trees. She was barefoot and stood next to a new truck. She looked country, she wore a faded blue shift, and when I hugged her there was the smell of her not washing. Her clovy woody flavors of sassafras and smoke and licorice gave me a hard-on, also knowing she wasn't wearing underpants under that old dress. Then we got in the car and when she bent over the ignition I saw the label in the neck and I realized it wasn't a hillbilly dress, it was new linen. She'd spent a lot of money on that dress.

It was Barce's car, a new black Cherokee, with four-wheel drive for his mountain. That's what Burry called his place, Barce's mountain. It took a half hour to get to on dirt roads. I fuzzed in and out of stories I'd heard before. Because Burry repeated herself a lot.

"Rene moved his studio here block by block from his hometown in Alabama. He bought an abandoned millhouse. Or maybe Texas . . .

"Jack, this is that place I told you about. A branch fell on the wire roof and pushed it down and the minks couldn't even go into the little yard. It's not even a yard . . .

"Farmer William is a slob. He leaves his old machines to rust outside. Rene leases to Farmer Mackey, who's gentle on the planet. Father says he washes his gravel."

I liked the way she drove. Her naked foot punched the accelerator going up hills and the tires spat gravel. She went too fast, we skidded on the dirt and the car rocked.

"I can't wait for you to meet Rene, he's a great old badger. Remember that's how you pronounce it. Rennie, the American way. Rene is loyal as winter. Father always says that."

And a bunch of other old-fogy expressions, too. And though I'd planned to ask her how Barce shot his first wife, now I realized it would just upset her. It would be traitorous. And I didn't want to either. I was going to be there with her instead of being an unhappy hypercritical asshole all the time.

At a rude stone gate we took a rutted path up through thick woods, actually two tire ruts with grass between. This became Rene's long driveway, an avenue of oaks, and at the end of them a small handsome Greek-revival farmhouse with white pillars out front.

The house was empty. People weren't getting there till later and Burry took me through pretending it was ours. It made you feel good about America and the future. My future, I mean. The windows were open. Two o'clock's timpani light showed the unevenness of the old plaster walls, and I couldn't take it all in, I was too stunned. Barce's wives had decorated the place, and it was all American and indigenous, nineteenth-century etchings and Hudson River paintings in chipped gilt frames, harvest tables with ring stains left by bruised berries in iron colanders, Indian-head paintings cut from tin, and none of Barce's gross anatomy series to be seen.

She showed me my bedroom with a narrow iron bed frame in it and her bedroom down the hall. Because it would be an insult to Father if we slept together under his nose, even if he didn't know we were doing it. So no sneaking.

We walked past the millhouse studio to the back pasture. There was a creek, and a board bridge over it, and Burry gave everything names, the plants.

"Nile's vermilion," she sang out in a Billie Holiday voice. "Fetlock dandelion." She went along a stone wall that was falling apart and pulled flowers from the cracks. "Vagrant cropsie . . . Mollie Leonard fescue. From before the Jews took the name Leonard."

"Burry," I said.

"It's a joke, baby."

"I know it is, but you know what? I was just thinking, just when you said that, I bet I'm the first Jew in this field."

"Oh Jack—" She dropped her hand with the flowers.

"It's true, Burry, isn't it? I bet it's true."

"Of course it isn't. Are you feeling insecure, baby?" She gave me a giant hug and hummed into my neck, and swung me from side to side. "Because listen, sweetie, if you're having self-loathing, that's not good, we have to do something about it."

"It's just culture shock, that's all," I said into the barn-dust smell of her scalp.

"You know what Blake told me today? She said you're great, and we should get married."

"That's because Blake would never marry me herself."

"Jack stop! I wanted you to hear that because when you get

down on yourself you can be a troublemaker, and Rene is one of my oldest friends."

"It's just a thought I had. That there's never been a Jew."

She swung her arm, sailing the flowers into the grass. "Well somebody has to think about the property values," she said.

I grabbed her hard, but she wriggled away, laughing. She fell in the grass and struggled to her feet. Then with a yawnlike animal shrug she yanked her dress over her head. It fell on high stalks and held there, and she was just in her black bra.

The dress made a transparent tent on the grass, and her muscular back sloped like an arrow into her high plush butt. She moved ahead of me through the safari grass, her flesh jostling with each step. Her skin was white and smooth like a mirror, and rays of hot sunlight danced off it into the speary grass. There was a pond. She stepped into it on black stones, up to her knees.

Seeing her like that tore at me, my stomach got heavy as a rock and my skin felt burned. When a girl's naked but wearing her bra it's even more of a turn-on than if she's completely naked. They'll do that in Italian movies. The bra in that situation is called an intensifier. This is something I actually know.

She untangled the bra from her shoulders and draped it on a rock, then gasped and went under. I lay in the grass and listened to the insect buzz. Short hard grass poked into my ear and the sun came right through my eyelids, so I put my arm over my eyes.

I woke up with water dripping in my face. Burry squeegeed her hands over her stomach and crotchpelt, then her thighs, throwing water down on me. She knelt on my chest. Her knees stuck up, she was like a kid with a pail on the beach. She reached back and fumbled at my zipper with her feet flatly planted.

If you tilted your head you could see a corner of the house poking over a tree. That meant they could see us.

"Not here," I said.

"Yes here."

I tried to get out from under her, but she pushed my shoulders down.

"Stop worrying about the neighbors."

Pondwater fell from her tits and in the sunlight you could see the lazy faint hairs that circled her bellybutton, you could see her squinched white belly making three generous folds. She licked her hands to put me inside her, then using her feet she began to push herself to and fro.

The daylight made me modest. I didn't look in her eyes, I looked in the grass. Her ankle was thick. First I thought it was the mud on her heel, or the angle. But I looked at the other one and it was the same. So: she had thick ankles.

Back at the house I took a nap and when I got up the light was shifting. I lay in bed listening to the noises of a country house filling up for the weekend. Cars came up the driveway, right under my window. People stretched and sighed as they got out. "Christ, I'm parched—" It was Blackie Roberts. He kept bellyaching for a while and threw his shoes on the porch.

I was about to go out when heavy footsteps went by my door.

"What a filthy lot of unwashed sheep," a man cried out. Then he went further and said, "Berenice! When are you going to get to those sheep?"

It was the Secretary. I waited for him to be gone, then the door opened and Burry came in. She had something to show me. We went to her room. It had more of Barce's simple style. There was a bed with dark wooden posts, and pineapples carved into the tops.

"Look at this. Peter brought it from the city."

I sat on the bed to read the *Daily News*. It had printed the cartoon of Sam Knowings, and there was already a controversy. The paper had hired a handwriting expert. And Vacca's lawyer was quoted saying the campaign questioned the authenticity but if he did do it it was because Vacca is the biggest Yankees fan around. It's something you learn in the law: I didn't do it but if I did do it this is why. I never got that. How can anyone say that? I don't mean as a lawyer, as a human being. How does that help you figure anything out? I guess Del McLean was right, I shouldn't be a lawyer.

Peter Sisley came in.

"Hullo Jack," he said.

"Peter," I said.

He sat down in a big wooden chair, and he was completely dressed up. He had on sky-blue bell-bottoms and a Nehru jacket, and the jacket was the same sky blue as the pants but with a darker blue paisley pattern in it. Under the Nehru jacket was a pressed white collarless shirt, and his shoes weren't really shoes but mouse-gray slippers.

"You look pretty," Burry said.

Peter looked down at his outfit.

"I got this last year. I've just been waiting for the right occasion. So I'll thank the ugly men in my prayers tonight."

Burry pushed the fingers of her right hand through mine. "Father and his friends called themselves that when they were young," she said. "The ugly men."

"Basically a bunch of straight rich white guys that need an excuse to queen it up," he said. "They'll all look at me funny till Blackie says, Oh, he's all right, he's one of us, he's a cradle Episcopalian."

"Peter, it's a tradition. From them all starting out and in poverty."

He laughed and drew a plastic bag from his jacket and began shaking pot onto a book. "That's good, poverty. And every weekend black-tie dinners."

"That was only when one of them had a book come out or sold a painting. Or if Father got a big appointment. Or like his speech tomorrow. Then they'd dress up."

153

"Oh great," I said. Because I was wearing jeans. I got up and went to the window, I sat on the sill.

"Even if they were only eating rice and beans." Burry's voice was faraway, furry with nostalgia. "When they didn't have a pot to piss in they put their nickels together for good champagne."

"I like that," Peter said. "Nickel champagne, the Early Quinlan story."

"I hate you," Burry said.

"Well really, Burry, I don't think they were poor."

"My little brother and I slept in the same room and the apartment was tiny."

Peter lit a joint and sipped hard on it. Then he let the smoke out. He held out the joint, but she turned away from it.

"Your grandfather was a New York congressman who owned a newspaper," he said.

"Right, a congressman. Public service pauperizes people. It's why Father has to do ridiculous things like write screenplays."

Peter walked the joint over to me at the window, and I had a hit. I exhaled, watching the smoke go up to the cracked ceiling.

"Burry, what am I going to wear?" I said.

"Oh you don't have to," she said.

"Really you can wear anything you want," Peter said.

But my heart was rabbiting at the idea of the ugly men. "Yeah and be a total loser."

"Maybe we can rent something in town," Burry said.

"Why not," Peter said, smiling. "There's always the 7-Eleven—"

"Burry you set me up," I said.

"No I didn't, baby."

"You didn't tell me anything—"

I walked the joint back to Peter. His chair was a white-hunter design, where the back reclines more if you move a rod to a different set of pegs.

154

"You confuse me, Jack," she said. "You're always telling me what a big outsider you are."

"Right. That's why I need a tuxedo."

Peter laughed. Burry placed her bare feet apart on the floor. She propped her elbows on her knees and held her chin, staring off. I touched her shoulder.

"Burry, somewhere in this house is a black suit. Now all you have to do is find it."

She looked up at me, then stood and left the room.

Peter let out a gust of smoke and held out the joint.

"Nice, Jack. I don't think anyone's taken her so seriously her whole life."

"That's the problem, Peter. Everyone underestimates her so she doesn't take herself seriously."

"I guess," he said.

I went to the window. Sheep were moving through the pasture not far from the pond. You could see what the Secretary was talking about. They were dirty and yellowish-gray. A lot of them looked like they were wearing old-fashioned lace-up boots that went to the knees. I guess they'd been walking through mud.

Burry brought back an old suit of Barce's and a white shirt from her father's stash. Politicians have a stash of white shirts in cardboard boxes. They use them like tissues. Stony even had one guy who was responsible for carrying the box, the shirt-carrier. It's a power thing, always have the crispest shirt. So I was wearing an official Quinlan shirt, and it fit O.K., the arms were just a little short. Peter lent me suspenders for Barce's pants, but the waist was much too wide and I moved around in them like waders.

We hung in Peter's room and then his friend Bill arrived from the airport, bringing Simi Winfrey. Bill was an architect in the

155

city. I guess it was important for Simi and Blackie to arrive separately, he was trying to keep the relationship a big secret, if only from his peers.

Peter teased me a lot about meeting the Secretary. He said it would be fine, but I was nervous, and I kept smoking pot. Simi was nervous, too. Her thing was French bottled water. Almost every sip she had to redo her lipstick, and her hand kept going to her hair, piling the dark mass up just right. She wore a blue jacket with the sleeves rolled up and black tights that stopped just below her knees. And her good little legs went down to forties-style sandals that had a high cork heel.

The house was filled with the smell of duck and pork roasting, and someone put on an Eddie Fisher record that boomed up the stairs. We went down at eight o'clock, cocktail hour. There was a table on the porch with a hundred bottles on it, and ice. Then an old red pickup with a split windshield came up the driveway and a lean man with long white corn-tassely hair slipped quietly from the cab. He wore overalls and a long-sleeved thermal undershirt. He nodded politely at each of us and walked through the living room and into the basement.

So that was Rene Rutledge Barce.

Barce came back up a few minutes later in black tie. I guess he kept his clothes in the basement, because he hung the over-alls on the basement door. A pad stuck up out of the bib pocket and you could see drawings on it, weeds and fish.

Burry introduced us. He was quiet and had a piercing stare, like a backwoods philosopher, that was the main thing about Barce. His skin was fine-grained and rosy, with the anger flowing out through every pore. He wore silver glasses.

"I like the paintings," I said, meaning the ones on the wall.

"You do? Of course this room is all of a theme."

I hadn't noticed, I hadn't even looked at them really. Talking about them was just my way of not talking about Barce's own paintings.

156

"They're all out of doors," I said.

He gave a little nod. "Landscapes. And fishermen. In every one there is a fisherman. A couple are hard to spot."

So I did the thing of going from one to the other.

The whole time the Secretary wasn't there. Then Blackie roared and people looked up. Quinlan was at the top of the stairs. He came down one at a time, chanting bullshit.

"Ban ban Caliban. Not a monster, not a man," he called out. People went nuts laughing.

"Ayn Ayn Annie Rand. Who used up the Spic and Span—"

And on like that, with everyone laughing and him pretending they weren't there, with his handsome, take-my-picture face. Then almost at the bottom he leaned out over the banister toward Burry. "Best. Did you wash. The sheep?"

He spoke in little bubbles of sound.

"Yes, Father." Then she put her fist into my back and pushed me forward. "Father, this is Jack."

He was so good-looking it was almost frightening. His hair went up like rock, like a mineral, and his eyes were small and steady and wide-set in the fine square face. "Hello, Mr. Secretary," I said, but he only looked at me for a second before he started spanking the banister again.

"Jack Jack Saranac. All the boys go quack quack quack . . ."

People laughed, and all the things I'd rehearsed to say to him, a little joke I'd thought up about not knowing whether to call him Secretary or Governor or Ambassador, it just died in my mouth. He could be an asshole, and he kept hitting the banister, giving himself time to think up more stuff about me.

"Jack Jack Kerouac— Plagiarized the almanac . . ."

Burry was quiet-squealing with laughter, and it came to me that I would never be as clever or talented as Secretary Quinlan, I just wouldn't. Even the way he held his shoulders and the way his hands moved, he blazed with a kind of talent. Even

157

the scar in his lip. Especially the scar in his lip. What if I went up to him and said, Mr. Secretary, I will never be as clever as you, would that shut him up about my name?

But of course I didn't, and we went into the dining room and Barce lit candles. In addition to normal candlesticks, he had a bunch of sculptures, old cement garden statues, cupids and those fat guys with fur pants that have a name, and he'd stuck long candles in the crooks of their arms or between their knees. The candles were fat and made torchy shadows on the walls, which was cool. Then the cook brought in the food and Blackie Roberts showed off this technique called siege-pouring he said a Sandinista had taught him, where you poured nine wineglasses at once. He drenched the tablecloth.

I sat next to Burry and on her other side was her father.

Blackie got up to say grace. He went to the head of the table, he put his hand on Quinlan's head.

"Lord, we thank you for the harvest. And pray for the timely surge of our brother's fortunes. It is September. The farmer sweats under the stars but Early's crop is still in the field. Subject to vermin and the elements—"

Then he couldn't go on. He put his glass down and covered his eyes. Quinlan patted him on the back.

"Hiccup," he said softly. "Hiccup."

Blackie looked up again.

"Let the vines sag. Let the leaves rattle on the belly of the pumpkins . . . And let us lead our lives with grace."

"Amen," Quinlan said, and Blackie kissed him on his scalp.

For a second there was a quiet graceful moment just like Blackie said. Everyone felt lucky, even me, I forgot about my total failure with the Secretary. But after that came a free-for-all for the food. Greasy duck breast was heaped on the plates and falling onto the tablecloth, etcetera.

The food was excellent. The duck had a blackberry sauce picked on Barce's land and the vegetables were local. There was good wine.

Burry tried again with her father. "Jack's a constitutional lawyer. He's an excellent lawyer."

The Secretary dipped his head. "Always a need for good constitutional lawyers," he said.

"Actually, some people say if one's not careful it's a lot easier to do bad than good as a lawyer," I said.

"More than other professions?"

"I think so," I said.

"Don't know about that."

His features were delicate and haughty. He was thinking I was a fool.

"If you think of how many real estate and political scams are basically brought off by lawyers," I said.

He looked away. "Focus on the doers. Not the surrogates. Lawyers didn't pull down Pennsylvania Station."

I had a whole answer for that but Burry squeezed my hand. No fighting, no biting. And a little later you got to move. I moved down between Peter and Simi. The cook brought in dessert, pies made from local peaches and blueberries, with good crumbly crust, and coffee she served you from silver.

Blackie crowded his chair in between me and Simi. His knuckles on her shoulder were greasy with duck. "Heart, what did you think of my prayer?" he said.

She turned her bright smile on him like a magazine cover.

"It's a rare special thing to see men express affection so openly."

"See, that's where you're wrong," he said. "The love of man for man is the strongest bond on the earth. It's stronger than romantic love. It endures. Just ask my wife."

Barce laughed a dry little laugh. "Women can never be ugly," he said.

"Who gets to be ugly?" Simi said. "Who and how?"

Barce stared at his coffee. The candlelight made his glasses into white disks.

"He must be married. He must have a future he can see."

"With a daughter he'd kill for," Blackie said.

Quinlan smacked a glass on the table. "Full engagement of one's powers. That's how Jack Kennedy defined happiness."

"Right," Blackie said. "The work's the only monument."

"And never, never be rich," Barce said.

Everyone laughed.

"Well not filthy rich," Blackie said.

"Not nigger rich neither," Barce said.

Well, they laughed more, Burry drooped her head laughing.

"What's that mean, Rene?" she said.

"Cadillacs in Harlem," Blackie said.

Quinlan scraped his chair back. "Imprudent. Spending—" He spoke in god-like fragments. "Windfalls. A body can't. Hold on to."

"There, that's nigger rich," Barce said.

"Careful—" Quinlan said. He got to his feet, his vague mirthful eyes hardened.

"Oh Early, the speech ain't till noon."

"That word has never escaped my lips," he said. "Not in four decades of service."

"Amen," Burry said.

The Secretary went out the French doors, his talent blazing, and I couldn't help it, I liked him.

Inside got too weird, Blackie was putting down other writers in a drunken way, so we went out. Peter and Bill went into the pasture. They were so high, they got spooked by the shadows of apple trees. Because it was a full moon.

"If only trees had eyes," I heard Peter say. "Then people would love them."

Burry took me into the garden. Her bare feet crushed the white pebbles and I studied the shadowy scoops she left behind her. We sat on a stone bench. A heavy gearshift clanked. Simple oval taillights glowed in the driveway: the old pickup.

"That's Rene going to his trailer in the woods," Burry said. "Oh, Jack, he liked you a lot."

"How do you know that?"

"He winked at me."

"I was waiting for him and Blackie to get going on Aryan bloodlines," I said.

"I know but baby, be big," she said. "You don't have to take everything personally."

In a lurch she hung her left leg over my right and put her arm around my neck.

"Don't forget they suffered," she said. "Remember what Blackie said about losing their gods and their friends."

Then I hated them. They talked constantly about their youth, and nothing we ever did would be as mythic as their youth. They would like it most if we pissed our own youth away, romanticizing theirs.

"Jack, what are you thinking?"

"About why they call him Blackie." So there, I'd lied to her.

"Jack—baby—close your eyes."

She fluttered kisses down my face. "Does that feel better?" I hummed.

"Don't you love being here in the moonlight near the gods, Jack, aren't we lucky?"

Her face filled with moonlight and her eyes were like jewels she just left out for you to steal. Then I felt guilty for all the things I'd thought about her and her father when really she was decent. She'd brought me here. It was cool here. Her father was aloof but O.K., the way he stopped them cold on nigger-rich.

"Jack, talk to me, you're thinking something again."

"I'm thinking about all the lying I've done," I said.

She took a sharp breath. "To me?"

"I lied for James Doyle, I lied right and left to Vacca."

"That's politics."

"I thought it was about relationships. Love, loyalty."

"It is. In the end that's all it is."

"But what about the means?"

"The means? Oh, Jack, calm down baby. In another month or two this will be over. Now what's our plan?"

"Our plan?" I said.

"Our plan, Jack"—she yanked me closer with her leg.

My guts felt heavy. My stomach turned to stone, my intestines, I was heavy as a statue.

"Your dad is going to win the election."

"That's only two months. You and I should think in years."

I looked away. Moonlight etched ridges and hard squiggles into the rinds of melons in the melon patch past the barn. I looked at the house. A woody old vine twisted hard against itself along the porch roof. Everything was neat. Barce had professional gardeners to do that. You ate good American food, you used your fullest powers like Jack Kennedy.

"Will we come back here sometimes?" I said.

"Of course. Jack, how often do two people come together like this? Sometimes it feels like a storybook. For a reason. I want you to listen to your heart. I want you to trust yourself."

I disentangled myself and stood and stretched. A tremble went down my spine. "But I don't feel lucky," I said.

"Oh Jack," she said. "I do. I feel very lucky."

I thought about my dad. Outside the left no one knew about him. Because my father was wrong about servants, about getting people to do things for you. You had to delegate chores or you would never get anything done. The Secretary understood that. That's why he had delegated tasks to me, the Valery-Michael. Suddenly I wanted to talk to the Secretary about that, about what I'd done for him. I'd never even shaken his hand.

Burry stood up.

"Jack," she said.

"I want to be with you," I said.

She nodded. Her eyes were quiet, real. "That's good. That's what I want, too."

162

I heard her breath going calmly. I heard every little thing, her dress moving against her sides, which I guess is what happens when something important is happening, everything slows down. I said, "I'd like to be married to you."

She made a little hum. "I'd like that, too."

That was how it was, too, deciding, and at once I felt better about everything. I didn't feel heavy inside, or trembly. We sat down and held hands like adults and talked calmly as if it were the simplest thing in the world. We talked about where we would live. Maybe near here. I could be a country lawyer and write books. Lawyers made a ton of money writing novels with legal themes. *Preponderance of the Evidence. Congress Shall Make No Law.* Bullshit titles like that. I could do that, and Burry would paint. Rene Barce had told her she had a gift.

"First you have to talk to Father," she said. "That's the very first thing, Jack. He's old-fashioned that way."

"All right."

Then just like that she started planning. Spring was her favorite season, and June her favorite month.

So June. And as soon as you say that other questions come. Like how many people, and where? A big hotel probably. And would she lose friends around it? People said you always did but she didn't want to. She wanted to invite all her old friends.

But she had so many friends. And who would buy the flowers. And who her dress. Burry held my hand in both of hers and moved them up and down against my leg like a pump of social pleasure.

14

I didn't really sleep, and a crow woke me up at daybreak. A rooster, I mean. It wasn't a sweet sound either, its voice was scrapy and harsh. I wondered if doing that hurt its throat. No. Probably not. They were made to do that.

When I got up again there were rude cries out the window that could have been a fight. But it was people playing touch football. James Doyle was there with some other campaign workers and Blackie Roberts and Peter, all the yellow hair men with cheekbones and the long lawn, like an ad set in old America. An ad only a Jew would make. But there I went, being bloody-minded when I should trust my luck.

I was marrying Burry, I was going to talk to Father. Then that rooster went again, as if agreeing.

Downstairs there was a huge pan of drying-out scrambled eggs and you could have that and bacon and leftover pie. Also, fresh-squeezed orange juice and grapefruit juice in heavy crystal pitchers with Saran wrap around the tops to keep them fresh. Then the cook came in and wanted to help me, with her Irish accent.

I got coffee and a toasted bagel and walked out on the porch. A hummingbird darted among the trees.

Burry was on the patio with her father and Barce. They sat in iron chairs, painted green. She was teasing her father about stuff. He was as dramatic as her, he threw himself back in the chair.

"If I found myself avec two bimbos on a bateau called *Monkey Business*? I promise you, Best"—he made the chair's feet clap on the flagstones—"I'd jump off the damn stern and start swimming to shore."

They all laughed, and I watched without their seeing me.

Quinlan's speech was set for the town of Antiochus at 1:00, and Burry and I went ahead of him in the Cherokee with James Doyle. The campaign was making a TV ad from the speech, and James sat in front, twitchy and quiet. Burry drove. She had on a blue silk dress your mother might wear, I guess the dress James had wanted her to wear at the convention. We weren't saying anything to one another, we were each carrying the secret, letting it burn down between us like a wound that would have to scar over.

I sat in the back between cardboard boxes filled with American flags on little sticks and round stickers saying EARLY NEVER QUITS. Because those were his initials.

James hung his arm over the seat. His jaw was tensed, the way it always was when he had an agenda.

"This cartoon story's very good," he said. "That story in the *Daily News*."

But I ignored him. I was going to talk to the Secretary.

"How many people know about the girlfriend picture?"

"Just you," I said.

Antiochus was small and pretty and tucked into a loop of the river. There were pretty Victorian houses on the high street, and leggy rhododendrons leaning out over iron fences. At the village green, boys were whitewashing the white board fence, but they were only doing a two-hundred-foot section behind

165

the platform for the TV cameras. It was a jewel of a green and right across the street was a narrow graveyard with tilting tooth-like gravestones thinned by two hundred years of shitty weather. It was perfect for a political ad, or a bed-and-breakfast, a place your parents would stay.

Burry wore black heels that James said were too vampy, so he made her sit first here then there and wanted to see how she held her feet. And no duct tape on the platform either, no wires, I guess because duct tape hadn't been invented in the 1800s. The Secretary was to speak without a microphone. They had a hidden microphone they clipped next to his boutonniere, so he'd look like a stem-winder, virile and blustery.

I stood outside the fence and when the speech began James came and stood there, too, with a sour expression. We each had a stone post to lean on. Flags snapped in the air over the platform, and the Secretary's hair went up into spears.

"I have come today. To share with you. Good people. A grand ambition." He spoke in those fragments. "Which only. With your support. Can I attain."

Long pause. The wind reached for his speech, but he flattened his hand over it.

"Sitting down. Last night. To write these comments. I thought to trace. The origins. Of that. Ambition. To chart its headwaters. And so found myself. Paddling back against the great current. Of time. To the. Waters of youth. The Mohawk. River. A great New York river. That cleaves Herkimer County. And most importantly. When I think of my boyhood. Separated me. Unhappily I felt. From Grandfather's house."

Another pause, and you thought you were in for a load of shit about the grandfather, how he walked ten miles to give a lady a nickel, and was injured in the World War, and then discovered lightning and the printing press, but Quinlan laid right off that.

"Now separation actually. Is a great and abiding principle. Of modern civilization. And one in whose development. This

166

republic. And this state. Can take some pride. The separation of powers. Of course. And the separation of. States under federalism. But more. The separation. Of. All individuals. Inherent in. The framers' words. And in our democratic. Institutions. And in the. Constitutional guarantee. Of being left. Alone."

That was his theme, the soul of a citizen of a democracy. The audience was completely respectful and polite with their little flags, and the Secretary was austere and respectful back. It came to me I'd gotten it all wrong. In the Walker campaign politics was about passion, conflict, and Stony said that politics turned people's fears and hatreds into hope. Now all that felt wrong, it was too open-ended and sweaty. Passion was passion, not politics. That's why I'd been so unhappy. Politics had called on my passions and then not been able to do anything with them. I'd felt used and lied to. Whereas for Quinlan politics was about order and respect, a public square to which you summoned people and asked from them only their best.

Then my mind fell. If it's about summoning people's best, what am I doing in the Valery-Michael following Joseph Vacca? So I started thinking like that, and my heart was bursting all over again.

"Jack," James said.

The speech wasn't over, but I turned. He was leaning against the column still, with his arms folded on the top, his chin resting on his forearms.

"I'm not going back to the Valery-Michael," I said. "I can do something else in the campaign."

"You're not in the campaign," he said.

My face burned, I felt as if he had pushed me.

"I never got you on payroll, Jack. And right now that's looking like a lucky thing."

"You're going to sell me out," I said.

James lifted his arms from the column. "Calm down, Jack. I want you in the fold, I have an idea for you."

"I don't want any more ideas."

167

Sustained applause. The speech had ended. The Secretary felt at his jacket, smoothed his hair. He stepped from the rostrum.

"Those memos you wrote?" James said. "On Vacca's reasoning? I showed them to the Secretary. The Secretary thought they were quite astute. Where you line up cases to show the obsession? And that they should be published. George Sides agrees."

The Secretary was stepping lightly in the middle of a fife-and-drum corps. They wore tricorner hats and were playing those famous Yankee Doodle tunes. Burry came across the green toward us. Her high heels weren't working on the ground, she buckled a little. She smiled at people in this friendly regal manner.

"George wants to talk to you," James said.

"I'm talking to the Secretary."

"Frankly I wouldn't bother the Secretary," he said.

"Then don't."

Burry and I walked back to the car together. People gave her room on the sidewalk and dipped their shoulders saying hello, it was almost feudal. She mouthed hello back or just smiled. A lot of times when we passed, she'd whisper shit to me.

"Clem, you better lay off them cows," she said. "Beulah, how'd you make it through the amnio net—" Because that was one of her jokes: amniocentesis was meant to catch people like that beforehand.

She didn't love the common man. Some individuals, yes, but she didn't see much of anything in the common man.

15

In the afternoon Burry took me to her father's room. It was in
a dormer that had been added later to the house, one of Barce's
many boxes. You went up a narrow set of stairs at the back.
Burry knocked and the door fell away under her knuckles.

I looked over her shoulder. Two windows in the same wall
opened over the fields. The room itself was small and tilted like
the bedroom in that Van Gogh painting. There was a tarnished
brass bed and wide floorboards. A large primitive oil painting
of a cow hung over the head of the bed. You could see it
reflected in the dresser mirror that hung opposite the foot of
the bed. Another cow painting was between the windows, a
black-and-white one, I want to say a Jersey. It'd be no sweat
if Barce tested me about the theme of these paintings.

The Secretary was in the mirror, too. I saw his spindly blue-
white legs slanting off the bed, and his white feet sticking up
straight, like a dead man. I backed away. But Burry grabbed
my wrist and pulled me over the threshold.

Her father was asleep. A legal pad tilted off his stomach and
his hand, holding a fountain pen, had fallen onto a pillow. A
black tit of ink spread out from the pen. His robe had come

169

open, a blue paisley job, and you could see his undershirt and boxer shorts. His half-glasses were perched on his nose.

Burry acted like everything was hunky-dory. She bent for the pen, and he opened one eye. He made a hum in his throat. He sat up, and the hum turned into a song.

"I'm a Yankee Doodle dandy," he sang.

"Oh, Father." She touched his hair. "I worry about you. Running takes so much out of you."

"Ahh— Best. The hand on the hip, I knew it, the hand on the hip."

She dropped her hand. "Elections are so cruel," she said. "Now where did you put that pen cap?"

The two of them began hunting through the bedclothes. I looked down at the pad. It was toppled against a pillow, but you could read it upside down.

Flashback. Afternoon. Brooklyn Pier. Jane Betters hands Rupe letter. Janey: auburn hair full lips light yellow sweater but aint a sweater girl.

Belovedness an illusion. Yet every great act arises f/ that belief.

I felt something cold on the side of my face and turned. The Secretary was looking at me, his cold blue eye. He reached for the pad and flopped it onto the nightstand.

"You'll get nowhere in life till you learn to read upside down," he said. "Who said it, Abe Lincoln?"

"Abe Fortas," I said.

"Father, you remember Jack," Burry said.

"Of course I remember Jack," he said. "Jack who believes it's so easy to do bad as a lawyer."

He smiled and I smiled back. Then he pulled himself forward and patted his feet on the floor. Burry knelt and found his slippers, he scuffed them onto his feet.

"Jack wants to talk to you," she said.

"Well then I want to talk to Jack," he said brightly.

170

The Secretary got to his feet and walked to the dresser. There was a native neatness to him, even in a robe. He didn't really have to comb that hair. A bunch of glasses were on the dresser, turned upside down. He slid one to himself across the marble and felt among a group of bottles, peering at the labels.

"Father, what is this—" Burry had pulled the door back from the wall. A rifle leaned into the corner with a sweater draped over its mouth, the barrel, whatever they call it.

"Is this Rene's?" she said. "Is Rene allowed to have guns?"

"Best, don't speak of property," he said. "Remember. The Declaration don't say 'Life, liberty, and property.' Jack can tell you that." He waved a bottle at me.

"Right," I said.

"Right. Says life, liberty, and the pursuit of happiness," he said. "What's that, counsel? Eh—pursuit of happiness?"

He laughed, and so did I, we were almost hitting it off, and just like that Burry walked out. She was gone, saying nothing. I heard her bare feet on the floor then the hard chub of her heels going down the steep steps.

The Secretary delicately unspooled the bottle cap.

"Secretary," I said.

"Early," he said.

"Early." The name felt weird in my mouth, small, cornerless.

He wagged a bottle at me, then not waiting for a response, tilted it with both hands. It chattered on the glass's rim.

"Always use two hands," he said. "Just like a pop-up. Just like your father told you. One hand is for hot dogs. Here—to the pursuit of happiness, whatever that is."

I wasn't ready for the drink. There was no ice in it so it burned my mouth, and when I swallowed the alcohol fled through my body and I had to sit. There was a chair against the wall next to the windows, a chair with weaving in the seat, rushes, bulrushes, I don't know the name. I fell into it, and the weaving sank and made a noise.

The Secretary lowered himself stiffly onto the bed. When his glass neared his chin he lost his cool. He dipped his head and like an eager cat his pink-tab tongue came out of his mouth to taste the liquid before it went into his mouth. In the light his black hair was mostly white. But thick, solid.

"Early I've been doing work for you," I said. "Reading up on Vacca."

He nodded, but his eyes showed no recognition. Maybe James had lied about that.

"He was a bomb thrower in law school," I said.

"Everyone is—should be, anyway." His voice came out clean, dehusked by the liquor. "That's why we send them to law school," he said affably. Then he stared right past me, out the window. The scar in his lip actually lifted the lip up a little, opening it. He took another sip, watching something.

I sat forward. "James feels, James Doyle, that I should make an article out of the memos I did on Vacca's ideas."

"But Jack doesn't want to," he said.

"Jack's not sure—" That sounded idiotic. "I'm not sure."

He peered outside again. He'd do anything not to look at you. The window was open but just at the top. Both frames of glass were at the bottom, doubled up. And you saw a million dead flies at the bottom. Then he turned to the bar, I mean the dresser. And this time he picked up the bottle with one hand, normal, and no bullshit about pop flies.

"Journalism—" he said.

"I'm not talking about journalism."

"Journalism quenches a young man's thirst for voyeurism. Righteous voyeurism—" He lifted the glass, and the same thing with his tongue, where it tabbed down like a cat. "Then he grows up, and he'd much rather have other people watch him."

"Politics is worse. No one thinks about anybody real."

Early glanced my way.

"Politics. The public face. Of politics. Is a carny show." He started going in those God-bubbles of sound. "A masque, yes.

172

But one designed to. Get the people. To shed their inhibitions. And speak their truth."

I drank off my glass. "But you had faultless political instincts."

He swung his head from side to side. "Nope. Never did. Historical instinct. That I had. Sense of the historical forces."

The robe fell open, and you got a whiff of his stale B.O., his big-speech willies. I leaned forward again in the chair, so the rushes, the crisscrossing, squeaked and gave.

"I got that cartoon," I said.

He blinked. "Pardon."

"That picture of the ballplayer everyone says is racist. Vacca drew it. I got it."

He held out a hand as if I meant to hit him. "Careful—"

"And I've been staying at the hotel," I said.

Early shut his eyes and yawned, or maybe not a yawn, his mouth opened and a long *Awwwnnng* came out, a sort of screendoor-spring noise.

"The Valery-Michael," I said. "Vacca's hotel."

But he had shut me out. He was wobbling his head from side to side, and the screendoor noise turned into a murmuring chant.

"I'm a Cock-a-doodle dandy," he sang. "I'm a Cock-a-doodle boy. Boyyy, boyyy boyyy."

It was a mumble and a song all at once. His voice blurred everything, and I waited for him to stop.

Then he was quiet. He retied his robe primly. I got to my feet and he held out his glass to me. I put a shot of Scotch in his glass and tilted some more into mine, too.

He sighed. "Damn sheep. Someone ought to wash them."

The sheep were in the pasture on the other side of a stone wall, maybe a hundred yards away. They were tranquil. Some lay on the ground having a rest, others moved through the grass, tearing up hanks. They jerked their heads to the side when they

173

yanked the grass. Maybe there were a hundred sheep, and they really were dirty. Dark mats hung off their undersides. There was crud in their tails, too. Brambles. They didn't seem to mind.

"I guess you can't process the wool till you wash them," I offered.

"Generally swim them through a tank." Early wiggled his hand through the air, imitating a sheep swimming. "Takes days for them to dry. Ergo. Keep them in a clean place. Then cut it off. All in one piece. Deburr it, they call it. And card it—"

He kept happily at the motions with his hands. That's the thing about talking to a traditional-type person. They don't want to ever talk sincerely about the personal matter between you, they want to talk about a third thing. Sheep.

"After that it's wool?" I said.

"It's wool right now," he said. "That's wool all right."

I looked back at the sheep and my heart chilled. Because you could see the pond, a corner of it anyway. Fifty yards past the sheep was another wall and then tall unmunched grass, the pond.

When had the Secretary gotten here yesterday?

I tried to make out the grass we'd flattened. No sign of it. I fell back heavily against the wall.

"Early, I'm in love with Burry."

"Is that wool? he says. Hell, that's wool right now."

"Berenice, I mean. Your daughter. We're together."

He pursed his lips and finally looked at me. "I thought she was with what's his name. Tharp."

"Charles?" I shook my head.

"Or that other. Little round Choatie. Mr. J. Walter Fatso." He moved his hand around. "The Hyannis beachball."

I chinked my glass down on the marble. "We want to make a life together."

Early stood up. He poured himself more firewater right on top of what was there and put some in my glass, too.

"What does he say? In *Lear*?" He knotted that robe for the

174

thousandth time. "And my poor fool is hung. No hanged. You should know this, Gold. And my poor fool is hanged!"

"I don't," I said.

"Ah, he doesn't know the greatest line in literature." His voice went off in a murmur. "And my poor fool is hanged! Lear says it. At the end."

Always talking about a third thing, never the thing at hand, that was the rule with him.

"*King Lear* is a tragedy," I said. "This is happy news."

"You sound like you're writing editorials in Grand Forks, Tharp."

"I'm Gold," I said.

"Sure." He laughed. "You're a dead ringer for Jack Gold. Pursuit of happiness. What is that? Huh?"

"Sir"—I started to answer, then I slumped. "I'm not as clever as you. I'm just not."

His blue eyes opened to take me in. I looked at my knees.

"Or as powerful. Or maybe as smart." I didn't say good-looking. That was a personal comment. No personal comments. "Still, we want to get married."

He had another sip and you could see him swishing it in his mouth, tasting the poison. That was something alcoholics did.

"You want my permission," he said.

"I don't believe in that."

"You don't," he said. "Well, I do. What about that?"

"Then I imagine this is an issue where you'll be on the opposite side from your daughter."

"Don't be a lawyer with me, Jack. Best and I are never at opposites."

"Burry and I have an understanding," I said.

"An understanding? Is that like a letter of credit?"

"We're getting married in June. June is Burry's favorite month."

"Reach me that, will you?"

He was pointing at the corner, the gun.

175

"I don't think that's such a good idea," I said.

"Oh you don't." He laughed. "Well listen, if this were the old days—" He moved past me to the corner. He tugged the sweater away, and the gun scraped down the wall. It bumped the far windowsill and rattled heavily onto the floor near my feet.

"Help me Jack—" He pushed down on my knee.

"Is that loaded?" I said.

"Calm down, I've never killed anyone before and I happen to be running for office."

I don't know why, I picked up the gun. Early reached out to take it from me but he was still holding his glass. So he didn't really have it, just had the stock in one hand and the barrel in two curling fingers of his drinking hand. In the end what happened, I took the glass from him even as I was letting go of the gun. An exchange. I set his glass on the sill, and he sat on the bed and admired the gun in his hands. He rubbed his fingers along the blue steel of the barrel and across the wooden stock. There was carving, a whole picture of a hunting scene in fine carving. I sat down, too, I tried to smile.

" 'Is it loaded?' he says—" Early smiled. "Russian fellow had this piece. Bolt action with a lot of history. Gave it to me after the first nuclear disarmament talks."

Anytime someone's talking about a gun, if they have the gun, you listen.

"Brezhnev's top arms man. Panofsky. Funny man, Panofsky. A wart right here like a pencil eraser. And carried an army canteen with vodka—" Early frowned at the gun. "Well a hateful business and we all knew it. So. Parted friends. And Panofsky said, Here, Early, for you. Lenin used this gun. A Rigby .30-.30. Lenin shot rabbits with it. Loved to shoot rabbits. Imagine shooting rabbits with a .30-.30. Communism in a nutshell."

He stood and me, too, right with him. Then he swung the barrel up onto the sash. It poked out toward Barce's mountain.

"I'd best be going," I said.

176

Early cheeked the thing and slid it this way and that. He bumped it right over the metal window lock and scraped it to the side. Just like some asshole shooting metal ducks. But it was in my way, a gate to keep me from going.

"Excuse me, sir," I said.

"He loves the girl but cannot bring himself to do the honest thing."

"You're standing in my way, sir," I said.

"Stop sirring me, Jack. Anyway you don't know that."

"But I feel it," I said.

"Right. He sees it feelingly. There's only one way for you to find out. But you're irresolute."

"Don't mix booze and guns," I said.

"Don't tell me—Hemingway."

"No, that's mine."

He laughed and bit his lip, looking outside. Such good teeth, square and white, strong. A politician must have good teeth. That's why Whittaker Chambers was such a terrible character, bad teeth. I felt myself slowly dissolving and drank down a lot of the whiskey. He dragged the barrel back along the window, bumping over the lock again.

I bent to go under the gun and he jerked his arms. "I know when a piece is loaded," he said, and then it went off.

The sound was so big I thought it would blow the house apart, and the recoil pushed Early back onto the bed. The gun thudded to the floor. It hit stock down, and from between the boards little pieces of dust jumped up. Even after things stopped moving, the sound kept filling the room. It squeezed out everything, a giant steel ball, hollow but expanding.

"Missed you," he said.

His voice was like a wire voice, the sound a wire makes. He reached for his glass. And this time no cat-tongue either, he bit into the drink.

I got the gun, I stood it back in the corner. I even put the sweater on it. I was trying to get matters back the way they had been, like a cover-up. No one ever says so but a cover-up is the most natural thing in the world. Everyone covers up. Dogs cover up. Animals. It's something you do automatically. Then people say it's the biggest crime.

"See, in olden days, Jack, a man didn't dither," Early said. "That's my sermon this morning."

Well, it wasn't morning, he was way off.

"I better go," I said.

"Oh hell, I've gone and bored you"—and he did the knot on his robe, just like old times. "Well, now you know what's what."

We shook hands with him sitting there. His hand was thin and sweaty. Our eyes met and everything was different. It came to me that he liked me.

"Goodbye, Early."

"Bye now, Jack."

Out the window all the sheep had run but one. It was down and kept getting up. It looked the same as all the other dirty sheep except it was trembling and it couldn't do anything with one leg. It stood up and calmly fell over. Then it jumped up on its front legs and tried to run and, bingo, over again.

"There's a sheep down," I said.

"Don't fun me, Jack."

Early stood up and looked. I glimpsed the whites of his eyes, he might have been scared.

"Egad, and I only meant to wing you," he said.

He put his hand on my shoulder, nicely almost, and walked me to the door.

"Listen, talk to Doyle," he said. "Doyle's a pro. He'll call the veterinarian. Don't ever pronounce that syllable. The *r* is silent. Vet-a-narian. Like February."

I laughed. "O.K."

"Only city slickers say vet-er-inarian," he said. "Rene knows where to find a vet. Last time this happened we had to go halfway to Penn Yan to find a chop-chop in the middle of the night."

He made a chopping motion with his hand. I wondered if that was when Barce shot his wife.

We went into the hall together like old friends, like ugly men. Then it came to me, that was a fraud, Early wasn't ugly. He sure didn't think so.

"Yeah Mr. Tharp. Comes to spend the weekend in his new clothes. Someday I'll show you what he sent me. I call him the ape."

I started down the stairs and he gave me a squeeze on the shoulder.

"You know it's never becoming to put yourself down."

"I guess," I said.

"That business about being clever or smart?" he said. "You should show a little loyalty to yourself."

"Thanks," I said, and went down the stairs.

"Don't ever try and play another fella's hand."

He was looking at me. We both smiled.

It was bullshit about the vet, a vet couldn't have done anything. I went out there with James, and the sheep was in shock or something. There was a red blush of blood on its side, it had come out through the filthy fur slowly, the fleece, which is where that whole expression comes from, getting fleeced. Also the golden fleece, same thing. Its round black eye looked right through you. For a minute we had the dilemma, do we put it out of misery, but then it didn't matter, the sheep died. I think it was scared to death. We scared it just standing there.

I said not to tell Burry, and James agreed. I went in to take a nap and lying in bed I heard James's cool voice under the trees, handling things.

Then the sound of the barn door grinding open on its rusted

wheel track. A rattling when someone lazy brought out a shovel, letting its blade drag over the gravel.

And later still, the squeak of the wheelbarrow. A circular squeak. A squeak every time the wheel went round, crossing the boards over the creek. *Cover-up. Cover-up. Cover-up*, it said.

When I opened my eyes again it was dark. For a second I thought I'd dreamed all that with Early and I was disappointed, I wanted it to have really happened.

Then outside my window there were voices and I got up and you could see the farmer, a beefy guy with his arm on top of the cab of his pickup truck, and reddish-golden hair in ringlets, and the same reddish hair on his arm.

James was talking to him. Barce was out there, too. The sheep was in the back of the guy's truck. It lay on the ridged metal bed, flat and stiff, and on the side that was up you couldn't see any blood.

It's nuts, but that night we had lamb for dinner. We had a fall meal. The cook made scalloped potatoes and roast fennel and leg of lamb, and it was excellent. No one said anything except Barce. He made a joke about Suffer the lamb. There were only eight of us at the table now, I was in the in-crowd and halfway comfortable. I called Rene Rene, and he called me Jack. But Blackie didn't seem to remember me from one hour to the next. And I didn't care. He was self-absorbed and useless.

After dinner we had a bonfire in a gully. The guys that prune and work Rene's acreage had piled old trees in a hollow and the fire went way into the sky. I thought I could tell my mom about it. She loves storybook shit like that. But where could I begin? I couldn't, I had so many secrets from her.

Rene passed around a bottle of cognac and Burry sang. She had a great voice I'd never really heard before. She sang old

180

blues songs, and when she didn't know the words she would just croon nonsense.

She laid her hands flat on the front of her hips and gave the littlest shakes from side to side, and I was helpless not to love her. The fire hadn't died back much when we went in to bed.

16

Larkspur had offices in a downtown building from the turn of the century, from a time when the literary culture was king and they published a satirical magazine called *Grubs' Parade*. I'm sure you've seen the Grubs' Parade. It's got all this extra detail on it, stagy iron mausoleum columns that are bigger than the building needs, a ballroom on the first floor. And right over the front door is a two-story green copper clock. But instead of numbers it says GRUBS' PARADE. The hands point at letters, GRUBS' across the top, PARADE across the bottom. It's really a bullshit building.

The clock is one of those things in New York that still actually work, and when I got there it said five to noon. George Sides had called me right after I got back, and we made an appointment. I liked the idea of writing an article on Vacca, and Burry kept saying how cool it was to be a writer. You only worked for a couple hours in the morning and screened your calls while you did. If you worked any harder, the writing was labored and lifeless. You only needed a few pieces of good clothing, to wear when you went out. That's why Blackie Roberts was such a slob, she said. Writers could be slobs if they wanted.

The Grubs' Parade has an old elevator just like you'd expect, and I got on and pushed 12. The gate was closing when a small guy threw himself through the gap. He just made it, and he stood there trying to hide his smile. You don't want people to see how much a tiny accomplishment like that does for your self-esteem, so he bit down on that feeling like he was biting on a lemon. I pushed 12 again. So did he.

"Where you from?" he said.

He was hip. There were his construction boots. Plus a little iron-filings goatee and a good billowy shirt. His face was red with a suntan, but it didn't keep him from looking a little ferrety.

"Yonkers," I said.

"Yonkers, America?" And he had a British accent.

I nodded.

"Brilliant," he said.

The same thing happened in the *Larkspur* reception area. Three or four people were sitting around on the beat-up old-fogy couch and armchair and the guy went up to each of them.

London. London. London.

"Balls," he said, and seemed about to leave. But he didn't, he sat on the couch arm.

A girl there showed me what was going on. She had a sheet with a tiny ad. "WANTED. Personal Assistant/Secretary willing to work American hours. 31/year." It was some kind of newsletter, with a crown on the front. I guess it was for expatriate English people, with small good printing on white air mail-type paper.

The receptionist buzzed me in and said George was at the end of the hall. The hallway wasn't straight. It curved past cubicle offices and it was lined with wooden panels with paintings on them, actually one continuous painting, a whole sylvan Persian fantasy. There were willow trees and turbaned bearded guys in harem pants, and goat-men. Nymphs came out of trees, bare-chested, a dot of red paint on each titty. The stream went all the way to George.

His was the one office with real walls and a door, and it was dark. The blinds were down, and George sat on his desk facing a blond woman in a conservative suit. She was English, too. So the ad was for George's assistant/secretary.

"After that I worked for Channel Four," she said in a hesitant manner. "A little production. Answering mail."

"In Oxford Circus," George said.

She shook her head. "London Weekend Television."

"Oh sure. Other side of the river."

So it was Anglomania, and then George saw me and slid off the desk. "Jack Jack Jack," he said, pulling me in, shaking my hand, almost like a lifeboat. Because he didn't like being one-on-one with anyone. I mean, man is a social animal, and so was George, George was very social.

I sat in a chair by the desk, and the office was Anglomania, too. It was private and masculine. The desk was large and clean, with a green blotter, and the chairs were covered with worn, cracked leather. And on two walls were old-time pictures of Indians. Just their heads.

"Now, Miss Laver, how do you feel about American hours?"

"Fine."

"See, we don't knock off at 5:00, we've got a global empire to run"—and George went quiet shaking with laughter. You could never tell how full of shit he really was, he made fun of himself before you even got a chance. Then he recovered and took her picture. Because he had trouble remembering names, he said. He had a Polaroid, and he asked her to put her name on the back. She left, completely frightened, with instructions to send in the next person.

"What do you think?" he said.

"A prig."

"But see, that's the joke, Jack. They all are. We're playing to type."

"I guess I don't understand."

George shot me his nervous half-smile.

"Hell, they're the only ones that you can understand on the

184

phone," he said. "Americans you can't understand on the phone. Also for me, Jack? It's a continuity deal. I just lost my assistant, who it just so happens was English. I don't need people calling up and saying, Where's George?"

I laughed. He could make you laugh. Because he took himself less seriously than you did, he knew he was a giant fraud. Then when I laughed George sighed thankfully and started walking around his room.

"Oh I know what you're thinking, Jack, it breaks all the hiring laws. Well Jesus Christ, I wrote those laws. In my kick-ass years? I helped write 'em, when I was a young fur-bearing creature," etcetera.

After that came the girl who'd shown me the ad, a pretty girl in a T-shirt and pearls, and George walked around flirting. He did this other bullshit thing, slipped in American questions.

"What is a fungo circle?" he said.

She clasped her hands. "Like a sewing circle?"

"O.K., good. Now who is Bert Lance?"

"I'm sorry."

"No no. No sorries. Good. How do you make bread pudding?"

She flushed and didn't say anything.

"Oh that's fine. Really. I've been getting some ringers. See, you don't even know what a ringer is, that's good, too. People come in here who have no sense of personal integrity."

He laughed hard and his cheeks got bright red. He turned to me to get me to laugh too.

She sat forward. "Am I done?"

"You're done. Excellent. I'd say yes right this second only I've got five more appointments this afternoon."

Then she left, and he winked at me.

"She's it. Dora. I'd hire her for the name alone. Dora."

He tried it out English.

"Notice how they talk, the good ones? Up and down, over and around. That's how you do it. Enunciation is a dying art."

He made his voice go around the syllables that way. "Up and down. Over and around." And imitating a British person, speaking super clearly like a Gilbert and Sullivan record.

"Up and down. Over and around."

He got a flat box from the counter and dropped it on the desk in front of me. It was filled with pictures of Joseph Vacca, Jr. I don't know where he'd got them, pictures from different phases of Vacca's life, when Vacca's hair was thicker and he carried weight. He had gone through lots of styles, he'd made clothes mistakes that made me like him more. For instance, he wore clip-on suspenders on jeans. Also striped suspenders. I never understood suspenders. Why don't those people just wear a sign, I don't have a sex drive.

Then George grabbed a spike off his counter and lifted off a fax. It was Vacca's schedule. James Doyle had faxed it, and George said he wanted me to follow Vacca around a little, bird-dog him, so I'd have some action along with the ideas.

"You want me to interview him?"

But he flew his hands in the air. "Oh no, don't do that," he said. "Just keep your eyes open. It's the little things he does that come back to you two days later that make him come alive in print. Little things."

A man came to the door, the guy from the elevator. George waved him in. He sat down with a disdainful air, and it made George self-conscious. He patted his tie and kept up his line of shit to me.

"Interview someone, you fall in love with them. That's the first law of journalism. You feel guilty saying what you think."

George turned to the candidate.

"Now, where are you from?"

"Denver."

"Denver"—George chewed the word carefully, as if it might actually be in England. "Denver," he said. "Denver?"

The man got his lemon-biting look. They had a lot of non-

186

verbal communication just in that second, and George laughed hard.

"Oh, Denver," he shouted happily.

"I'm from London," the man said, and I could see he liked George, George amused him. And the same for George, he liked the guy. Because he got ten times more self-conscious. He felt at his hair, he walked around the desk and going past me he spanked a photograph.

"Argyle socks," he said. "That is the dirty secret of the American power structure."

"I can't write about socks," I said.

"Of course not, if you could it wouldn't be a secret."

George laughed, and the English guy got up and came to the desk. So both of us were staring at the picture, and George held forth.

"They hide this one in plain sight, my friend. Everyone says they hate the WASPs, then they idolize them to hell. You look at all the idiot stepson WASPs in the big jobs. You look at that one at the *Times*. The one that drives a sports car? He has a club and a white three-piece suit, so the Jews make him a big editor."

A laugh hit him like a wind and he had to hold on to the desk.

"Well I'm sorry he hasn't earned the right to wear a white suit. He's a show-off. He's a face-man."

The other guy and I just watched. George's stomach heaved a little as he subsided. His face was red.

"See, I can't even explain it," he said. "That's how big a secret this is."

I tossed the picture back in the box.

"I'm not smart enough to do this article," I said.

"Oh yes you are, Jack. I'll give you everything you need."

He sighed, getting serious, and went to a closet. He got out a cardboard box and was sorting through it when the phone buzzed. George dropped the box. He was about to get the phone when he stopped dead in his tracks. He turned and stared at the guy from London.

"Not on your life," the man said.

The two of them had all this silent communication, and finally the guy grimaced and stood up. He walked to the desk and lifted the receiver.

"Yes," he said.

"I like that, surly," George whispered.

The man looked at George. George made a cutting motion on his neck.

"Well. I'm afraid he's not here. Right . . . Yes. Roger."

He spoke in a low precise way and then hung up. George smacked his hands in delight.

"You went to public school, didn't you?"

"You're supposed to be at lunch with someone called Hiltie Brennan. He's waiting at Ho Chi Minh City."

"Oh, that's right, hell—" George got his jacket from his chair. "Listen, when can you start?"

And not waiting for the answer George brought the guy to an alcove. He demonstrated the stapler and the pencil sharpener and told him who to talk to about the computer.

"Now look, I don't even know your name."

"Danny Smith."

"Danny Smith. Danny Smith. Listen, we'll do like the blacks do, we'll blacken you up. We can call you Martin. Is anybody named Martin Smith?"

"Balls," Danny Smith said.

George just glowed. He went back to the box on the floor. Hiring the guy made him light on his feet, and he lifted out tape recorders and played with them. He couldn't figure out which were working, so he pressed two on me.

"Listen, Jack, don't take notes. That's the first law of journalism. You miss everything important."

Danny Smith stood in the doorway and watched with a droll

188

lemon-biting smile. So they were thick as thieves, and George gave more rules as much to him as to me.

"Also, I want to know how tall the person is," he said. "Height is destiny, who said that? And find out what his house looks like. How many acres. Your reader is going to be very competitive about his house. Square feet. Furniture. Teeth, car. Jack, come out with me. Oh, what else—"

He shook Danny Smith's hand then tipped toward him helplessly to touch his shirt.

"New and Lingwood, am I right?" he said.

But Danny gave him a dead-eye look, and that is how we went out. We walked past other people waiting to be George's assistant and out to the elevator.

"Do you like him? I could tell you liked him," George said. "I bet he's from some fancy family. I can smell it."

"George, I'm not going to gossip in this article," I said.

He shut his eyes as though I'd stabbed him.

"Of course not," he said. "I don't want gossip. All your reader wants is character. The trick is bring the scuttlebutt in as commentary. Let the facts be your friends."

He laughed hard, but by then I was used up. I was going to do it the way I wanted and so what if he didn't like it.

But he didn't ever stop, and on the elevator he pressed 6 and 5 because he said there were modeling agencies on those floors and if we were lucky we could pick up some office furniture for the ride, some Danish modern. We got lucky on 5. Two blond girls got on, calm mannequin girls with little tits who held themselves still.

I was so worn out from George, and then it threw me how calm they were. Things were clear to them, you could see that. They stood there untroubled and they had a values system that worked even if it wasn't going to save the world. But did they even get to choose it? Did they have to think it through, or was it just given to them?

George loved having them. He smiled at them and said things

about the weather, flirting, and winked at me and took deep inhaling breaths of them. Then when the elevator stopped he held the gate. He did a whole gallant gesture and he had them eating out of his hand. One almost smiled and the other said, "Thanks."

We paused under the clock to watch them go up the street.

"There are some upper-branch-leaf-eaters for you," George said in a little reverent murmur.

Then he turned to me with a solemn great-expectations expression.

"You insulted them not looking at them."

"Bullshit."

"Oh yes Jack. They love being stared at. You're giving them their sunlight staring at them."

"They scare me."

"Of course they scare you. That's cause you want too much. You're Jack Gold, Jack Gold wants too much. Someday you'll see how little there is to get, and you'll stop wanting so much."

He laughed hard. I smiled.

I was feeling O.K., too, till I got to Times Square. I changed to the 1 train in Times Square and there was a band playing on the platform, South American guys, those ones that play indigenous instruments, reed pipes. They play them very fast and their long black hair hangs down around their sharp Latin faces. I zoned a little watching them.

A tall guy in the back moved the pipe across his mouth with great speed. You couldn't see his eyes but he sounded everything, upbeat notes, down ones, and things in between. All in a little space of time in a tune. It made your heart flood. And you heard his breath behind every note, you heard the actual man, his voice. Then the train came and I dropped a dollar in the box. It was jarring to step back into my life. For a second I didn't know why I was doing it, George, the article, fearing the models, any of it.

17

I followed Joseph Vacca everywhere he went in the city for two weeks. I went to three Knights of Columbus halls and four Jewish seniors' centers and set my two tape recorders up at every stop. Vacca noticed them. I would see his cold-hot gaze go around the room and stop on the upright piano or under my chair, wherever I'd put them. Before long I figured out what was wrong with the machines and only used one. But Vacca kept looking for it.

After a few days I didn't even turn it on. I'd long since lost track of the tapes.

On a Monday in mid-September, Vacca held a noontime rally on Wall Street. It was a rainy day and I got there early. The narrow blackened streets of the financial district are more like alleys. They're worn down and chambered and illogical, like from a time when human beings were different, shorter and darker, more brutal, which they still are down there. The cobblestones were stained blue-black by rain and you had to study them so as not to slip. It wasn't even raining hard. Greasy solitary drops fell down as if from the bottom of a lid.

The traders had beaten me there, the Wall Street guys. Probably four hundred of them had gathered in Exchange Square but instead of joining the tiny rally inside the barricades, they'd stayed outside to heckle. The traders were there because Vacca was running against Wall Street. He'd come out for a special tax on the securities industry and then during a Q and A in Buffalo, he had called investment bankers "moneylenders in the temple." *The New York Times* devoted a whole editorial to that comment.

The traders were out of control. Anything that happened they jeered. A woman with big tits going by, a Vacca poster falling. I guess these are the guys that come up with the jokes. When someone gets arrested for putting someone in the furnace, or there's a bizarre sex murder, these are the guys that invent the jokes. They do what Burry always says, listen to their heart, and the jokes come right out of them, because they lead lives of violent meaninglessness. Well you know all that.

I sat on the Exchange steps with George's tape recorder, and then Vacca's car slid in alongside the barricades. The traders went nuts. They jammed against the car and rocked it. They cried, "Eggman! Eggman!"

That was because of an ad Vacca had done where he talked about his grandfather, an egg-candler.

The redhead came out with his head down, Blanchard, and held the door. After a minute Vacca came out with his head down, too. He hurried up the steps and his hair was flat on his scalp as if the rain had found him. But he hadn't been in the rain. He'd been in the car, sweating.

Another car door opened on the crowd side, and a new guy pushed his way out. He was only a kid, but big. His black hair was super-short on the sides and he wore a small black mustache that was almost Peter Sellers. The main thing was how unafraid he was. He punched the air with his fist daring the crowd. They shut up a little, then he waded right through them and the police had to move the barricades to let him pass. I mean, he was big, he couldn't angle himself through.

192

He chugged right by me. His suit bunched up on his keg thighs. You could see his shirt creasing against an undershirt.

The traders kept chanting through Vacca's speech. It upset him. Someone would heckle him in a new way, *No balls!*, and everyone else would start chanting, *No balls!*, and he'd stop, or get the words wrong.

I didn't listen to the speech. I'd stopped. It was all about right and wrong and the enduring moral values. If you actually listened to it you didn't feel right about anything. You began wondering how much of your behavior would legally qualify as sodomy or venality or another category from the Bible. You'd get pictures in your head. I would imagine a thorned vine winding itself tightly around Vacca's white flabby flesh and drops of blood falling one by one on to a begrimed marble floor lit by a high dome with just a hole in the top that let the rain in.

He never said any of that. That was just the feeling.

But the speech's ending was upbeat. It was a long metaphor about a grass-stained sandlot baseball that we'd all grown up with and polished with our sweat and had only cost $2.99.

As Vacca got near the end he started to rush it.

"Something has happened to America since our fields of youth. Today that ball has been used only once or twice and left out overnight while the kids watch MTV. Dew mildews the leather, rain swells the yarn. It's muddy and busted and forgotten . . ."

A man in the crowed yelled, "Waah-waaah." Others took it up, and within seconds all the traders were crying.

Vacca stepped back. He wiped his forehead with the droopy sleeve of his jacket, and his face was white. I didn't think he was going to finish. The new guy went up to him, the big guy with the red-apple cheeks. I don't think he was more than twenty-five. He leaned against Vacca's shoulder and said stuff. Vacca nodded. Then he said something else and Vacca jerked around to look at him in disbelief.

For a second Vacca seemed like he might crumple. He was spooked and angry. He walked back to the mike with an absent look. He stared out over the crowd and didn't hear the jeers. He reached for the microphone.

"You—you. You people—"

He stammered and then his voice twisted down hard.

"You are the root cause if ever we needed to name one. Whole towns go bust upstate when you change a decimal on your computer— You came up with a meaningless expression for what you do, the bottom line."

He was almost coiled around the microphone, and the crowd was still.

"You laugh at me, but I've seen you. You're not looking when you go down the street cause you're on the phone, you have to get through before Chicago closes. You're probably getting brain cancer with those things. They say it isn't proven. Give it five years. You're killing yourselves into the bargain."

Then Vacca stood and took a giant breath. Like a guy in a movie filling his lungs and saying I'm a new man, a guy on a hillside in a white shirt. He batted the microphone with the back of his hand and started down the steps.

As he plunged past me he said, "Two boxes. Where's number two? Gotta have two, don't you?"

When he got to his car someone threw an egg. It wasn't going to hit him but Vacca did this martyr turn. He threw his hand over his head and the egg caught his elbow. It splattered over him and then he slipped. Later the papers said the egg knocked him down, but it didn't, Vacca fell on the slippery stones. The big guy ran after him and helped him up. But Vacca didn't go right into the car. He took off his jacket first and laid it across the redhead Blanchard's arms, like, Let's preserve the evidence for the Warren Commission.

All that night I thought about what Vacca had said to me. I felt as if the real Vacca had come out. Not the mechanical Vacca, but a passionate man I could halfway relate to.

I guess I don't understand journalism. You hear that thing about a fly on the wall, that a journalist should be a fly on the wall, watching. But that was bullshit. Say you're in the room, you can't focus on anything when there's a fly on the wall. You watch it. If it doesn't move you wonder if it died there. Then turn it around, think of the fly. It's trying to home in, to lick stuff off your hands. Or more likely it's trying to get out, banging its head against the glass. It's desperate. I'm just saying it's a whole relationship.

On Thursday Burry was having a dinner party for the autumn solstice, a pagan celebration she called it. We had chocolates for breakfast, some guy who had taken her to a party at something called the Society of Colonial Dames had sent over a big box of them. Then that afternoon I bought her a green-and-black velvet dress for a lot of money. I put it on plastic.

The department store where we got it is famous, it's a place my mother used to stare into the windows of but be scared to walk into. Burry acted like we belonged there. Even the fitting rooms felt fancy, a little regal, and I went in one with her, I got down on my knees and ate her out. She had her foot up on a chair so she could see how the velvet fell across her leg, and she turned out her knee so I could angle my face up there. With the heavy velvet it was like a feudalism fantasy, a vassal and queen thing, and the salesperson kept coming to the door and saying, "Hello. Hello. Are you all right in there?"

And Burry would say in a clear voice, "We're fine." The salesgirl got to be like the lady-in-waiting.

I went from there to the New York Public Library. I was looking up clips on Vacca. But when I actually sat down at the computer I typed in Burry's name instead. You're not supposed to do that. I mean, it's probably against the rules of modern relationships. They're supposed to be built on trust. The psychologists on the radio say that, also those yellow-covered paperbacks that tell you how to be in a relationship that girls are always reading. I was just curious.

There were a lot of articles on her. There was a party where they'd honored Maddie Lister and Burry had done a performance piece by giving a tableau vivant of a painting. She'd clad herself in grapes and sod. There were a couple performance pieces she'd published and little bullshit interviews she'd given saying she'd never met a man that was smart enough for her. One magazine had a picture of her and Blake Roberts. "Aristobrats," the headline said.

I was lost in it all when the library bell clanged. Then I walked up to Burry's place to help her set up.

She was making eggplant Parmesan, but because eggplant and tomato are so yin she was building a giant salad, too. I swept the living room, and she gave me the garbage to take out.

I looked through it putting it down the chute. That's something else you're probably not supposed to do. Like if you find a diary you're not supposed to look at it. The only time it's all right is if the person sends you to their desk for something and a letter is sitting there and you can't help seeing. Or if the diary's open on the kitchen table. The trash seemed akin to that situation, so I didn't stop myself.

There were long spooling stretches of virgin dental floss, all unused but for one little bit at the end. There were a bunch of paperbacks, including *All Quiet on the Western Front* and *Ulysses*. Almost-new bottles of perfume and shampoo that I guess she hadn't liked. New magazines. The not-completely-used jar of coconut oil that we'd been taking to bed. It was hardened and white, you could see the hungry digmarks her fingers made in it getting clumps to rub on my ass. Also money. She'd thrown out a bunch of pennies, nickels, too.

You're not supposed to do a whole investigation without telling the person, the way Nixon misled Alger Hiss, made him

196

think they weren't out for blood when they were, so I brought the money back into the bedroom.

Burry laughed at me.

"What does it come to, fifty cents? Jack, you're so materialistic."

I sat on the bed. I was actually thankful for her reaction.

"Nature hates cheapness, Jack. Nature kills the cheap."

She kept going, and I just had to listen. That a healthy animal responds to the earth's abundance with an abundance of spirit. A skinny deer doesn't survive the winter. That you can't ever be cheap in love.

She was getting dressed. She took off her T-shirt and weighed her tits in her hands, she went up to the mirror.

"See how big my breasts have gotten, Jack. Remember how they used to be?" She found my eyes in the mirror.

"Sort of."

"Of course you do, baby. They were smaller. My body has changed for you."

And the same with her hips. She pushed her jeans down and smoothed her hands out over her hips, saying they had gotten more womanly. All because of our love, all because of what we gave to one another.

A dozen people came and the party was O.K., it was fun. There was cheap wine like any dinner party I'd ever been to and people drank a lot and talked about movies and current events. The food was off the way food is off when one person does everything.

At eleven o'clock a few people left and the rest of us went to the bedroom. Umbra, this model, finally arrived, and David Cope, the critic for *Follies*, got out some dope. They call him Jinx because of what he can do to a play or a book. Burry said if he likes something it's worse because he never sounds genuine saying anything positive. People figure the play is shit.

Umbra and Blake Roberts and Mica Barce, who is Rene Barce's daughter from his first marriage and is skinny and wore a black, gunnysack-style dress, all lay around the bed smoking dope like in a decadent seraglio painting. Umbra was beautiful. She had a long foxlike face with a mouth like a split plum, and Burry had told me if you talked to her she was actually pretty smart.

I got pretty stoned, too. Probably I stepped back too far. These are the glowing good-boned faces I'd always seen in pictures, I thought. The people in black-and-white pictures in magazines my mom had sneak-bought when I was a kid.

People being languid in boats, on beaches, on great lawns. People with grace. With money.

Jinx Cope held court, harboring the same fantasy as me, if everyone got stoned enough a couple of girls would go to bed with him. He's one of those fat guys who get women to curl up around him. It's a whole angle. They have teddy-bear paunches and they're always a little fucked-up but they've got a ton of potential. They're geniuses, so it's going to be worth the woman's time to take care of them. You see it on the left. Just listen to one of those guys talk feminism sometime.

"Jinx, I don't want you coming to the *Larkspur* party," Burry said. "I'm doing a performance piece for George and you'll make me self-conscious."

"That would be a first," he said. "But I'm not invited."

"No one's invited yet. Blake have you gotten your invitation?"

"No. But I thought George always got rap singers."

"This year it's me," Burry said.

"Rap music is great art," Umbra said. "It's really, really difficult. Have you ever tried to write any?"

She looked around the room, she looked at me.

"No," I said.

"Well you should try. I have. Then you would appreciate how hard it is. It's as hard as any other poetry."

198

Jinx said, "George is off me because he fixed me up with Bucky Miller and I didn't like her."

"I know Bucky," Umbra said. "She puts Sweet-N-Low in her Scotch."

"That's because she's a chemical girl," Mica said.

"Chemical girl!" Blake said. "Chemical girl."

She kept saying that, then she went to her bag for a bunch of photographs. She wanted Umbra to help her pick the right one for her book. The pictures got handed around. They were of Blake in all these poses, sitting, legs crossed or knee drawn up, gazing at you. They turned you on, with the white leotard top. Blake said that was the point.

"Why a phone?" Jinx said, holding up a picture.

"Oh, that one's for my dad," Blake said. "My dad always says, when a photographer comes in the room pick up the phone. He learned that covering the civil rights movement. It's so you look like you're actually doing something if the picture shows up in a history book someday."

The room suddenly felt stuffy and I had to get out of there. I went into the living room, and that headline came back to me. Aristobrats. It was a lot more true of Blake than Burry.

What if I was a rat. Could I be a rat that was curious and just check out civilization? I thought about it. What if the rat wasn't hurting anyone, just wanted to watch for a little hour. He stayed at the edge of the room not trying to eat the big fucking wheel of cheese or the duck breast. He was perfectly still. Then they noticed him. Would they have to kill him just for that? Or would they let him go?

And other paranoid ideas, the paranoid style in American politics, etcetera.

I had to change the channel so I went into the Secretary's office. The door was open, and the light went on with a thunky old-fashioned pushbutton. There were framed antique maps of all the countries he'd served in, and the desk had a manual Alger Hiss–type typewriter and piles of books. If you actually

199

wrote something and wanted to go to the next line with that typewriter you couldn't, the rolling-pin part didn't have room to move there were so many books.

The Secretary was all right. The Secretary was from dirt, just like me.

There was an iron bed with a quilt on it against the far wall, and I decided to lie down. Then I saw a letter lying on the desk. On spiral-bound drawing paper, with big handwriting and a sketch of a gun.

"James, Rifle registered to Alice B. She bought for me in East Tex (hog hunting in hollows). Also: Burry Q liked this pad. Please give to her. RRB."

Clipped to the note was a sales record from Somewhere, Texas, $1,100-plus for a Rigby bolt-action rifle, made out to Alice Barce.

I sat down on the old iron bed thinking what a royal fucking fraud Early was. Lenin's gun. I got out a cigarette to kill the panic.

He could have sold me anything. He could have sold me Lenin's fountain pen, Lenin's ink bottle with original Lenin ink.

But I'd believed him, that was the thing, that was what freaked me out.

So just don't keep calling everybody else a fraud. Because Vacca was a fraud and George, too, and the Foundation for Fair Uses (of Power) was a fraud. James Doyle and Simi Winfrey. Victor Bandy, and who did that leave who wasn't a fraud, no one.

Right then somebody else could be lying down somewhere and saying, Jack Gold, what a fucking fraud.

I rubbed out the cigarette in a glass on the windowsill.

Here, meet Lenin's house cat. This is Lenin's rubber tree plant.

I'd bought it. Because I loved Lenin. No I didn't love Lenin. Who was Lenin. Because I loved Early.

18

I woke up with someone massaging my shoulders.

"We've been trying on makeup," Burry said. Her face was covered with warpaintish makeup and she was hung all over with African jewelry, a nose ring, too. It was like in *Playboy* where they get natives to daub mud on a naked white girl and put patterns in her skin. I looked up her nose to see if it went through the nostril. No, clamp-on.

We went to her room and the girls were painted, too, but everyone was going. It was three o'clock and the women were leaving with Jinx and trying to ditch him at the same time, while he clung desperately to his vision of a ménage.

"I'll get a cab to Tenth Street, and Mica, you come with me and we'll drop Umbra in SoHo—" Blake said.

"But Mica's on Third Street, and I'm in Tribeca," he said.

"Right, you're in Tribeca. It's ten times easier for us."

"Why is it easier for you?"

"Because you're going a lot farther."

"It's on the way. We'll get a nightcap on First Avenue."

They kept trying to come up with polite plausible reasons to ditch him, and he always had a logical answer. Then finally they left and I saw where Jinx had that pad of Rene Barce's drawings in his hand. The same pad from Rene's overalls.

I sat on the bed. Burry went around the room putting out candles.

"You're so quiet. Baby, what are you thinking?"

"That I like that smell." Because there was the smell of paraffin.

She blew a candle out right next to me.

"Burry, what did you give Jinx?"

"Some pictures Rene gave me."

I felt so thankful that she didn't bullshit me. "Are you selling them to him?" I said.

She sighed, she went to the mirror with a towel. She leaned into the mirror wiping off makeup. "Jack, I am so broke."

"Burry, when we're together, can we go somewhere anonymous?"

"You mean when we're married?"

It was the first time either of us had mentioned that since we'd decided.

"When we're married," I said. "A place with ordinary people. Not just famous fathers."

"You're always so hung up on people's fathers," she said. "I think it's Oedipal. It's not about them, it's about you."

"But all your friends have famous fathers."

She threw the towel into the bathroom and left the room, she came back in with a garbage bag. Her brow was dark, pitiless. She began really cleaning stuff up.

"All my friends?" she said.

"No, but Mica Barce. Blake."

Burry let the bag drop limply at her side.

"How can you even say that," she said. "Blake is my best closest friend. She's struggled really hard. I've told you that. She was in therapy a long time and one therapist really fucked her over, and only last year she found someone who's helping her deal with some really paralyzing issues around her father not wanting her to succeed. And the result of that is a beautiful beautiful book."

"You said she gave her diaries to the editors."

"Jack! You promised you'd never mention that."

"I'm only repeating it to you."

"It's the context. It worries me you'd just come out with that so easily. Anyway, it's her first one. Give her a chance."

"Who else gets that chance?" I said.

She gave a sobby sigh and left the room. I heard her tearing the tablecloth off and shaking it with a whipping noise. I went to the doorway. She was gathering butts in her hand.

"Blake's never been nice to me because I'm a nobody," I said.

"Oh, Jack, be big for once. She doesn't trust men."

She drained the wineglasses into two wineglasses. She consolidated all the butts in an empty wineglass.

"Father was a complete nobody. He was a doctor's son in Schenectady. He was a complete outsider till he married Mother and got his first job in D.C. Then people made room for him."

"But now you don't know anyone like that."

"I know you."

I slumped against the doorjamb and shut my eyes to slow things down.

"Maybe I'm supposed to be like one of those ballplayers that are always thanking baseball. Those Dominican players? Well, I'm sorry Burry, I can't always be thanking baseball."

Her hand swept across the table, and a glass flew into the wall. A blot of wine went down the wall with bits of glass, and Burry started to cry. She sat down and covered her face.

Neither of us said anything, then I got up.

"I'm due at a Vacca fund-raiser in four hours," I said.

I went into the bedroom and lay down, then Burry came to the doorway. I heard her standing there, upset.

"Father warned me," she said. "He said you're naïve, Jack. That you don't know how the world works."

"O.K."

"I'm telling you that because you don't have a clue what it's like for women. You're so fucking righteous about giving everybody a chance, you've never had to consider someone like Bonnie Raitt or Jane Fonda. Women who wouldn't have gotten anywhere without the tiny advantage of a well-known father. Virginia Woolf."

"I was talking about how people pick their friends."

She walked over to the bed.

"But you said a hateful thing, Jack. You said nothing ever came to me but for my father."

"I didn't say that."

"That was the energy in your words, you were resentful. Father noticed that, too."

"What else did he say?"

With a sort of grief, she dropped onto the bed.

"Oh, Jack, I only told you that because I see it myself."

I got up on my elbows. "Tell me, Burry."

"Nothing else. Just that you're really really smart but you lack self-esteem."

"I know. He told me that."

"And that people who are that innocent can be dangerous."

I shut my eyes and lay flat. "Let's go to bed."

"I knew I shouldn't have told you. Jack?"

"It's O.K."

She turned off the light and got into bed. But I didn't sleep, and Burry wasn't sleeping either. I saw her eyes moving.

"What else?"

"I'm just making a list of women and fathers. Anjelica Huston. Deborah Harry—" She tabbed the names on her fingers—"Paloma Picasso, and Freud had a daughter, too. Oh, and Cokie Roberts."

Three hours later I got up and shaved using Burry's pink leg razor. I let myself out without waking her. The place was beginning to smell. Sodden lettuce mixed in the air with red wine and rotting chickpeas.

Downstairs they had just cleaned the street. Wet streaks went down the asphalt and bits of trash were squeezed against the curb. I got a cab on Park Avenue, and its cradly suspension put me to sleep going through the park. The driver had to wake me up.

The address was an old apartment house on Central Park West that was supposed to make you feel proud to be part of New York. The lobby had a mural. On the left wall Indians were selling Manhattan, in the middle Olmsted was landscaping Central Park, and on the right girders were going up on the frame of the Empire State Building. Victor Bandy would say they were all crimes. I bet even Central Park had some crime behind it.

The fund-raiser was in the penthouse. Jared "Mike" Michaelson, a former deputy mayor, was hosting it, a group called Lawyers for Vacca but that everyone called Jews for Vacca. Fifty people were there, mostly tanned balding men, the kind of guys who brag about how little sleep they get. Five hours. Six on the weekend. Four and a half hours. That's another great thing about New York I almost forgot, grown men lying about how little sleep they got, feeling proud of that. Someday they're going to put that in a mural.

I got some coffee and looked at the park. The apartment had a glass wall. Giant potted bamboo plants curtained each end of the wall, four on each side, and the view was in the middle. From thirty floors up the park looked as square and regular as someone's back yard. The bamboos had an elegant tilt and stopped right at the ceiling. I bet some servant had to get on a ladder and clip them.

There was tumult near the door and Vacca arrived. Everything had changed in just a few days. His numbers were up from the dead, the papers said his new TV ads were warmer. He held his head at a new angle.

The new guy from the campaign came up to me, that big guy, and his face was pink and scrubbed-looking. Even his mustache looked clean. He was the type of individual who uses a washcloth with a lot of soap every morning like it's a sign of virtue. Well, probably it is a sign of virtue. You like it when the person you're talking to is that clean. I liked it.

"Harris Feinberg," he said, extending his hand. "Everyone calls me Honey."

The suit was tight on him, and you could hear it pulling against his body. It made little squeaks.

"Jack Gold."

"Gold Gold Gold." He shut his eyes and held his hand to his forehead. "Any relation to Paulie Gold. On House Armed Services staff?"

"No."

"Oh well." He laughed. "That's the only reason they sent me up here, they needed somebody to do Jewish geography."

"Then you ought to get your boss to lay off the Aquinas when he's in a synagogue."

Honey stepped closer. "But is it good for the Jews?" he said.

He laughed hard and I laughed, too.

"I've always thought that's the worst thing Jews can say," he said.

"Selfish," I said.

"Sure. It's almost as bad as intermarriage." He laughed hard again and slapped me on the arm. "Eat something, Gold, you're making the fish nervous."

He was giving himself permission. The fixings were lavish, almost like a Jewish wedding. Brioches and caviar and smoked

206

fish with pearl onions fitted in their jaws. Grapes, peaches, melons. A guy in a chef hat was making omelets. Honey reached for a croissant and dropped it on a plate, he took a bunch of grapes, too.

"Say, what are you writing about us anyway?" he said.

"About the way he thinks," I said. "About the paranoid style in American politics."

Honey's mouth opened wide in a sort of embarrassment. "Well I hope you put something about Early in there."

"Like what?" I said.

He rolled his eyes and shrugged. "I can think of a few things."

"The guy has a cocktail at the end of the day," I said.

Honey seemed shocked. Then he got a pained brotherly expression. "Not you, too, Gold—"

"It's generational," I said.

That made him laugh. He shook his head and reached past me for a crescent of melon he bit right into. A short guy put his hand on Honey's shoulder, and he turned. The guy was handsome, with Kennedy hair.

"Hey Mike"—Honey used his left hand to pump hands. "Jews for Vacca and there's bacon."

"Canadian," Michaelson said. "The best."

He pulled a woman over by the elbow.

"Beth, you know Honey Feinberg?"

"Hey Beth." Honey reached to give her a left-hand shake.

She was tall, dark haired. It was the woman from the hotel. She wore the same face powder as she had when I'd followed her, she held herself that same modest way.

"How long you in town?" Honey said.

"Six more weeks," she said.

I moved back among the bamboos, I felt faint. I got another cup of coffee and I didn't hear the noise of the crowd. Honey made a cranking motion in the air. "Let's do it," he said. Michaelson started shepherding his friends to seats. They made a little theater in the round for Vacca, and Honey walked him to the center, between the bamboos. He had his hand on Vacca's shoulder and muttered something in his ear, the same as he'd done on Wall Street when he scared him. Then he patted him and stepped to the side, right in front of me.

Vacca stood there quietly a few seconds. He seemed troubled. He turned to the window then back to the little crowd. The good china looked like play-china in his large hands.

"Big buildings make me a little woozy," he said. "Till I was eight I don't think I'd seen a building that was taller than ten stories. I'd certainly never been in one. I'm saying I know what it's like to come up in the world. I don't have to kick myself to remember, this is Manhattan." He put the cup down on an end table. "With all its Manhattan airs."

The room stirred, but Vacca held up his hand.

"That's all my campaign is about," he said. "A little more of the common man's wisdom in the affairs of state."

"Good," Michaelson said, from a leather-and-steel sling chair.

Vacca relaxed some. He jammed his hands in his pants pockets and stood with his feet apart. He waited again before he spoke.

"My story is an American story. It's not the only American story, but it's one I'm guessing a lot of you know. My grandfather came over on a boat. This country rewarded him, yes. It also confused him, it belittled him. People told him he wouldn't get anywhere unless he got rid of the vowel at the end of his name. He thought of changing the name to Vance."

Someone laughed, but there wasn't any humor in it for Vacca. He looked down, clamping his mouth against the emotion.

"They told him his hands were too big, that he talked with his hands. He did what we all learned to do, hid them away—"

Vacca awkwardly pulled his hands from his pockets. He held them out in front of him. People were just listening.

"You might think it's sad or pathetic, but my grandfather

took this republic at its word. Because even as it insulted him, this country dazzled him. Its vision of fairness. The commitment to people like him that it seemed to want to forget but could not. Because that promise had been made in a solemn moment—"

Vacca broke off, and his face was broody.

"There's one story he told me I don't know how many times. He was walking past a fancy restaurant. He had just lost a job. Its big picture window was steamed and clouded from revelry. He paused and looked inside. At all the happy people. People different from him. People blithe at heart . . ."

It was a good speech till Vacca came to that cliché. After that it went downhill. Grandfather had struggled but he left a small poultry business to father, etcetera. And from that right into the business values of the room: the genius of the self-made man.

When he was done there were questions. A youngish guy asked something about tax law that Vacca went all the way into, having a little argument with the guy, quoting federal code, boring the hell out of the room. A man near me asked about abortion.

"I'm against it, plain and simple," Vacca said, but followed up with his usual hedge that never made any sense to me.

"The polls say Quinlan is way out front," said a bald guy on the couch.

"I know," Vacca said. He turned to look at Honey. "I know. This is Harris Feinberg. He can tell you about the numbers."

Honey stepped into the clearing. He punched a pair of heavy black-framed glasses onto his face then felt inside his jacket. He got out a piece of paper and unfolded it.

"Hey, wait a second, how could I forget?" Vacca said. "My sister's here today. She's a trainee at Chemical. Let me introduce my little sister. Beth—"

He held out his hand toward the corner. The tall woman was sitting on a bench. She looked down at the floor but made a little wave, like, Let me keep my privacy. People laughed. I tilted the empty cup to my mouth.

"O.K. Here are Wednesday's numbers," Honey said. "First we look at downstate double primes. People who vote in every election. Their mother died that morning, they vote. Yes, Early's way out front there: 53–45. But move to the primes"—he lifted the page—"the gap closes, it's only 50–47 Early."

He made a sucking noise with his teeth against his lip, and then I saw what he was looking at. It wasn't polling data, it was a fax of his phone messages. There were four While You Were Out slips, back to back, xeroxed, so he was winging it, and I liked him even more.

"We get better news when we break out the sometime voter," he said. "That's almost 40 percent of the electorate."

"Honey—" Vacca said.

Honey twisted around to look at him.

"Speak English," Vacca said.

People laughed.

"You're supposed to call him Honey. Don't ask me how Harris became Honey."

Honey used the heel of his hand to snug his glasses against his nose. "What this means—we pull a few Catholic and ethnic voters and hang on to upstate, it's a photo finish."

"Chancy," the guy on the couch said.

"Right." Honey's cheeks flushed. He stepped toward the group. "This race ain't for the faint of heart. If no one took a chance we wouldn't have gotten Ronald Reagan. Or J.F.K."

"Joe wouldn't be here right now," Michaelson said.

"Amen," Honey said. "And brother, I've got that feeling."

Something came over him. He shut his eyes, he swayed a little. His tongue touched his mustache, leaving it wet and bright. His head lolled. The crowd went still. They were New Yorkers, they were used to people taking off their clothes on the street or crawling up in rags.

Honey began to stomp in place.

210

"It feels good," he groaned. "It feels like a squeaker—"
Vacca clapped and let out a wolf yelp. The redhead Blanchard
made a sharp whistle. Honey marched across the floor with the
same swaying tuba rhythm and hugged Vacca hard. Vacca's
face was flushed for once.

Everyone else got into it, too, yelling encouragement, and
that was how it ended. Honey strutted out of the place rolling
his big shoulders. Michaelson slipped in behind him, guiding
him so he wouldn't knock over any sculptures, and then it was
a line dance. People made a line. Blanchard held Vacca from
behind and moved in bunny hops.

I got some orange juice and sat down on the couch. The sister
had disappeared. Well, Vacca was still a fascist. Think of the
clever way he'd turned a democratic story into a paean to small
business. Or the way his people jumped up when he jumped
up, in unison.

The place began to empty and I stretched out. I thought about
my own grandfather. He'd come on a boat when he was eight.
My mom had a picture of him in the weird clothes boys wore
then. Like a dress almost, I guess they call it a frock, with a
bow at the neck, and lace-up boots, and a grown man's hat that
fell to his eyebrows. Ezra Reshevsky. We called him Hezzie,
but he'd named his dry-goods-later-patio-furniture business
E. W. Reshevsky. E. W. What was that about? As if no one
would figure out he was Jewish. I lay my head on the armrest
and thought about Hezzie, how optimistic and terrified he was
at the same time. An hour later the guy with the chef hat shook
me awake.

19

Writing the article took ten days. I tried to get into a groove: I wore nice clothes just going to my desk, and every day I had lunch at a Cuban-Chinese place on Broadway. You sat at the counter and ate pepper beef with yellow rice. They had the staples in banks of steel drawers set into the wall. They would pull out the drawer and spoon out black beans, then shove the drawer back in. I guess there was a heat source in the wall.

Most nights I went to Burry's and I was glad to get away from writing. Because the drill was, you sat by yourself and had weird fantasies about someone on the other side of the city or the state. You spent all day having an argument with yourself about their state of mind and put three-by-five cards on the wall with different things they said on them. It was like being a nut-fringe assassin, an asshole that keeps a diary and writes, "I burned incest today." Or he studies documents for the imprint a ballpoint pen makes on the next page to build a whole theory.

Finally I was too sick of it to read it another time, so I printed it out on good paper. I opened a beer and bundled my newspapers and all the rough drafts of the article, I put them out on the street.

In the mail there was an invitation to the *Larkspur* party. It was fancy, a starched white hanky with the time and *Grubs' Parade* embroidered on the corner, also the RSVP number, and all in rainbow hippie stitching. I felt so proud to get it and I wondered if I could show it to my mother. She'd run her hands over it, she'd ooh a lot.

I came back upstairs and it beat me what to put the article in. All I had in my desk was a big white envelope from the Center with some report inside. I dumped that out and then I saw the report we'd done on the Haitian refugees a year and a half before. What happened, I'd gone down to see the Haitians in the refugee camps with these other people, we had this whole task force. The Center, PEN's Freedom-to-Write Committee, a couple other groups.

That was a long long time ago and I didn't want to look at it, I pushed it down in the trash. But doing that seemed worse, and I got it back out. I looked through it a little, and it made me feel weird.

I remembered everything. I remembered this guy Albert Verre we interviewed. He'd been tortured because of his radio broadcasts. He was so young and unbending. He looked at you plainly and didn't say much. There were scars on his legs and arms he showed you. He wore this super-clean white short-sleeved shirt, and you were just another person he was meeting as he went along in his life. He wasn't going to lie to you.

When he dies he's going to be that way, his head held at the same angle. I read more of it, and I felt so weak. It wasn't even the report. I'd done what my dad used to say, telling me to slow down and not be emotional. Name things precisely, Jacob, or I won't understand you. We'd done that. We had the straight-forward testimony from victims of torture, and we'd gotten Albert and another guy to draw little pictures of the devices the police used, the way they would tie their arms and legs around logs, their arms behind their backs.

So even if you read it two years later the experience of those

213

people crowded up through the words, honestly, and I started getting emotional. I thought, I'd done that, even in my fucked-up fluorescent life. Then my eyes blurred and I was really crying, tears went down my face and fell on my shirt, I couldn't help myself.

O.K., good, have a cry, I said, just like someone on television. I put the report back in my desk to honor it and drank off my beer and walked around the apartment a little, to get some closure. Carmen Frankel always used to say that, process and closure. But it was the opposite, it was like something had fallen, because that feeling kept coming. I had another beer and put on a CD to get a grip, but I'd just get weepy again and have to sit down and the next thing I'd be sobbing. I'd just be sitting there shaking and couldn't even hold my head up. I don't understand it.

It was more than the Haitians, I was thinking of who I'd been, Jack Gold, deputy director of the Center. That I was that person, O.K., sure, a nobody in a fluorescent cardboard-wall job and my jacket didn't fit me right, etcetera, and I was naïve and lacking in self-esteem, blah blah blah, so anyone who wanted could sell me a jacket telling me Bob Dylan had been the last person in the store trying it on, and my friends said I was a bullshit artist. But I'd done a report that was a good and decent thing. It was clean, I wasn't trying to get attention or get laid. And when I did I'd known it.

It's good for a person to cry. Women will always tell you that, trying to justify it. That it's biological and relieves tension. Man isn't the only animal that cries, dogs for instance. But I got to where I couldn't stop. I took a shower and I started crying in the shower. I'd think about that report for a split second and it would come back over me. I didn't know why I was crying so much, because of my old life that I'd thrown away or because of the Haitians.

And if for the Haitians, why? Who were they to me? It was

214

like that guy in *Hamlet*. The guy in the play within the play is crying and Hamlet can't figure out why the guy is so broken up. What is Cuba to him? It was the same with me, except I was both guys, the guy crying, the guy wondering.

Later I took a walk in the park and my appetite came back. I ate two slices of pizza at the corner and decided I wasn't going to call Burry. Then I got up to my place and it was dark and empty and it seemed a lot scarier not to call her. My place didn't feel familiar, it felt threatening. So I called, and she said to come over, she had something to tell me.

Burry had a fruit jones so we went out to the Korean on Lexington and she filled a steel wire basket with fruit. I just stood at the front of the store watching her, trying to decide whether I hated her or loved her. An all-news radio station was playing. They had a report saying Early Quinlan hadn't gotten the hospital workers' endorsement, which he had been counting on. I don't think Burry heard, and I wasn't going to tell her.

She brought a knife and a big wooden bowl into the bedroom and made fruit salad on the bed. I lit candles and we ate with our hands. Juice went down her wrists and made trails almost to her elbow, but she didn't care.

Then I loved her all over again. I loved the way she held the mangoes to her neck in the store because she said when they were ripe they gave off heat. The way her tits crowded the armholes at the side of her too-tight dress and she glared at people if they looked hard at her.

She pulled my head to her with her sticky hands and said in my ear, "Baby guess what, we're pregnant."

I looked at her. "We are?"

She nodded. "How does that make you feel? Happy, Jack?"

"More surprised."

"I know, me too. I saw the doctor, he says every time an

215

egg gets fertilized it's a little miracle. But are you happy?"

"Are we sure?"

"Why do you think I'm eating all this fruit? I'm craving things. This afternoon I had to have licorice. I haven't eaten licorice since I was eight years old."

I lay down with my head in her lap. She put chunks of mango into my mouth and I licked her fingers.

"I'm due in May," she said. "We'll get married in January and I'll be just beginning to show."

"Don't we want to think about this?" I said.

"All you do is think." She cradled my head in her messy hands. "If you think all the time you never do anything."

"But we can undo this, too," I said.

"That's not for me."

She lifted my head from her lap and got off the bed. She set the wooden bowl on the floor and reached for a bottle of imported water. She sloshed the water over her hands, letting it fall into the bowl.

"We'd wear it forever on our souls, Jack. We would."

She went to the bathroom and came back out with a towel.

"The thing is I'm getting old. I'm almost thirty. My eggs are drying up."

"And this way it's best for Father," I said.

A soft wail rose from her. "You keep trying to force me to choose between you and Father."

"You do."

She dropped into the armchair, she used the towel on her hands, pushing it between her fingers.

"You're being a lawyer, Jack. Like saying who would I throw out of the lifeboat? We're not in a lifeboat, you're both in my life."

We were quiet and the room got cool. The window was open and the air came in just in that second and made the candles flicker. I got up and closed the window then sat on the bed with my feet on the floor.

216

"You've changed from the summer," I said.

She nodded. "Everyone says I'm growing up. I'm glad, Jack. I don't like being the person I was. It was nuts. Anyway, you've changed, too. You're quieter, more guarded."

"Give me that towel," I said. She threw me the towel and I wiped my hands. "Because nothing's ever private," I said.

"That's politics. I always hated that. You live in a fishbowl, then you get used to it. When I was six Father had to leave my birthday to go to a party for George Ball, that broke my heart."

"So this one we get to choose," I said.

"You're choosing. You're choosing not to be with me."

For a minute there was just silence. In books, people always say there was silence for five minutes, even ten. They say it about Nixon and Whittaker Chambers. I don't believe it. One minute is so long when it's two people not saying anything, it's almost too much. Then she got up and took the bowl to the kitchen. She came back in and put out most of the candles.

"I made that smell for you, the smell you like," she said in a quiet voice.

I got into bed, and she took the last candle into the bathroom. When she came back out she was naked and holding the lit candle. It was like winter, how clean her face was, how clean everything is in winter, chaste. She stood there with the candle-light just showing her face and the pale tops of her tits and nothing more.

"Jack, I can feel you turning. I want you to try and stay in the good feelings. Fatherhood is a wonderful giving thing."

"I'm not ready to join the great white race of fathers."

She laughed and sat on the bed, she mussed my hair.

"Baby, you have lots of time. Almost a year. You can do everything you want. You can go canoeing with your boy-friends, you can fantasize about having all the other girls you want."

217

Her voice went up, toward mirth, and she blew out the candle.

The next day I wanted to drop my article off at *Larkspur* without having a whole bullshit relationship with George Sides, but no, the receptionist called George's office and he said for me to bring it back.

The *Larkspur* office was in a little frenzy. Everyone was at work on the annual party. The phone was ringing, people were running in all directions, and George's office was the way he liked it, jammed. I stood just outside the door. George lay across his desk with his shirt off getting a massage. His suspenders hung down on the side of the desk, and a small man in a black kimono with white Chinese-style letters on the lapels moved around the desk, he'd drip a tiny drop of oil on his back then work it in hard. George shut his eyes and moaned and gurgled and meanwhile he was conducting business, like all those stories of L.B.J. getting an enema while conducting domestic policy.

Danny Smith sat in George's tilting leather chair with his feet under him on the seat, and some kid, an intern I guess, stood inside the doorway with a printout on continuous-feed paper he'd look for names on. George was asking him who'd RSVPed. The guy scrolled the thing and it spilled over his shoes and across the floor.

"Ann Spadafora," George said.

Riffle churn riffle. "Yes."

"David Putney Ida."

Churn riffle churn. "No."

"Bucky Miller."

Riffle. "No."

And so on till the assistant went out and I went in. I put my envelope on the radiator across from George's head.

"Jack," he said. "Just who I wanted to see, Jack Gold."

218

He grunt-reached for the envelope and held it in front of his face, turned it this way and that, that old envelope from the Center with the name crossed out.

"This looks good, this is very nice," he said.

I laughed, but George looked up at me earnestly.

"Listen, that's the first rule of publishing. If it's in a fancy envelope it's horseshit inside. That or a lawsuit."

He laughed and dropped the envelope back on the radiator and the masseur, masseuse, whatever, slapped him to make him stay still. He put his head down on the desk.

"Now help us with our party rules, Jack," he said in a gurgle. "Where are we?"

"Four," Danny said, holding a fountain pen over a pad.

"O.K. Listen, no dogs," George said. "Last year we let a woman bring her little dog and it got hurt dancing and they put it to sleep."

"No more dancing dogs," Danny said.

"The people were dancing. The dog was underfoot. I'm serious—" George looked up at Danny with delight. "I had to write a smarmo letter to her quote-unquote roommate, another female, because she threatened to sue."

Danny dropped his feet to the floor. "Don't be homophobic."

"I'm not homophobic. Anyway what's homophobic?"

"You know what."

"No I don't—" George turned his head to me. "Jack, what is homophobic?"

"Don't encourage him, Jack," Danny said.

"Hating gays," I said. "Afraid of gays."

George got up on his elbows. "See, I would have said it was the other one, the open spaces. Which I'm also not afraid of. So how can I be something I don't know what it is—"

"O.K., five," Danny said.

"All right, I don't want them coming in leather," George said. "Leather cummerbunds? Leather tuxedos? No thanks mister."

219

"Who's them?" Danny said.

"I'm not playing that game, Danny. When they monkey with a perfectly good outfit. Can't they just say, O.K., tonight I'm wearing black tie."

"You can't enforce that," Danny said.

"You don't enforce it, you just get someone to write it in a column." Right then my envelope flopped off the radiator onto the floor. "After that they come however they want. At least they know they're breaking the rule. That's what law is all about. Jack can tell you this. All law's consensual."

"I'm done with the law," I said.

"Well good, Jack, you can be a journalist."

I went all the way in and sat on the windowsill.

"No," I said. "You have to mind people's business even more than a lawyer. You only see what's wrong with them."

"Shit don't smell till you touch it," Danny said.

"What?" George lifted his head in shock. But he made Danny repeat it ten times and kept gazing at him with delight.

The masseuse was done, he gave George a little slap on the back and started putting stuff away. Then George leaned off the desk to get my envelope. He hoisted himself up to a sitting position on the desk, half-naked, in no hurry to get his shirt on. So it was like we were in a men's-club locker room, and George had a bear gut, a white round belly, and thin black, old-guy hairs whorling over his titties. The masseuse left and George lifted his undershirt off a chair and slowly put that on, pushing my envelope right through the armhole along with his hand.

"Well, I hope this has some clinkers in it, Jack. Some pebbles in the snowball." He shook the envelope by his ear. "A little broken glass on top of the wall."

"I'm no good at journalism."

"Don't say that. If I was as young and wild as you? If I was a wild fur-bearing animal"—George turned to Danny—"see,

Jack is young, Jack has energy and a ton of motivation. Plus he doesn't have any friends."

Danny laughed.

"Oh thanks," I said.

"Jack, you know what I mean," George said. "You're young and judgment-proof. It gives me an ulcer to piss anybody off."

"You're about to piss off Rene Barce," Danny said.

George sighed and lifted his shirt off a chair. "The painter. Anatomy and all."

"I know Rene," I said.

George looked at me and I was surprised at my voice, how proud I was.

"We're telling how he shot a lamb for dinner on his farm." George laughed. "First his wife, then a lamb."

"It wasn't Barce," I said.

"That's what we heard," George said. "Ran out of food and shot his lamb with an English hunting rifle."

"Somebody lied," I said.

"I don't know." George frowned. "Who can say. We print what people tell us, and sometimes people lie."

He tried to stab a cuff-link through one-handed. He'd folded the cuff and was pressing his wrist against his thigh.

"See, Jack, this is what I tried to tell you about, the story of journalism. The only time people don't differ on facts is when no one cares what happened. That's just the law of events."

"Maybe you should write a letter," Danny said. "That's what we tell people who disagree."

"Write a letter—ha!" George barked happily.

I turned and looked out the window. Parting the blinds you could see the Lower East Side, the tar-paper roofs and the huddled, thrown-together black tenement buildings, and also a bridge, that gray Erector-set one over the East River. The view spreading out from George's window was the whole long-suffering Jewish Lower East Side, full of moody griefs and humor, and now and then exaltation.

The river gleamed like a coin in someone's open hand.

My grandfather came up right there on yonder river. My eyes got blurry and I thought about my grandfather, E. W. Reshevsky. Why did he say E.W.? Because he was naïve. Just coming over had been naïve, believing in America. He would tell you the stories about steerage in this untouched way, twelve days at sea and the people who died, the baby born and died on the ship and the kid who drank vodka. The golden land. But now somehow I had that same idiot belief worse than him.

I turned away from the dirty glass. George was looping his suspenders over his shoulders, red ones with two black stripes, no-sex-drive suspenders.

"I have to go. I haven't slept in two days."

"Oh hell, Jack, you're probably right to get out," George said. "This is a terrible business to get old in."

Danny laughed hard.

George turned on him. "The legs go at thirty-five."

"What'd you eat for lunch today, George?" Danny said. "Dolphin with composed butter at Jimmy's Belasco?"

George slid off the desk and got to his feet.

"Jimmy's is over. We went to Tatterdemalion."

"George has not paid for his own lunch in fifteen years, Jack. There's your story of journalism. Who got the tab? Arnold?"

George turned to me. "Do you know Arnie Sheldrake?"

I shook my head.

"O.K., Arnie Sheldrake. Arnie was a reporter. A good one, too. He covered takeovers for the *Journal* and was smarter than Satan, he knew the deals better than the bankers. So." A sigh went through George the way a horse shakes. "He crosses the street to Goldman and I can't blame him, he was making fifty-seven five and said fuck this. And now he makes so much he can't relate to anybody—"

George clapped his hands, his cheeks brightened. The story was inspirational, a kind of Horatio Alger tale of corruption.

"It's like play money to Arnie. The sonofabitch thatched his

222

house. He took the goddamn slate off. Then this summer he had to air-condition the gazebo. It traps heat, he says."

George fished with his feet for his shoes, small black loafers, and slid them on.

"And I can't say where Arnie ever believed that stuff about the public's right to know in the first place," he said.

"And you don't write about him," I said.

George sagged against the desk and clutched his heart.

"Et tu Jack," Danny said.

"Oh I ought to fold this place right up," George said.

But when he said that Danny laughed and then George started laughing, too, like an in-joke, and that was how they were. They never stayed too serious, they saved you from that, and they would make fun of what anyone made the mistake of saying in a genuine moment. You couldn't be any other way with them.

After that Danny Smith went to a cabinet behind the desk and got out a bottle of cognac and three small glasses. They were those little heavy glasses that are actually a lot more glass than space for liquor. He sloshed cognac from one glass to another and handed George a glass and me one, too.

I didn't know why we were drinking, but I drank.

"Drink," Danny said to George, like it was medicine, and George stared at the surface of the liquor.

"Drugs and alcohol don't do it anymore," he said. "Don't touch the inner man."

But he drank anyway.

"Only thing does the trick now is new clothes." George ran his hand over the front of his shirt. "Egyptian cotton where you can almost smell the little Chinese fingers on it, making their blinding little stitches. Don't say it. Homophobic. Well, Christ, I know I'm homophobic."

The drink put him in a fresh mood. He grabbed at my envelope on the desk and tore the top off.

"New clothes and good reporting, that's all that does it. Oh,

Jack, I hope you lanced that boil, What's-his-name." He snapped his fingers and turned to Danny. "Who is that one I can't abide—"

"Honey."

"Right, Honey. Honey Feinberg"—George shivered with excitement. "The byline on the Wednesday food column. I see him on television, I want to tear off that Groucho Marx mustache, that electrical tape job. I want to fix a lamp with it, Jack, before somebody gets electrocuted."

"Honey's smart," I said.

"Hell I know he's smart. Listen, this is a man, whatever else he is—" George dropped my article on the desk. "This is a man who doesn't know how to dress for his weight. There's a way to carry that weight and dress fine. It's not a bad weight."

He was so excited he started to cough, then he put down his glass. "He found a sausage maker not a tailor," he said. "Don't say it, homophobic."

I was going to learn a whole lesson from him, Don't take anything personally. I said, "George, it's been a pleasure."

George got his lopsided smile and held my arm. "Oh hell, Jack, we forgot to make a toast," he said. "You can't go till we make a toast, we've insulted the gods—"

He held out his glass and we touched glasses.

"To former journalists," I said.

"Hear! hear!" Danny said.

I drank off my glass and left it on the desk.

20

A storm hit and I sat in the Cuban-Chinese place watching water lash the picture window. A hurricane had bounced off North Carolina. They had that hammering-plywood story on television every other minute, and my mom called. She freaks out whenever there's bad weather up here, or a disaster. Disaster's the grist for her mill. When a plane crashes at La-Guardia she calls me. Or if some friend I hardly knew when I was eight years old gets cancer, she's on the horn.

I told her about writing the article and you could hear her heart get lighter. She said she'd tell my dad I was taking a break to do some journalism. A break. I know what that means. Why did I go to the best law school in the country if I wasn't going to do anything with it? She said my dad hadn't been feeling well, and we both know he doesn't care for journalists. Journalists misrepresented him when he did his big Multiplier Effect report about money spent on Reagan's defense buildup, big on the left anyway. Also, he says that journalists were the running dogs of the Red scare in the fifties.

Lapdogs, pariah dogs, watchdogs. It's hard to say anything about journalists without comparing them to dogs.

An hour after I'd finished with my mom, my dad called back. He had a whole sanitized lecture.

"My anecdotal evidence suggests there aren't many able practitioners, Jacob, so with one credible article you should stand out in the field."

I.e., one article. No more. He never says what he feels.

But I didn't like being a journalist either, and the next day I spent a lot of my *Larkspur* pay without having it yet on clothes. George was going to give me $3,500. I blew nearly a grand. I got a dark green cashmere jacket for the winter and a black shirt with a print of whales, also black suede shoes. I thought I'd spend my way out of ever becoming a journalist.

Burry said she felt alienated from me, and I went over to her place in my new jacket. She made pesto, and when she got out red wine I figured the whole pregnancy thing had gone away. But I didn't say anything, and she was careful around me, too. She told me about her dad's meeting with the *Times* editorial board. Later I went into the bathroom and spread open on the side of the tub was a book called *My New Body: A Woman's First Experience of Pregnancy*.

In the morning I woke up with a red-wine hangover and thought maybe I'd dreamed that part. But the book was still there. I took a shower and when I opened the door I smelled coffee. Burry never drank coffee.

She was still in bed, and when I went into the kitchen James Doyle was sitting at the table. That was the way he was, quiet as dust. And wearing a whole political outfit, too, navy suit, striped tie. With a bunch of papers spread out around him.

"Good morning, James," I said.

"Hello, Jack. There's coffee."

He waved at the stove. I got a Department of State cup with a gold-edged seal and stood by the window. The sun was out. The storm was over, and in the sky over Central Park a flock

226

of birds dipped and wheeled and flew back up. They did the same wheeling pattern over and over, in unison.

I reached for the *News*. They'd endorsed Vacca for governor. Energy and ideas. I put it back on the table.

"Sorry," I said.

"It isn't worth five thousand votes. The only endorsement that matters is the *Times*. We'll get the *Times*."

"Burry says it went real well," I said.

"That it did."

He set his coffee cup down on the paper, he was careful to set it right back on the ring it had made the time before. He turned toward me, he put his hands on his knees.

"Listen, Jack, congratulations. Burry told me the news confidentially, she says you're engaged."

We shook hands, and he held my hand an extra second.

"You're very lucky, I think you both are very lucky."

"Thanks," I said. That's the trick, don't take anything personally.

"Listen, I don't know if Burry's told Early. I haven't. But I want you to know the Secretary's people will get behind you in a big way. You don't need to worry about a job. Early knows everyone. I mean a good job, just about anywhere. A good firm."

"I'm done being a lawyer."

"Well, O.K. But what? I mean, do you want to work on the Hill or for an agency? Really, Jack, this is a lay-up."

"That's O.K.," I said.

"Burry said you're looking for a house, we'll help you find a house."

"We're not looking for a house."

"That's fine, too, Jack." He lifted his hands out to the side, palms up, to show he was easy. "We're team players. We watch out for each other. We pinch-hit. We run for each other, we keep things in the family."

I had dry mouth, I got out my cigarettes.

227

"But," I said.

James pushed his chair back. He frowned, you saw his tongue moving in his mouth.

"There are no buts, this is straight as it comes."

"You want me to say in *Larkspur* that Vacca killed a sheep."

James rubbed his face, then he couldn't help it, he laughed.

"George says you love Vacca."

"No. I just don't hate him is all."

"Well listen, it doesn't matter, that's fine. You say whatever you want."

He stood and poured himself more coffee. He saw something in the surface of the coffee and got a spoon, lifted it out. He put the spoon in the sink. There was something he wasn't saying.

"You know Burry's very special," he said. "She's real decent, and you're smart as they come."

"Thanks," I said.

"Don't thank me, it's just true."

He sat and put the cup right back in that same circle.

"There's something real delicate we should talk about."

"Here it comes," I said.

"Jack, relax. This is delicate, but Burry has told me in the strictest confidence—" He stopped and frowned. "Listen, I just want to dialogue with you about abortion."

I turned a burner on the stove and bent with my cigarette, I blackened the end and filled my lungs. The cigarette went in right on top of the coffee, I mean the drug of it.

"You know how the Secretary feels about this issue," he said. "A woman has the right to choose. He's been very out front from day one on this."

I went to the window. I felt faint and my head swam. The birds were still going over the park, the same circle, a little wider. It was almost like an exercise, like they were teaching some of them to fly.

"He gets a bum rap, but he has. But Jack it's obviously an issue you never want the rubber to meet the road—"

228

I turned back from the window, reached for a chair, and sat down. I had this brilliant idea that I could explain shit to James, I could make things clear to him and me, too, at the same time. "James, I've worked for a lot of do-gooders," I said.

"Right."

"When I was a lawyer. I mean, I still am a lawyer, but this is before—well, it doesn't matter. I'm talking about people who thought you could make rules to improve things. That in some way behavior could be altered and improved through intercession."

"O.K.," he said.

"I mean, it's a belief built into democracy." I stopped again, off track. "There's this whole legal expression, does everything come down to cases? The agreed-on answer to that is no, it doesn't. Everything isn't its own case you have to deal with on its own terms. So that in fact you can come up with rules, and that way everyone will behave. The personal is political, and so forth."

James nodded a lot, nicely. "Go on," he said.

Sweat went down my rib cage, and I understood I'd gotten nowhere. I had another hit off the cigarette and grabbed an ashtray. Burry had lifted it on one of her many social errands, some engagement party, with "21" in gold on the bottom.

"All I'm saying is, I think they were wrong. Because the funny thing is, everything does come down to cases. You can make all these rules, abortion is good, abortion is murder, but in the end all that matters is the individual. What they're feeling. And trying to keep some things personal."

James dropped his hand on the table.

"Doesn't this fall into the category of things we learned in college?" he said.

"I guess I'm just saying I make a shitty lawyer."

He laughed. "You sound like a good lawyer to me."

"Well then, the easiest way to say all this is, it's none of your damn business."

I went to the sink. I rinsed my coffee cup, splashing it clean, not really washing it, then I turned it upside down on the drainboard. I dumped the ashtray out, too.

James shifted his chair around, facing me.

"Jack, you know what? You're too smart for politics." He held up his hand. "Wait, don't jump down my throat, it's meant as a compliment. Some people are so smart they can't do politics. They can't do simple arithmetic. For instance, Early's base, you look at any of the polling data, his base is almost 50 percent Catholic. That's just a fact. And those people, for whatever reason, they believe in taking responsibility."

"What about privacy?" I said.

He didn't blink. "What about the pictures you took?"

I sagged. "Burn them."

"They're in a very safe place. They could be very helpful."

"James, it was his sister."

He scraped his chair back. "Whose sister?"

"Vacca's. I saw her at a fund-raiser last week."

"Then what's she doing in the room?"

"I don't know. She's here on some bank program. So maybe she stayed at his room instead of going back to her aunt in Queens. They're a close-knit family."

He got up and put his cup in the sink. He was calm.

"Well, I don't think that's really the point, Jack."

"I fucked up," I said. "I fucked up and I wish I could have that back."

"O.K. You know what? We both did. We both fucked up. And guess what, we're lucky. It isn't hard for us to say that. We can walk away. But the Secretary can't make excuses."

I nodded and left the kitchen. He followed me into the hall, the picture gallery.

"Jack, everything's going to work out all right," he said.

"Why don't you put her picture up here?" I said. "It's part of the story. The Early Quinlan story."

I guess I was moving my arms, I was pissed off. James stood back.

"Jack, I don't want you to start worrying about any of this. It doesn't have to be in your DNA to screw everything up."

"Right," I said, then I walked out.

21

When I got home I realized it was my birthday. Twenty-nine. My mom had left a message on my machine, and I checked the date in the paper. I'd been thinking it was the next day. The mail came with a card from my sister in Boston, a musical card that when you opened it up played a whole song, the happy birthday song. It didn't stop.

Burry called and I didn't pick up. She said she got upset when there was any conflict between me and James, she wanted to talk about it. But I didn't know what I could say to her.

I had a birthday beer and cleaned up my place. I boraxed the sink and bathroom and put two sick plants out on the street so someone else could do better by them. Burry called again and I screened again. But the next time the phone rang I picked it up.

"Is this how a relationship in New York ends?" she said.

"My place is a mess. I'm working on it."

"Jack, your voice is dead. James said you walked out on him."

"I need a day by myself."

I had this plan to stay occupied. I read the paper in Strawberry Fields, then I took the subway to the Village, to the Foundation for Fair Uses (of Power). You have to wait for the guy to come in from the sidewalk and run the elevator for you. I guess it's a full-employment thing. But Ralph Lopez wasn't there, so that plan was screwed and I walked all the way back to my place.

At night I stopped at a video place on Broadway for porn. This time I got the porn straight up and didn't invent a whole cover story dragging Kurosawa into it. A cover-up.

The movie was feminist porn you were supposed to feel good about watching, like you were making the world a better place by beating off. It was about a housesitter, this college girl, but none of the homeowners' friends knows they're gone. So they all show up. Another mix-up. The accountant, the doctor, and so on, they come over. The girl runs the show, and they all land next to the swimming pool, a pile of them. That was the best thing about porn. Everyone got naked. You could be anybody, you could be a judge or a teacher, you could be the head of a public-interest law firm, but if you were in the movie you were going to get naked, no two ways about it. Even if they came in uptight and dressed in a three-piece suit being an asshole, you knew what was going to happen: that person before long was going to be stripped naked and moaning and legs spread, everything else. It was pretty fair that way, it was hard to think of a more equitable arrangement.

Afterward I felt washed out and useless. I thought I was getting away from my mood. But I just sank further into it. I missed Burry.

In the morning I decided to find Joseph Vacca. It had been ten days since I'd seen him, and I needed to update the article. Vacca's headquarters said he was visiting a school in Harlem, so I took the subway up to 125th Street and walked ten blocks to this elementary school. It was sunny, but whenever the breeze came the air was cool, and the lifeless hangover of beating off twice fell on my shoulders.

233

They had the schedule wrong, because when I got there the school tour was over and the press conference was wrapping up. There were more reporters around than I'd ever seen for Vacca. They trailed him across the street to his car, and he stood with one foot in the door continuing to talk issues. And right behind him Honey Feinberg stood in the front door, spinning another little group of reporters.

I didn't even listen to Vacca, I watched his black eyes, how fleshy the sockets were and the way the droopy flesh under them formed charcoal-rubbed circles. There was a way the newspapers always described Vacca's looks, commanding or intense. Now I understood it was just a way of not saying he was ugly. Really he was kind of ugly. He wasn't like the Secretary, a golden boy with wavy black hair and that glamorous scar. No, Vacca was a different bug. He was hard to love.

The reporters left, but Vacca didn't move. He hung in the door and looked at me.

"Jack Gold—" It was the first time he'd ever said my name.

He turned and put his hand on Honey's shoulder. "Guess who's coming to dinner," he said.

When Honey saw me he forgot about who he was with. He came around the car door and stared as if I were a mirage.

"It's Gold," he said.

"No scenes, Honey," Vacca said.

Honey swallowed a couple of times, then he came right up on top of me. The edge of his mouth was wet, almost foamy, and you felt all the oniony heat coming off his body.

"Baboon," he said, and dropped his hand flat onto my chest.

His eyes were shut, his face was all pink with feeling. I guess he'd seen my article. Somehow he'd gotten hold of it. That happened in journalism all the time. People passed things around. Charles Tharp and Simi were always telling one another stuff.

"What's with you?" I said.

234

"Dirty red-ass baboon."

"Honey," Vacca said sharply.

He got in and pulled the door shut, and the redhead Blanchard leaned out. "Let's go, Honey, we're twenty minutes behind." The driver started the car, and Honey reached woodenly for me. He gathered the shoulder of my jacket in his fist, twisting it so it bound around my shoulders.

"Hey calm down," I said.

"Baboon—"

Vacca rolled his window down. "Let's move it, Harris."

But Honey was in a zone. He was holding my jacket and gazing off.

"Harris. Get your fat ass in the car."

Honey flushed even more. He turned and pushed me onto the front seat. He was strong, but I went with it. I don't know why. Because I liked him, because he acted like my brother.

There wasn't room. Blanchard and the driver were already there, and with me and Honey cramming in that made four. The car started going, but Honey couldn't get the door shut. In the end he crunched onto my lap and pulled the door closed. His head was tilted at an angle against the ceiling right over me. Taffy strings of spit filled the corners of his mouth.

"Great breath," I said.

He breathed on me, long draughts of stale breath.

"Fuckface," he said. "Filthy red-ass baboon."

"You're crushing my cigarettes—"

He mashed into my chest. "Ass. Hole. Ass. Hole. Ass. Hole," he chanted.

"Honey, calm down," Blanchard said.

"Listen, Harris, what did I tell you," Vacca said from the back seat.

"Honey, let's talk," I said.

They all broke up in laughter, all but Honey.

The car was moving fast down a big Harlem avenue, one of

235

those blasted-out boulevards with no one around and new names on them, political names, and every once in a while a nomadish person walking over the landscape.

Vacca tilted forward. "I told you, Harris. This is nothing. This is bullshit," he said in a quiet voice.

"The hell with that," Honey said.

I twisted to see Vacca. His big white hand rested on the seatback, and he looked at me neutrally. He had half-glasses on, reading glasses. The asshole had the whole back of the car to himself.

"Harris, it's a New York story," he went on. "This shit is dog bites man in New York."

"What story?" I said.

Vacca pinched me on the cheek. "You."

"You haven't seen the *Post*?" Blanchard said.

But Honey shoved in between us. "Red-ass monkey," he said. He strained hard, making a sound like he was taking a shit.

"I told him this would happen," Blanchard said.

"Sure you did," Vacca said. "But he didn't hear you. They don't teach New York stories at the Republican National Committee."

"You don't have to yell," Honey said.

"I'm not yelling. Can't you tell, I'm humming." He did a little hum, like "Jingle Bells." "Humming, Harris. Anyone can hum. That's humming. If you want yelling, I'll show you. Now, Harris, let's drop loverboy off."

"Loverboy," I said.

Everyone laughed. Honey cried out, "Starfucker. Red-ass starfucker."

"That's my business," I said.

There was more laughter, Vacca's the loudest, and suddenly I hated them, I hated their whole little nuclear family.

"Let me out—"

I pushed Honey at the dashboard. I guess I put too much in

236

it. Because Honey's forehead smacked into the windshield with a cracking noise.

"Pull over," Vacca said.

Honey rolled back against me, dazed, heavy as a mattress. Two giant circles of sweat met in the middle of his shirt. Vacca had to reach over the seat to get the door handle. Then I rolled Honey onto the redhead Blanchard and slid out. I was wobbly on my feet. The fucker had broken all my bones.

A whole Harlem vista unfolded before me: a new municipal sidewalk, a clean extruded path of raised whitish concrete. And all around it nothing. Tall weeds and broken bottles, ungainly trees. They call them ghetto oaks. Stony always talked about the ghetto oaks, springing up with vigor in brick ruins, and this is where Stony had grown up, probably a half mile from here, next to Morningside Park. I started tenderly down the street. Fifty feet ahead a charred mattress draped over the curb. Coils came up out of it, blackened but intact.

"Gold!"

It was Vacca's voice. I ignored him. When he said "Jack!" is when I turned. He was leaning out the window, he had a hard smile. It came to me that he thought more of me for knowing about Burry.

"August 6, 1959," he said. "Your birthday. That was you in the hotel, I never forget a birthday."

"My birthday was yesterday."

He frowned. Then they were gone and I kept walking. I came to a bodega and looked at the *Post*. The gossip column said Burry Quinlan was rumored to be engaged to Jack Gold. There was a picture, too. You saw Burry head-on and me beside her. We were on a cobbled street, the flash lit us almost like a portrait. It was one of Morgan's cake pictures.

My cigarettes were all broken. I pulled them out one after the other, dropping them in the gutter. Honey had smashed them all to hell. Red springs of tobacco came out of tears in the paper. I crunched the pack, tossed it into ghetto grass.

22

When I hit Central Park I kept going south straight through. I didn't follow the paths, I went over the hills, through the woods. I imitated Vacca, I hummed. Humming people were healthy people. Burrs clung to my socks and thorns cut my arms, like in the Bible. Well it's probably not in the Bible, but you know what I'm saying. Then the park ended at Fifty-ninth Street and Sixth Avenue and I went to a phone.

Morgan's card was still in my wallet from that time at the courthouse, now it was curved and softened. A woman answered. The Somebody Somebody Gallery.

Is Morgan there? Let me get him, she said. No thanks. I got the address, a number on Broome Street, and took the subway down.

SoHo was quiet in that snotbag streets-of-Paris way, with the dark cool streets and the people walking around with their quiet purposeful lives. Nobody saying anything, nobody going insane, just a lot of swift civilized eye contact. Old friends passing in the street with just a nod. People who are married having affairs and everyone understanding. What Quinlan said in his Labor Day speech, separation, self-reliance.

The gallery was in a four-story industrial building painted

muddy green. It had a new skirt of black steel plating at street level and the staircase going up to the front door was of the same material, black pressed steel, with anti-skid cigar shapes going in two different directions. The gallery proper was half a story up from the street. It had clean, giant windows, but the second-floor windows were filthy and crusted with darkened cardboard boxes piled against them like an Arthur Miller play.

Through the windows the gallery seemed empty, an acre or so of blond wood floors with sunlight smashing off them. Along the walls were televisions, probably ten large black TVs at even intervals. I opened the door and there was a woman at a desk. She put her book down and stood, and she was pretty and tall, with long brown hair like the naked woman on a Tarot card.

I was checking out her body, but you couldn't. She wore black tights and a baggy gray sweater that hung down over her ass and had cost her an arm and a leg. Girls who dress like that have tits, it's just an obvious fact. They don't want drool guys like me focused on their tits.

She was watching me right back. She had this whole calm goofy way about her, with big teeth, big lips.

"I want to talk to Morgan," I said.

She started across the bright floor toward the back. "O.K., Jack Gold," she said.

"I'm Jack Gold. How do you know?"

"You look like him."

Well, she was a bullshit artist, so I relaxed a little. I followed her and said, "What's Jack Gold look like?"

She gave me a cool assessing look then went on her way. But she'd turned all the way round, a three-sixty. Just the way she looked at me she lifted my anger, but you still couldn't see her body.

"Like a Fuller brush man," she said. "Except instead of brushes when he opens his case there's a swarm of bees."

"You're full of shit," I said.

"You were in the paper. Morgan told me about you."

"He's a liar. What did he tell you?"

"You lost your job when his picture came out," she said.

Then she did this thing with her hair. A hank of it traveled down her face onto her chest and she flicked it back over her ear. It seemed halfway sincere. She wasn't trying to work out her complex with you.

"That's not all," I said.

"Talk to him—"

She sprung a door in the wall, but I lingered. There was a way she made you feel, not like a bundle of nerves, and she didn't have an agenda. Then I wished it were a different time. The 1950s, or the fifteenth century, and she and I could step out of our tangled lives and just walk away together, that whole romance.

"He's upstairs. You're going to want to shape-shift past the garbage there."

You went up this iron staircase and dim light came through the dusty window, and the upstairs was trashed. Maybe there's an Arthur Miller play called *Before the Flood*, or I'm thinking of the Jewish joke about the businessman who makes a flood. I'm scrambling things. But this place was like an insurance scam, with flattened cardboard boxes on the floor and charred footsteps over them and water damage and machinery piled up in the corner from what Carmen Frankel used to call middle-late capitalism. Large chains and toothed wheels and motors in a black dry-greasy pile no one had touched in years.

Morgan appeared in a doorway with an Indian blanket for a door. He was unshaven, and his hair hung down in strings. His white T-shirt made his white arms look whiter.

"Hey Jack," he said, and I went right by him.

The whole back of the second floor was a loft, the artist's-loft stereotype, one big room with a sink and a bathtub in the middle of nowhere and the smell of photochemicals. But a woman had been there, you could tell. The futon on the floor was neatly made. A pale yellow cloth was wrapped tightly over it.

Morgan went past me through another blanketed doorway and that was his space. Brown paper bags were lined up along the walls, ordinary supermarket bags filled with negatives. His negatives were curling over the edges.

A television was on there. Morgan felt among the video-cassette boxes stacked atop it and, lifting one, shook out a pack of cigarettes. He held the pack out to me.

"I'm not smoking a peace pipe, you put me in the paper," I said.

He sat on a couch and lit a cigarette. He rubbed his strange squinty eyes and looked at the television.

"I don't own that picture, Jack. I sold it to you, remember?"

"You made prints."

"I don't own the copyright. You do. Who'd you give it to?"

I came all the way into the room, I sat on a table littered with camera parts and pretended to watch the television with him. I didn't know what I was doing there.

"You give it to *Larkspur?*" he said.

"No," I said. "I don't know."

Morgan offered the pack again, and this time I lit a cigarette off his. C-SPAN was airing a Congressional hearing. I used to write about that. Hearings are the greatest proof man has found of the existence of democracy. That's in Victor's book. Well, Nixon had probably thought so, too, when he held up the Alger Hiss film for the reporters. What if he thought he was doing the right thing. Yes, this will destroy someone but I'm standing up for sacred principles. What if he was only naïve?

"Or *Larkspur* bought it for James Doyle," he said. "It's the same account."

"What's that mean?" I said.

"Hey, you read that thing. *Larkspur* carries water for Quinlan. People say that's where George Sides gets his money, Quinlan's rich pals."

"Who?"

He squinted with smoke in his face. "I don't know. It's just what you hear. Or that George was going to shut it down last year then he didn't. He got a bunch of money and now he's like *Stars and Stripes* for Quinlan."

I drank a lot of smoke. "He got sued."

Morgan pointed his cigarette at me. "See, you know more than I do. Who paid for the picture?"

I looked around. Morgan had pinned blurry pictures to the wall of people moving. Their backs or the sides of their faces. Fires burning in cans on streets. The homeless.

"You work for the papers?" I said.

"I'm trying to get out of that," he said.

We each got another cigarette. He lit them off his first one and crushed the butt in a silver film canister. He nosed the canister across the floor to me with his black sneaker.

"Well, I got to go," I said.

He got up, too.

"Hey listen, congratulations," he said. "I forgot to congratulate you. You're getting married, right?"

"First I have to ask the Secretary," I said. "He's pretty traditional."

He held out his hand. It was the first time we'd ever shaken hands.

"What if he says no. You elope?"

"I guess. Sure. We elope." I hadn't thought about any of that. "We leave New York and don't come back."

"The geographical solution," he said.

"Well, it's a solution."

He smiled. "It's not a solution. That's an expression. For a way of not facing your shit."

I walked out, but he came after me.

"Listen Jack, I want to show you something."

He dropped his cigarette and kicked it past a giant spool of twine, blackened rotting string, probably ten miles of it, with

242

just the end hanging off and grinding into the black floor. Then he went down the stairs and at the bottom he stopped and turned.

"Listen, you could do me a big favor. If Mona says anything about she can smell cigarettes, they were yours."

"Who's Mona?"

He pointed at the gallery. "Mona covers the rent. It would be a big drag if she thinks I even smoked one cigarette."

For a second his face was tortured and almost hungry.

"I'm not lying for you," I said.

He pushed open the door and the light made me blink. Morgan walked ahead of me to the desk. The girl was there, Mona. She sat reading a book with a long title, like a self-help book, a book with a yellow cover. All those yellow-cover books that teach girls how to fix their relationships. They probably had a shitty relationship, Morgan and Mona.

She moved out of Morgan's way as he pulled out drawers. "Don't destroy my desk, O.K.," she said.

She put down the book. She made that goofy smile at me. "Jack, why do you smoke?"

"I don't know. It calms me down."

"You know why? Because it lyses your spirit."

"You read that in some book."

"So what. It lyses your spirit, it deadens you, Jack. Nicotine chemically breaks off the little impulses that try to wake you up and make you who you are." She did that thing with her hair again, flicking, like she'd done it a million times. "So you never know, and that's the tragedy."

I laughed. "You're full of it," I said.

But just the way she said my name, I liked, and I walked the cigarette to the door and threw it into the curb.

"Good, now litter," she said.

Morgan laughed. He came away from the desk with two remote wands. He waved one at the first television.

A VCR came on with what looked like a home movie, set

in Central Park. The camera jumped and moved, I guess the person holding it was running. His breath came in long wheezes. It didn't sound like Morgan. Three guys ran ahead of him through the park. They were in a meadow. Not young guys either, and in shitty clothes, black guys. There was a cracking noise. One of them pointed a gun at the bushes.

I looked at Morgan. He was white-faced, biting the edge of his thumb.

"This is a good part"—he motioned at the screen.

The man had shot a rabbit. Another man lifted it by the back of the neck from under a bush. It was dying. It kicked out its legs and blood went down its fur in a pretty way, blood dripped off one of its kicking, gray-brown rabbit feet.

I looked at Mona. She was turned in her chair, reading the book.

The men started arguing about whether it was disrespectful to photograph an animal dying. While they argued, it died. The man with the gun said a prayer you could barely hear. The rest of them kneeled and mumbled along with him.

Morgan surfed the remote at the other televisions. They all came on with the same picture, and then the men stood up and one said, "I ain't skinning no rabbit."

"They're homeless," I said.

Morgan nodded, he muted the TVs.

"I just give them the camera. We're doing a show. Called *Above and Below Fifth Avenue*. It's opening next week."

He had that scared helpless look, watching me. He said he was going to have little TVs on top of the big ones, and the little ones would show a tape of rich people at some party. He wanted a tape the rich people made the same way, by their own hand. He explained the whole thing. It was the longest I'd ever heard him talk.

I turned away from him to the television. Someone had gotten the rabbit's skin off. He was working a stick through its body, like a spit, from its mouth in. But Morgan turned the TVs off

244

all at once. I had no choice but to look at him, and he was ugly, with those blunt features, that stringy hair.

"The *Larkspur* party's Thursday night," he said.

"It's not on Fifth Avenue."

"That doesn't matter."

"Everyone lies, don't they?"

Mona laughed. She had put her book down, she was watching us with a neutral expression. Gray eyes, small but watchful.

"It's the idea of Fifth Avenue," he said.

"I don't take pictures," I said.

"You don't have to, just give them the camera."

"Why don't you do it?"

"Because they throw me out of their parties. You know that." He slouched there, watching me. "I make them feel sick, or worse, I make them feel dumb. They like you. You make them feel smart."

"I'm done with politics," I said.

"This isn't about politics."

"Morgan," Mona said.

He looked at her with annoyance, the annoyance of an old shitty failed-artist relationship.

"It's nothing if not about politics," she said.

He sagged. "It's about representation. Just like the way the papers represented Jack today," he said.

"O.K.," she said.

"The specific politics isn't what matters," he said.

"Everything matters," she said.

As much as anything, I was jealous of their fight, a real fight, and I didn't want to be there. I went out the door.

Morgan came after me. He stood holding the door while I went down the stairs. I thought I was just going to walk away, but I had a weird tremor, I thought about the Haitian report with the little drawings of people being twisted around logs and steel drums, I thought about my drawings way back when of the man on the stage, the man going up into the air, whether

245

or not he would hit his head. Pictures rushed past me. Then I felt bad I hadn't said goodbye to that Mona.

"A camera's magic," Morgan said. "People like to touch it, pass it around."

Give anyone the opportunity, they start lecturing you. I bent at the gutter for the cigarette butt.

"Tell Mona I picked this up."

"O.K."

He nodded and let the door close, a wide bronze sheet of afternoon glare, sealing them off.

23

The *Larkspur* party was October 23, and that was the night the season turned completely to fall. The air was cold and wet and I stood outside Grubs' Parade in a long line of people in evening clothes whose faces were speckled with the rain. The line took forever moving along the wide sidewalk, and everything was grand and old New York: the people's nervous voices, their clothes and the ornate streetlights smeared yellow against the sky, the steam coming up from the grates and wrapping itself like muslin over a limousine's grille.

There was all this bullshit at the door with girls in black velvet dresses looking at your hanky and taking your coat. I kept the camera bag on my shoulder, a black nylon bag with Morgan's video camera in it. Morgan had brought it to me at my apartment that day. I took it, but I hadn't made him any promises.

Then you parted heavy green-and-red velvet curtains over the doorways and you went all the way inside George Sides's vision of New York. Massive bunches of dried flowers hung by ribbons on the cast-iron pillars of the hall, and tables were piled with fall fruits. Here and there about the floor were giant blue-ribbon pumpkins carved into jack-o'-lanterns. Not ordinary pumpkins but saggy ones from the front page of the local news-paper. And at the front of the room an all-women's band was playing, women dressed up in tuxedos and playing big-band numbers. There was going to be entertainment all night. Burry had been working at her performance piece for days, it was about her brother, the Republican. It was what I always said, she was serious, someone just had to call on it.

The push of people against you was exciting and the hectic smell in the air was like the smell of crossed wires. Or maybe charred pumpkins. It made you feel lucky to be there. That was the look in people's faces. No one wanted to be anywhere else.

I looked good, I knew it. I had on a new shirt and black tie, a whole fucking cummerbund I'd bought, my good new jacket.

They were making martinis in official triangular martini glasses, with the little onion or the olive, so I got a martini and looked for Burry. I ran into Danny Smith near the stage. He was wearing an earring and a black turtleneck, not even a tux-edo, and he said Burry was backstage.

But then when you tried to go, a bouncer said you couldn't.

I wanted to tell Burry about the camera, I wanted to talk to her. So I had another martini and a third one, and that was when the gin hit me. Things got looser, I wandered up near the stage. The women took a break and George Sides was there. He was wearing a white three-piece suit and he had an entou-rage of adoring friends, maybe not an entourage but hangers-on. You heard him saying aphorisms.

"Live right, publish left, it's what anyone that claims to have any integrity in journalism does," he said. "Just no one has the guts to say it."

So everyone was getting loaded but I didn't go up to George. I was afraid. I'd been calling about my article, but he hadn't been answering my calls. There was only one issue of *Larkspur* left before the election. I wanted my article to be in it.

The entertainment started. George liked low culture, and the first out were pop-lockers from Times Square, five skinny black guys in black Tyvek track suits. They pop-locked and moon-walked and spun upside down on their shoulders while one of them beat on the bottom of a plastic construction bucket. Then the oldest, least-skinny one did gangster rap. But you could hardly hear him because he didn't have a microphone. I don't think George wanted him to have one, because the rap was very aggressive. So it was censorship.

He came to the front of the stage and shouted. And it didn't matter that you couldn't hear the words, the crowd loved them.

Then they left and a Borscht Belt guy came on, a comic with a hairpiece. I should know his name. I bet my parents have a record of his, one of those guys who instead of saying "tit" will say "her left side." But the thing is, the joke is as rough as any tit joke. It's worse than any tit joke.

One of George's assistants brought the mike back onstage, and George stood near the stage and with every joke let out a kettledrum laugh. The guy did his nontit tit jokes and people hissed, but George laughed and so did his entourage.

Jinx Cope came up, the guy from Burry's party, the critic. George put his arm around him.

"David, don't ever praise," he said in a too-loud voice. "It's the first law of journalism. All happy families are alike. All good reviews sound alike."

One of the hangers-on brought George a note. He read it and crumpled it with a theatrical gesture, he flew it to the floor. He looked around and saw me, then he rolled his hand, summoning me.

"Jack!"

I went over and he didn't look at me.

"Jack Jack Jack. Listen, friend, your wife wants you."

"I don't have a wife."

"Right. O.K." He had his nervous half-smile. "Future wife."

249

"I don't have a future."

We both laughed, George harder than me. Then I said, "George, when are you going to use my article?"

"Jack, hey—I've been meaning to talk to you about that."

"I need money," I said.

"Hey listen, Jack let me tell you something. Do you know what those pumpkins cost? I bought them pumpkins for you."

I looked at the pumpkins. "I can't use them."

"He can't use them. Ha—" George made a barking laugh and his cheeks shone. "They're not for using. Jack. Jack. Listen, my friend."

He reput his arm around me.

"When fortune smiles on you, the deal is, relax into it. See, you already know that. You're drinking a martini. Listen, I tried to call you. I guess your machine wasn't on. The article is very good, it's close, we have to talk about it."

He pointed me to the stage door and waved to the bouncer.

But I had to wait. The comic was finishing up and the all-women's band was crowding up to play again. People jeered the comic off, and he pushed ahead of me into the passageway. The hall struck off narrowly into the side of the building, it had plywood walls and bare bulbs hanging down. The comic went sourly down the passage and stripped his tie and issued a stream of expletives about the crowd.

Two women crunched past me to get to him, women in their forties or fifties, blondes.

The dressing room had been used for coal once, or storage, the brick walls were sooty. Someone had undertaken a half-hearted effort to fix it up for the talent, with makeup mirrors and folding tables. There was bullshit show-business food, too, a big foil-covered cardboard disk with a pineapple in the middle and meats folded like hankies around it. The pop-lockers were wolfing food and putting their suits into nylon shoulder bags like mine.

Burry was at the back. She sat in a canvas chair, and her

250

stuff was around her, bottled water and scads of folded, fretted-over pieces of legal paper covered with her writing. She wore the green-and-black velvet dress I'd gotten her. It hung way down off her shoulders. And over the tops of her tits and her shoulders she'd put little sparkles like angel dust on her fine white skin. She looked so beautiful. Dark makeup chiseled her eyes into the sharp bones of her face.

She rose and grappled my neck in a lifesaving hold, and I felt wobbly.

"Jack, where were you? I looked for you everywhere. Father was here, too, Father wanted to see you. Then he had to go to another event and they put us in this slum and now my voice is shot."

She touched her throat. I was dizzy and felt for something to sit on, the edge of a packing crate. She sat, too. She reached around on the table for a mango, and the bones in her shoulders jutted glamorously.

"Doesn't that make you happy, Father and I were looking for you and I'm wearing your dress?"

"Yes."

"Oh, Jack, you're drunk. You're drunk, aren't you?"

"I'm scared."

She pulled my hands into her velvet lap alongside the mango. "Baby you're drunk and my throat is f'cocked."

"That's Yiddish," I said. "You're speaking Yiddish."

"Oh, Jack, it's because of him—" She waved at the comic.

I caught her hand and held it. "Burry, baby, listen to me. I'm feeling dangerous, like your father said."

"Baby, you're not dangerous, you're drunk."

She lifted a sweating highball glass from the table and rolled it across my forehead then along my cheeks and my neck, bringing me down. "Is that thing in the paper still bothering you?"

"No."

"Jack what did James tell you? It was somebody young, it was a stupid mistake."

"Right."

"These things happen. People learn stuff and they can't help it, they blab. Like if the President gets sick. Listen I'm going to get that guy fired from the campaign."

"Don't," I said.

Burry felt blindly around on the table. Her hand came back with earrings. They sparkled madly, pendant crystal costume earrings. She hung them on her ears with one hand, not taking her eyes off me.

I lifted the bag into my lap and unzipped it, I poked the camera out.

"What is that?" she said. "Oh, Jack, you can document my performance."

"I was going to give it to people and let them use it. A friend is doing an art project about haves and have-nots."

"That's good. That could be funny."

"It's art, but it's also political," I said.

"O.K., but first document my performance. Blake was going to do it but she flaked, she had to meet her agent. Take my picture here."

A tide of nausea rose in me, I set the camera in the bag on the floor.

"In performance you document everything. The entire context. Get them—"

She pointed at the pop-lockers. They were leaving. George's assistant had given the oldest, least skinny of them an envelope. The guy held it in his white teeth and pushed open a fire door. Cold air came from the street and made me feel better.

"Burry, let's be brave and ugly and go," I said.

"But honey, I'm going on in twenty minutes."

"You're sick and we don't have to be here," I said. "It's a carny show. Just like your father says."

"My father?"

"He talks about the carny show," I said. "It's one of his little

252

themes. About politics. If we don't leave I'm going to fuck things up."

Burry looked at the fire door and seemed to think about it. "I guess we could make an announcement," she said. " 'Her father's campaign needed her, so Ms. Quinlan . . .' "

"I don't want an announcement."

"Oh, baby, you're so sensitive." She picked up the mango and tore off the top. "Now you know how it feels having your name in the paper."

"It's not the paper, it's everything. It's how we are together."

"But I promised George and my father," she said.

"Your father doesn't care," I said.

"Jack, that's hostile. Why are you saying that?"

"What is George paying you?"

"Oh, Jack, you're so drunk." She held my shoulders. "This is something I get to do. It's an opportunity. You're upsetting me. Now don't be icky-materialistic."

She did this thing with the mango, massaged its sides and ate it from the hole she'd torn, sucking and stripping more of the skin down from the top. She bit down to the seed. Then she held it out to me, with yellow-orange strings coming off the seed. The sweet pulp cut through my nausea.

"You know, Jack, I have never had a private life. I never had a choice. Now that's the way I am. I'm always going to express myself publicly."

I thought about the way she spoke too loud at the movies, that that would always bug me.

"Who will listen?" I said.

She cried and flung her arm. The mango hit my cheek and bounced off my shoulder and skidded twirling across the floor. It stopped at an old brass fire extinguisher. The comic stood up and clapped. "Bull's-eye," he shouted in his thick asshole voice. "Young man, get out while you have your eyes."

Burry was crying, she sat there covering her face. I reached for her hands, but she pulled away.

253

"I'm sorry," I said. "I hate this place and I feel like I'm about to pass out."

"If you were of a different class you would have hit me," she said.

"Burry, I'm sorry."

"I'm serious. Why didn't you just hit me? Where did that come from, Jack?"

"Because I'm scared," I said.

She lifted her head. "Oh, look at you, look at your new shirt." She grabbed a glass and tissues, she dabbed at the mango spatter on my shirt and lapels.

"And now I've gone and lost my voice—" She held the glass against her throat.

"I'll get you some juice," I said.

"Jack, that's the worst thing for me right now. I need a doctor. You know this is because of our baby in me. I need you to find John Ellen."

"The guru," I said.

"He's a doctor, Jack, please don't say that to him. He's a healer. He's here, John Ellen Rohr."

She said how he'd patched up all these people at the last minute before they went on: her father before a speech he gave at the Organization of American States when he had laryngitis, the Kennedys during campaigns, Luciano Pavarotti, Salman Rushdie before a reading.

"He does show business and liberals. He did Fidel Castro at the U.N. and Michael Redgrave at the Walter Kerr."

"John Ellen," I said.

"Call him Dr. Rohr. Sweetheart, don't futz it up."

John Ellen Rohr turned out to be a tall thin guy with a silver ponytail and a fringe beard. I found him by the bar, George Sides knew where he'd be, and he reached for a tumbler and

254

had the bartender fill it partway with brandy then made me get a roll of toilet paper from the bathroom. Toilet paper was as sterile as anything you could find in a hospital, he said.

Ten minutes after that the band broke again and George got up onstage in his white suit. He waved his arms and clapped.

"A distinct pleasure and a genuine privilege, wait I've got that backwards, a distinct privilege and a genuine pleasure—Ladies and gentlemen, Burry Quinlan."

She stilted out on heels, and George hugged her. That was when I thought of getting out the camera to document her. But it wasn't on my shoulder. I'd left it somewhere. Well fuck it, I thought, Morgan probably has a grant.

"No pictures, O.K.?" Burry said.

She held herself up with the mike stand, her red hair shook like metal. In front of people, she was beautiful. With an audience, I mean.

"I'm sorry I'm a wreck. I'm sick and I autoprescribed, which you're not supposed to do."

People laughed. She bent and, freeing her heels, kicked them to the side. She was barefoot. People crowded the stage, guys whooped as though she was going to take off her clothes. Because it was performance art, and in performance art girls are always taking off their clothes. "Take it off," some asshole yelled. Burry brought her hands to her chest, cupping her tits. Then she pulled her hands away, and she was giving him the finger. So just like that she took control.

"You people are all so sophisticated I was going to do something new for you. I wrote this, called 'Lover in a Cage.' "

She flapped a wad of paper. A flashbulb went off and she tilted her head, voguing for the camera.

"But I'm trashing this." She ripped it in half, to cheers. "I saw my father tonight and I remembered my first performance piece, the one I did for him when I was ten."

She dragged a speaker to the center of the stage, she tilted

255

it on its side. Then she sat down and pulled the mike stand down so it was horizontal. The heavy silver bottom tilted up on its edge like a wheel. Her eyes were soulful, dreamy. "Father never read to me. Mother read. Father was busy. One day I decided to read to him. Mother told me the name of his favorite book. *Paradise Lost.* I found it and learned a lot of it by heart. I met him at the door, and this is what I sang." She stood up, she dropped her head to get ready. "Be nice, I'm going to forget some words," she muttered. Then when she lifted her face she was in a sort of trance. Her shoulders hung like a rag doll's. Her voice came in a girlish croon. Not even imitating a girl, inhabiting her.

> *Marching from Eden towards the west*
> *The marish bride and serpents merge*
> *Sucking the something carnal breast*
> *To sap the black bituminous urge*

"Those aren't the words," a man shouted.

Burry's eyes opened and she walked to the very front of the stage. Her arms fell at her sides.

"Maybe you don't know it, I'm giving everything," she said.

George came up and put his arm around me. "Say, 'I love that girl,' " he said.

"I love that girl," I said.

"No, Jack." He bellowed, "I LOVE THAT GIRL!!!"

Everyone stopped talking. Burry beamed. She dipped her shoulders deeply, showing the tops of her tits, then she bent her head again to go back into her talent.

> *The something virgin's black and bruised*
> *By laws that argue many sins*
> *She scales the ark in Satan's shoes*
> *In Albany, by leave of kings—*
> *And something something very far, oh shit, wait.*

She stopped, trying to remember. She draped her arm over her head, and I saw where she'd shaved her armpits. She said she was never going to do that, but she had.

And if the serpent bruise your heel
His eyes bestuck with glamorous darts—

"Slanderous darts!" that same guy yelled, but this time people booed, and Burry kept going in a girlish singsong.

Take me to the county fair
Past days of heaven . . .
Schoharie County Fair

The song sort of fell apart. Burry's chest heaved. Then she had her normal voice again with all the hoarseness returned, quiet.

"I said that to him at the end of dinner. And that night he didn't go."

She curtsied and started off the stage, bending for her shoes. George Sides ran up. He caught her and held her and brought her back. He reached for the mike and squeezed her tight.

"Burry Quinlan," he said, and you could see her mascara running, she was crying.

George lassoed his hand over his head.

"BURRY QUINLAN!" he said. "BURRY QUINLAN!" in his loud vaudeville voice.

He wouldn't let her leave, and people began clapping harder. She covered her eyes and held her face against his chest, so it was this whole tender scene.

Then her mood changed and she pulled the mike back. "I'm sorry I didn't do better material—I autoprescribed, which you're not supposed to do when you're pregnant."

George held her out from himself, he held her and looked at her face.

"My dad's going to be grandfather and governor at the same time. Where is Jack—"

I was going to go, but her eyes found me, they buttoned me into that spot. Makeup was raccooned over her cheeks and I didn't try and dodge her, I nodded.

"Another announcement"—her voice rang through the hoarseness—"my father needs you. November 7, vote Early, vote often."

People were laughing, then everything fell apart and Burry's friends massed the stage.

I went into the men's room. The camera bag was hanging on a hook opposite the sinks. I must have left it there when I got that toilet paper for Dr. Rohr. Someone had hung it up for me. I lit a cigarette but after one drag I threw it in a urinal.

That was when I got sick. I lay on the tiles in a stall and every time I lifted my head there was a new pair of shoes in the next stall. Always look at the shoes, Victor used to say that in my old life. The life I'd gotten in exchange was a snare and a delusion. I began to love my old life now that it was completely gone.

I kept retching but there was nothing to show for it, just a coil of yellow martini-olive scum in the toilet. So I lay there and felt sorry for myself. I.e., don't die here, you're in a snob crowd and in love with someone whose values you hate. She shaved her armpits so her father could win the election. Cock-a-doodle-doo.

24

When I came out, the air had gone out of the party. Half the people were gone. The band was playing and people were dancing, but no one was standing around talking. Someone pulled me around by the camera bag.

"Jack—"

Simi Winfrey's hair was piled up like a cake. She wore a black coat with tails that went down to the backs of her knees and slim black pants that stopped right above her ankles, in men's blue pinstriped suiting fabric. Her small feet were on high heels that looked like a human-rights report about footbinding. Simi was completely comfortable in them.

"I'm supposed to find you," she said. "No one knew where you were and everyone else left. Charles had a car."

"All right."

"They all went to Burry's. Oh, Jack, I almost forgot"—she held both my hands and stared at me with a mouth-open look, as if I were unbelievably handsome—"congratulations."

"For what?"

"You don't have a clue, do you, Jack. Listen I have to take you to Burry's."

She hung on my arm as we got our coats, and I gave myself

a Dale Carnegie lecture about why I should go to Burry's. It was fine to be marrying someone with different values. It happened all the time, it didn't mean you couldn't keep your own values.

"Jack, what is wrong, why are you trembling?"

"I just puked," I said.

She held me closer. "I know the feeling, vomiting is completely underrated. Let's just wait here for Blackie."

The steps of Grubs' Parade were empty. The street was clean-feeling, from the rain. Simi didn't let go of my arm, and I watched a guy across Broadway putting up posters on a wall. He used a long-handled brush. First he dipped the brush in the glue, then he flopped the poster up onto the plywood over his head with it and in one swift motion positioned and tacked the poster, again with the brush. Then he dipped the brush in glue and slapped the poster down all over, smoothing the bubbles out. All with the brush and not with his hands.

Blackie Roberts came out of Grubs' Parade just in his tux. He plunged past us going to the curb. He put his arm up for a cab. We got in together. First Blackie got in, and I held the door for Simi. We squished in against one another.

He dropped his big arm on Simi's leg but stared off grumpily.

"What happened?" Simi said.

"He says he's tapped out," he said. "But the sonofabitch made promises to everyone and he seems to have squirreled a fuckload of cash."

Simi's eyes brightened. "Oh God," she said.

"A scoundrel of the first dye," Blackie said. "His father was a fireman. He says it was his grandfather but it wasn't, it's his father."

"I know." Simi turned to me. She felt at my bag. "Jack, what is this?"

"A camera."

"Now I know you're having a baby, the only people who get

260

these have kids. They take pictures of them in the bathtub."

"It's to video Burry. We're documenting Burry's performance."

She laughed hard. "They even change diapers on video."

We stopped at Fourteenth Street, and a man came out to do the windshield, a black guy in T-shirt with a squeegee. The driver said no, but he did it anyway. Afterward, when the man tapped at the window, Blackie got pissed off. He sat up and rolled down the window and stuck his head and shoulders out.

"He told you we didn't want it," he said.

The guy yelled something, and Blackie shouted something and lurched back into the car.

"Tell me something, logically," he said. "Why don't all the white people put their money together and move?"

"William, roll up your window," Simi said.

"I'm serious, doll. Buy some other nice place, let them have America. They'd probably like it more themselves that way."

"Jack doesn't like this. Now close the window."

"What are you going to do with the Jews?" I said.

"Jack!" Simi said.

"They can come." He got the window. "We'd get lawyers on this."

"Jack's a lawyer," she said.

"Not anymore," I said.

Simi looked at me doubtfully but kept her big dazzling smile. "What are you now?" she said.

"He's a photographer," Blackie said.

"Blackie, give me a cigarette," I said.

He gave me one, and he was too drunk to light the match, I had to light the match.

"I worry about you Jack—" Simi squeezed my arm.

"I used to do that, feel sorry for other people," I said.

"Not feel sorry, *worry*. I worry about you."

"That, too."

261

"Well, I know you'll do the right thing," she said.

Blackie held out a silver flask. I think it was bourbon. You could feel the screw threads of the opening on your lips.

Burry's place was jammed. The Scandinavian wooden furniture was stacked in the living room to make a dance floor and someone had put on James Brown. Everyone's outfit was sweaty and messy, they weren't wearing their cummerbunds anymore, their ties were off and the women's dresses were open halfway down their backs. Burry was dancing with Jinx Cope. She reached out for me and kissed me on the forehead. Her shimmering beauty was a snare and a delusion.

I went into the kitchen. I laid the bag on the counter and lifted the camera out. Morgan had said which buttons to hit, but I hadn't listened, and I tried to remember. Do the right thing, that's what Simi said. O.K. But right for who? When someone tells you that you should run the other way as fast as your legs will carry you.

Charles Tharp came into the kitchen holding out his hand. "Jack, I want to be the first to congratulate you."

"You're not," I said.

My hands were occupied but he kept his hand held out. He had those red lips and soft glossy eyes. So we shook.

"I knew it when I met you," he said. "You and Burry would be great for one another. She needed someone to help her put on the brakes. And you—"

"Me too," I said.

"Right, you needed her, too. Here"—he took a cigar from his jacket—"do you smoke cigars?"

"No."

"Well, you should definitely start smoking cigars."

"O.K. Listen, do you know how to get this on?"

He picked up the camera. "What is this?"

262

"It's to document Burry's performance."

He was good with machines. The red light came on, and I went to the refrigerator for a beer. He pointed the camera at me opening the beer.

"In performance art this is all part of the performance," I said. "Me drinking a beer is part of the performance."

Then I started out of the room.

"Jack. Here."

"Get those guys—"

I pointed at the Presidents on the wall. He laughed, and I went out, slipping past the dancers into Burry's room.

Peter Sisley sat on the bed in his erect aristocratic way. He was separating seeds from stems on Burry's *I Ching*. He had a new haircut. His blond hair was cut sharply at the sides. He squinted at me and smiled.

"Hello Jack," he said. "Or do I know you? I can't remember whether I'm allowed to know you or not. James keeps telling me different things."

"You know me."

"Well good, I'd much rather."

I lay down on the couch across from the foot of the bed. Peter had a little assembly line going, three joints lined up on the table. He moved the latest joint in and out of his mouth and set it to dry, then he picked up a burning joint and sipped.

"What have you been doing with yourself?" he said. "You've been in trouble, I know. You've been in tons of trouble."

He laughed.

"Peter, what does *Larkspur* do for the campaign?"

He exhaled, then proffered the joint to me.

"Now I'm trying to figure out which hat I'm wearing. Am I wearing my campaign hat?"

I inhaled. "I'm no good at hats."

"Well, I don't know. You hear all kinds of rumors. About George Sides and Early's friends."

"Tell me the rumors."

He got up to take the joint back then sat back on the bed, refolding his long legs.

"Oh, for instance that Blackie got equity in *Larkspur*. See, Jack, I'm not good at conspiracy theories. I don't have the temperament. My old boyfriend said it's cause I'm entitled. I don't know what that means. I believe the truth is simple. George Sides likes us so he says nice things."

Peter took a deep hit, and Blackie Roberts came in the room. He stood in front of Peter with his feet apart and seemed to waver a little.

"Brother Sisley," he said. "Where is Early?"

Peter pointed at the bathroom door with the joint. Blackie turned in that direction then back to him.

"Brother Early got tired," Peter said. "Brother Early is taking a long bath."

There was a little wisp of mockery in his voice.

"What's that supposed to mean?"

Peter paused. "We're two points up with two weeks to go."

"Early doesn't look at numbers," Blackie said.

Peter got up to hand me the joint. "I don't think this brave experiment has seen a more ardent consumer of raw polling data than Early Quinlan," he said. Because "brave experiment" was an expression Quinlan used in his speeches.

"Wrong. And vicious," Blackie said.

But he sat resignedly on the bed. He drew the flask from his tux jacket and held it out to Peter then me. We shook our heads. At last he drank from it himself.

Peter took the joint back.

"See Jack, to me it's always a question of what does anyone really want to know," he said. "Because if you want to know something, then it's yours. They should call it the right to believe."

"Like an ideology?" I said.

He wagged his head, he was focused on a faraway point.

"Maybe. But what if you don't want to know? I saw in the paper they say there won't be another lunar eclipse this big for 141 years. Now can I just say I know that because I read it? I don't know that. It's a question of what you want to believe."

"You're stoned," I said.

He laughed and glanced at Blackie, who was leaning against the wall.

"I'm sure if anyone was interested they could find a million sleazy connections," he said.

I laid my head on the couch arm, and then Simi came in.

"I have it," she said.

She had a yellow, paper-covered book in her hand. She lay down on the bed, propping her shoulders against Blackie's side. She held the book up and turned fiercely from page to page. The cover said *Chemical Girl*, by Blake Roberts. But it wasn't done, I mean it wasn't published. I guess it was a bound galley.

" 'His face is chipped from obdurate stone,' " Simi said. "That's on page 21. But on page 40 you're 'blue-eyed and devastating and corrupt as compost.' "

I looked around at Burry's room as if for the first time: the figurines, the candles, the miniatures, her own little drawings. Everything vibrated and swelled with pity. I felt a grief and pity for Burry, for her world. I tried to kill that feeling by looking at the fabric under my head, by tracing lines in the paisley. Paisley came from mango, Burry always said that.

"This is my room, love."

I looked up, and Burry had come in.

"Here lies my lover, Jackson Gold." She was doing an accent she sometimes did, an English accent that was also American. She said she was making fun of Americans who had gotten permanent English accents after a year there.

Charles was following her with the camera. She picked up my head in both hands, cradling it against her stomach. Then she laid it back down on the couch arm.

265

"Here is one of my closest friends on earth, William Roberts."

She picked up Blackie's head and hugged it and rolled it against her stomach then dropped it, too.

"And this is Simi Winfrey, reading my closest friend Blake's book. How is it, Simi?"

"Beautiful."

"This is Peter Sisley, who I love dearly."

And the same with his head, and Charles taping. Peter cupped the joint next to his knee, hiding it.

"Peter, where is Father?" she said.

Blackie leaned off the bed. He swatted at the camera.

"Can we have a moratorium on the rap music for a second?" I guess he thought the camera was a boom box. He jabbed at it, and Charles held the camera away. "Let's have something melodic. I don't care if you put on that bald chick—"

He fell off the bed onto all fours, and people had to help him up. Then he sat back on the bed against the wall, and Burry turned to Peter.

"Where is Father?" she said, this time without the accent. She had her hand on her hip.

"He was tired," Peter said in a thin voice. "He decided to take a bath."

She walked purposefully to the bathroom door and put her ear against it. Her eyes were big.

"Father," she said. "Father. Father—" She made a hard little drumming with her fist.

"What's with the camera?" Peter said.

Charles held the camera out. "Jack brought it. To document Burry's performance."

I didn't care. Now it had Father on it, Father in the bath.

"Father," Burry kept saying, and everyone was watching her. She was alone in a circle of sadness, knocking on the door. My feeling for her rose, grief and desire, sympathy.

266

I got up. Burry looked at me gratefully and made way. I opened the door.

"Wait, Jack." She held my wrist, but I went past her, then closed the door after me.

Early Quinlan was in the tub. He had his clothes on and the tub was dry. He was reading. He'd piled towels behind his back to make it comfortable, and how could you blame him, the apartment was such a carnival.

He glanced amiably at me. He put the book down on the rim of the tub. It was *Baby and Child Care*, by Dr. Spock. I sat on the closed toilet seat. He reached for a glass that he'd perched on the soap dish and lifted it toward me as a form of salutation.

"Hello, Jack," he said.

"Early."

He sipped from the glass and stared at his feet, at the faucet. His great American face was pale and his hair was limp with sweat, it didn't go up strongly. His shirt was off, and he had on a sleeveless undershirt that was gray with sweat in the middle of his chest. He balanced the glass back down on the soap dish. It struck me he was scared, scared of me, scared of losing. White whiskers went off his shoulders.

"It's a carny show out there," I said.

He nodded. "The banshees are out. Man needs a little privacy. Now." He stopped and smiled. "To what do I owe this rare pleasure?"

"I'm a little stoned."

"That's all right. That can't be helped."

"But I have to say, I never got your politics."

His face flushed, his mouth closed primly. "I don't believe you know them."

"You were someone we always watched. On the left, I mean."

"Jack has come to get things off his chest."

267

"You went so many different ways," I said. "Whoever had power—"

Then I stopped, I lost heart, and Early held up his hand.

"The ones that don't change are the ones you can't trust," he said. "What do you want, a stone or a human being?" He liked that line, and his eyes brightened. "I'm a man of my times. What do you think they call all the books, Ixy Nixon and his times. The Pied Piper and his times. Jack Gold and his times."

He lifted his hand and made a motion of turning a row of dials in the air, one after the other, then he laughed. No one was ever going to name a book *Jack Gold and His Times*, that's what he was saying. But who was he, he wasn't a genius or an oracle you went to for answers. He was someone clever with a tough hide. Then my anger collapsed against me and died, and I only felt sad for myself.

Early slapped the rim of the tub.

"So Jack. You've come to make yourself an honest man."

"In politics, they all lie. In your campaign."

"Well, look the other way."

He hummed in his throat.

I thought about my father, how he used to take me downtown. We'd eat in Chinatown and he'd show me the big government buildings, monuments to do-good government. He was so proud of them. Even though he was a big outsider and survivor he believed in them.

"I'm thinking about the official buildings my dad used to show me," I said. "With the words on them. Justice. Fairness. Every man his due. For the people to read."

"I told you already." His face was mirthful, handsome again. "An impressionable young man like you. Should learn. To look the other way."

He fumbled in the bathtub beside him, by his shoulder, and lifted a bottle of white wine. He was agile like a juggler, hoisting it by the neck, swinging it around Indian-club style. He had a cat's balance. Because he could do anything drunk, I bet he could drive drunk or deliver a speech. He was better drunk. He filled his glass and then held out the bottle to me. I took a mug from the sink and he tilted wine into it.

"To us," he said.

"To our club," I said.

He gave me an affectionate smile. "Yes, to the private club of the two of us."

"Nothing's private," I said.

"No, only everything is," he said. "Everything's private. Life's unfair. That should be on your buildings, Jack. Learn those lessons and it's all pretty clear sailing. The people that don't learn them get written about. They're the people they have to escort off airplanes."

"You sound like a Republican."

He put his hand on the tub rim, and the book fell to the floor.

"That's just politics. Politics is a lovely fiction. But it will never hold. More than a thimbleful. Of a man's. Grief. Or joy."

Whenever he gave a speech he started speaking in little fragments. I drank down my wine and put the mug in the sink. I filled it with water, then a feeling started on my skin, like a cool wind, an awareness.

"Early. You put my picture in the paper."

He waved dismissively, but his face darkened.

"You did," I said.

"You're big on honesty, Jack, I will tell you something very honestly." He drank off his glass and set it on the soap dish with great delicacy. "Life ravages you. It breaks you open like a crab. You've seen a bird catch a crab?" He looked frankly at me. That scar was grayish. "It breaks it open and picks its insides. That happens to everyone. It's happened to everybody I know. The trick is to use life faster than it uses you. They're supposed to tell you that at the outset."

269

He sighed with a little shiver. "Which is why you must commit. Otherwise what is there?"

I looked away. A cloud of lonely feeling blew onto my mind. I felt it on my body, like water.

"We're not right for each other," I said.

Early slapped the tub. "She is right. You are not. You are troubled. You are out of touch with reality, you boil with resentment."

He announced that in a loud even voice, and then the door broke open. Burry flung herself to the floor at the side of the tub, like opera. She grabbed his hand and her feet stuck out to the side of the spilled edges of the dress, black on the bottoms.

"Best," he said calmly.

"Oh Father, you wear yourself out. I'm going to put you in bed."

"What are you wearing, what is this?" He was looking at that dress, the neckline.

"Father, you probably have a temperature," she said. "Oh, this election is awful."

He reached for the glass and used her shoulder to pull himself up. First he sat on the tub rim, then rose experimentally to his feet.

"I was just saying this to"—and he jerked his thumb in my direction—"elections are merely a plot device. They promote good feeling. The people desire a happy ending."

She got her purple kimono off the bathroom door and helped him step out of the bathtub. She tugged the kimono's short wide arms over his, she tugged the front over his heavy chest, and I took that moment to slip out.

Burry's room was crowded. Most of the party had gathered there the same way that people in a village gather outside the headman's hut to see the headman. Charles Tharp had the

270

camera on and focused on Blake Roberts. She lay where I had been, on the couch. She pushed her hair back and gazed into the camera.

"The answer is, I've been working on this book all my life," she said. "This book came to me when I was a child. I had it as a dream before I had any idea what form it would take."

Charles dropped the camera and nodded solemnly. "That's good," he said. "But they're not going to be shy, Blake, they're going to push it. They'll ask point-blank, Is this your father?"

"That's crazy, of course it's not my father. It's See Wainwright's father. And yes, I'm See and I'm also her father. The only real-life person in the book is me. I'm in all my characters. I'm even in the character of New York that's in the book. If the characters weren't in me I couldn't write them."

"Good," Charles said, and I thought, Now you can say that in Morgan's show.

Early Quinlan came out of the bathroom and everyone turned.

"I was reading Pliny the Younger," he said. "What quarrel can subjects take up with a sovereign power. Be it territorial, financial, or pertaining to the rights of persons. Before the creation of *habeas corpus* but not much more—

"HABEAS CORPUS!!" he thundered excitedly.

He wasn't like our little club. There was a way he got when he was around other people, he was helpless to be any different. Peter Sisley got up from the bed. He put his hand on Quinlan's shoulder.

"Let the Darwinists prattle about the opposable thumb," Quinlan said. "*Homo erectus* did not truly begin to walk on two legs till he had arrived at the concept of *habeas corpus*—"

He moved out of Peter's hands, he reached for the armchair and plopped into it.

"GIVE US THE BODY!!!" he said.

People laughed, and Quinlan held out his glass. Burry filled it from a tall plastic water bottle. Then there was a lull. People

271

were waiting for the next joke. Charles lifted the camera almost like a sign of respect. Quinlan abruptly extended his legs and, gripping the chair arms, lifted his heels a few inches from the floor.

"Did I show you my ottoman?" he said. "Ancient historic ottoman. Made by Iroquois, out in Wyo."

He kept his heels in the air, legs scissoring with the effort. His face strained.

There was nervous laughter, and then James Doyle came into the room. He shouldered through the crowd and bent to Quinlan. You didn't hear what he said. Quinlan put his feet down and rose from the chair with a little murmur. The two of them started out.

Near the door Quinlan stopped suddenly and swayed a little. James reached for him, but when he did that Quinlan handed him his glass of water.

"Oh, Hickory," he said sweetly to the air. "Course I know where hickory is. Hickory-dickory! Right after lunch."

He slumped out of James's hands. He braced himself up another second or two, head cocked to listen to that voice. At last he stretched out gracefully, feet together, in a way that reminded me of a mermaid.

25

After Early Quinlan lay down there was a lot of confusion. James Doyle got him awake by dashing his face with water and Burry helped him to his feet. Then they called a car and James said to clear the room, and he was angry so it was chaotic. Charles had put the camera away, he'd set it down on the couch, and as people started crowding out I sprung the tape and took it into the bathroom. I smoked a cigarette sitting on the toilet in the dark. Then I heard someone calling my name, Blake, I think. I shoved the tape into Burry's trash and got into the bathtub.

I could sense Early's presence around me in the towels, his B.O. and his sweat, his success. Early Quinlan was a success, but look what it did to him, he was more a concept than a human being. Someone knocked and I pulled the shower curtains across.

The next thing I heard was someone vomiting. It was dark, I'd fallen asleep. The person was tilted into the toilet. His shoes skittered around on the tiles. When he whimpered you could tell it was Peter Sisley.

After a couple of minutes the door opened sharply and the light came on.

"You're a pretty picture," James said.

"Leave me alone."

"I do. Then you piss on the Secretary."

"Oh please, James, what's Blackie told you now?"

"You do it all the time. You thought it was funny last week what Daphne Sherman said about intellectual chameleons."

"It wasn't what she said."

"You were laughing."

"I told you before, it was what she was wearing."

"Well now I'm pissing on you."

"Oh put that little thing away."

But a struggle followed with Peter rolling away on the floor and James trying to stand over him, and James was laughing hard. I'd never heard him let go before. He made a high squeaky sound like a kid's bathtub toy with a stainless steel valve. You know those toys where it doesn't matter if it's air or water, the valve passes it. Then he calmed down and pissed in the toilet.

"I thought you guys do that to each other for fun," he said.

Peter didn't respond. He was right next to me, sagged against the tub.

James washed his hands thoroughly. Soaping, rinsing, toweling, the whole bit. Well, I would, too, if I touched that prick.

"Now Peter. I talked it over with the Secretary. I'm sorry to say this, your services will no longer be needed."

"Bullshit you talked it over with the Secretary." Peter pulled himself up against the tub. "James, there are two weeks left in the campaign. I thought your political instincts—"

"My political instincts are fine. They say that we're battling a massive tide of resentment and that Peter Sisley is history."

"James. I would ask you. James. Please." Peter's voice quavered. "James, it is terribly terribly important to me that I keep this job. I've worked hard at this, and it means almost everything. You know where I was a year ago."

"Just about where you are now," James said. "Why'd you let them use that camera?"

274

Peter was quiet.

"I heard Jack brought it to record Burry," James said.

"Your little ape told you that."

"Where's the tape?"

"Do I have a job?"

"Talk to me. Where's the tape?"

Peter used his elbows to pull himself up further against the tub. His elbows jutted the curtain in at me.

"We've got it," he said.

"Where?"

"It's with my things."

"Give it to Burry. Your last official act."

James left the room, and it took Peter a little while to get to his feet. He held on to the sink and then bent to the faucet. He gargled a lot and blubbered his lips in the running water.

"Hello, history," he said to the mirror. "How is history feeling today? Do you think someone's going to make history?"— a whole patter, trying to cheer himself up.

Then he turned off the light and was gone.

The next thing I knew it was dawn. I pulled the curtain and there was a gray rinse on the floor from the beginnings of sunlight.

The tape was right where I'd left it. Then when I got it out I started going through the rest of Burry's trash. It came to me there would be something in there to prove she wasn't pregnant, a Tampax, tissues clotted with blood. But there was nothing, no smoking gun.

Light was filling a far corner of the bedroom like salt, and everything was clean, I mean a lot cleaner than you would have thought. Her room was halfway put together and Burry lay on her back in bed, her arm framing her head. The light had found her lips. They were red, they seemed the only color in the room. I lifted the camera gently off the television. I was going to be super-quiet and leave, but then I felt weak and sat down. You had to admire her lips, you had to admire her face. She was happy here, this was her place. I was the one that had chosen wrong and then I started to cry.

Not making any noise or anything, but I couldn't get up.

"I thought you were gone," she said. Her eyes were open, but she lay there.

"No. But I better go," I said.

"Why?"

She sat up naked, she didn't even pull the sheet around her. It was like seeing her body for the first time. Long, white, feminine. She had a strange, beautiful body. I looked at the floor.

"I feel I'm in the wrong place. If you choose the wrong door? That whole idea. The wrong door."

"When? Today?"

I shook my head.

Her face changed, and she reached for the sheet. She wound it around herself.

"Do you trust yourself to know that, Jack?" she said.

"I'm pretty sure."

"Because if you didn't it would be really unfair. Unfair to both of us."

"I know."

"But you sit there. You don't do anything. Sit here, Jack."

I went over and sat on the bed. She held my hand.

"Let's just try and stay inside the good feelings we have for a minute." She entwined our fingers. "Because I think we're lucky. We're really really lucky."

"When you're lucky you know it, like if you get out of a burning house. You say, I'm lucky."

Tears started down her cheeks. "You're tortured inside."

"I guess."

"And that's why you tortured my father. You always had to get under his skin."

276

I got up and went to the chair for the tape. "This is yours," I said.

"Jack, you're not leaving. That's not brave."

"Well, I'm not, I'm not brave."

"You were brave at the Valery-Michael."

That made me laugh. "No I wasn't. The opposite."

"Jack, sit. Don't go for a second. Let's try and be clear."

I dropped the tape on her *I Ching* and sat. She held my hand and for a minute things were calmer.

"We'll go to the country," she said softly. "We'll stay at Rene's and get back in sync."

Then before long I was stressed again. It filled up in me like feathers in your lungs, and just trying to breathe.

"I have to go out," I said.

"Jack if you just got a little help, I feel like everything could be O.K. You could change."

"You always said not to change the person you love."

"But if you want to, Jack? To adjust? If you saw somebody maybe you would accept yourself more for the things you are instead of always fighting."

"What things?"

"Who you are, who you can be." She stroked my hand. "There are sliding-scale places, you wouldn't have to pay very much."

"But what are the things?" I said.

She gazed at me. I felt hatred, and she could see it. "Say some of the things I am," I said.

She was frightened, she wiped tears from her face. "Jack."

"Just two."

"You're smart, you're nice, you're handsome."

"I'm not handsome. That's a lie."

"Oh, Jack." She laughed through her tears. "You're handsome to me."

"I don't think I'm that nice either. Really. Tell me, Burry, honestly. Don't worry about my feelings. James thinks I'm a fool. That's fine. If someone would just be honest to me I think I'd feel a whole lot better."

"You're Jewish. You're leftist."

I shook my head. "Those are just adjectives, they don't say anything."

"Jack, you're so angry."

"That's something."

Her voice changed. "You're selfish, Jack. You act like a big leftist but you're out for yourself."

"Who isn't?"

"Not Father."

"Your father most of all."

"But he doesn't bullshit people, Jack. You're a bullshit artist. You bullshit yourself, you bullshitted me."

I nodded and she started to cry again. After that we both cried for a while just sitting there.

"You wanted everything. Now you don't," she said. "You just bounce off people, don't you?"

"You're not pregnant, are you?"

Her face corded with rage. "You want permission to go, Jack, don't you? You want some bourgeois excuse to feel good about yourself so you can go. Well guess what, I'm not going to give it to you."

Tears came from her squeezed-up eyes as if from a sponge. But it didn't feel accurate or true, her crying that much. What did you ever see in me that you're crying so much? Did you even ever love me? But I'm not going to talk about love, it's not something I know anything about, I've been a failure in that area. Only when I sat there I looked at her neck, a place I used to rest my face. Now it was just a girl's neck, a girl I didn't know if I even liked anymore. That was how cold I felt.

I stood up. I looked around at her room, seeing if I was leaving anything. "I did that tape to sell everyone out. That's the reason I did it."

"I know," she said.

"You knew that?"

She didn't look at me. "I was going to let you," she said.

That tore at me and I had to go. It was getting light. I had a desperate feeling that if I didn't go that very second I'd miss everything, an appointment with someone who was waiting for me right that second, or maybe a month from then, an appointment with my life.

Out in the hallway the party was still bedlam, frozen bedlam. You had to pick your way over destruction, over cushions spread out for people to crash on and bottles left rolling on the floor, and the heavy beer/wine smell in the air, and finally the avenue of pictures of the old Secretary.

I took the stairs down. I ran, turning myself on the landings by grabbing the yellow railing and spinning myself centrifugally right onto the next flight with the camera in my free hand. When I came to the lobby I scared the doorman. That same Polish guy was asleep in one of the big leather chairs. He jumped up with a guilty look and first thing he reached for his hat.

Like, don't ever not wear your hat, that's the policy. Well, fuck the policy. Fuck all policies.

The brass door was locked and he had to undo it for me. When the bolt clunked is when I felt lucky. I dug in my wallet and pushed what I had, a ten, into his surprised white glove.

26

Central Park was cold with dew that made the pigments blur and blaze, the hues. I'm thinking of the part that isn't the color but the shade of the color, the brightness. It had gotten to be fall, and color had come back. Leaves that had fallen to the blue asphalt were flame color and the blue jay's tail feathers looked sharp as a piece of glass.

When I walked up to my apartment building Morgan was there. He was sitting on the concrete stoop with his back against the glass wall and a newspaper draped over his knees. It was 7:30 already. He wore the same rust-colored jacket he'd had on the first time I saw him and his mouth was just a line, like a cigar-store Indian, and it clamped a cigarette. He looked like hell. His face was white and his hair was stringy. The cigarette was cold, it had gone out. He was a guy who really knew how to wait, you had to admire that.

"Got a smoke?" I said.

He lifted his jean cuff and felt inside his sock. He had two or three loose cigarettes there, like a prisoner, and he got one out and smoothed it with his fingers, reviving it, before handing it to me. I lit it and he relit his.

"How'd it go, kimo sabe?" His voice came in a croak.

"They did just what you said, they shot one another."

His mouth opened in a grin I'd never seen before. His teeth were funny, they were set apart from one another, almost jack-o'-lantern.

I lifted the camera off my shoulder and swung it to him.

"I lost the bag."

"O.K.," he said, and turned the camera around on his knees to get at the chamber. He snapped it open and shut a couple times, then slung it onto his shoulder.

"Got the tape?"

"Burry has it. You can talk to her."

He stared at me, he looked me up and down as if trying to make out where I'd hidden it. I dug in my pocket for my keys and he got a little desperate, his eyes were wet and open.

He stood up, flicking his cigarette into the street.

"Look Jack, I'm the one that will get into trouble."

"I don't care about getting into trouble."

"Do you want money?"

"Fuck you, Morgan."

Because we hadn't talked about money. The only thing we'd discussed was if it worked he'd give me one of his old cameras, a still camera.

"Jack, what do you need, I'll put your name on the show."

"That's O.K."

He was wild. He walked around the sidewalk in a distracted circle. His face was pained, he scuffed the sidewalk.

"Look, if you're thinking about holding up George Sides for dough, you can't."

"I'm not."

"Good, cause he's gone belly-up."

"You're full of shit."

"He eleven'd yesterday. They're saying here the party was just some tax thing."

He bent and scrabbled at the newspaper.

"That's O.K.," I said.

I was thinking it was illegal of George, then I thought that was bullshit, you could do almost anything legally if you only got someone to say it was the right thing. I opened the door and Morgan came back onto the step and reached hungry-eyed for the door. He didn't come in, just held the door, respecting my distance.

"Would you talk to Burry for me?" he said.

I shook my head and he winced, looking away.

"Now, Jack, where are you going?"

"I don't know. Maybe out of town."

Morgan nodded. He seemed resigned.

"The geographical solution," I said.

I crunched my cigarette on the door and threw it into the street. Morgan stared after it. "It's not a solution," he said.

"Now I'm going to crash," I said.

He nodded, but he didn't let the door close, he watched me walk to the stairs.

"Hey, Jack? If you're worried about invasion of privacy? Don't. I've got a lawyer you can talk to."

"I'm a lawyer."

"You're a lawyer—fuck no! You?"

I nodded, and he smiled. He hung in the doorway, waiting for me to change my mind. When I was on the third floor I heard the door close.

I lay on my bed still in that suit and my black suede shoes and thought about where I could go. Out West, a place where things were simpler. California. I'd visit Phoenix. My brother's a doctor in a place called Mesa. He's done real well. He bought a big house on like a mountain, and my parents moved out to be near him and his kids. It's a whole little clan. My dad got a ranch house with a little swimming pool and dwarf fruit trees in the back they water the hell out of. He did the whole American thing. He got a white gravel driveway and a "rockscape" by the pool and white, heavy-pile wall-to-wall carpets so they go crazy about you leaving your shoes at the door. I've been there once in four years. They've even converted to air-conditioning.

Every once in a while my dad sends me pictures of his house with the fruit trees hung with fruit, with bright orange and yellow globes and my mom eating a peach by the pool after her laps. And of the lemon tree, too, all bestuck with lemons.

That much good fortune hasn't stopped my father from beating up on the United States. In the little folded letter that comes with the pictures he'll talk about what he's been reading then in the next sentence start in on all the injustice that's made manifest out there.

What the white man did to the virgin forest.

What the white man did to the Navajo and Hopi.

What the white man did with uranium.

Etcetera. My dad can sure beat up on the white man. Meanwhile, he isn't any good at personal communication. He'll get going about economic justice and not give a shit about you. Not think of his audience, not be able to come up with even two adjectives to describe you, not think of what will happen from him saying you really should go to law school. I guess he's bitter. His friends say, Your dad is dry, or he's aloof.

But that's really a charity operation, my dad can be a real sonofabitch.

Still, I thought I'd sleep on my parents' foldout or use my brother's spare bedroom while I figured things out. My brother's a great chef. That's his passion. He's always making Mexican food and recipes with tofu and fancy olive oil on his restaurant stove and pronouncing the names of everything right, and when you sit down to eat he talks about the food. Well, I can do that, I can talk about food.

Then everything went white, like the end of a home movie, and I was asleep.

Three hours later I sat up straight. It was 11:00 and I walked out of my place and took the subway downtown. I was still in evening clothes. People were looking at me on the subway as if I were glamorous.

The elevator at Grubs' Parade wouldn't go to the twelfth floor no matter how hard I pushed the button. They'd turned off the 12 button, so I took it to 11 and walked up. *Larkspur*'s front door was locked, and I walked around the narrow hallway looking for a back door.

They'd put all this stuff in the hall, the building had. I guess they were replacing ducts. The hall was filled with bright open-ended aluminum boxes. The boxes had these flanged edges so they could be tied into one another, welded, whatever. Most of them were straight, but there were a few made to take corners, angled and shiny. I stepped around them, and there was the back door of *Larkspur*, open, and you could see the painted passageway with its scenes of life in the grottoes.

I stopped because there was a screeching sound. I didn't want to turn the corner to see. It was like a monkey screaming, where you couldn't say whether it was happy or sad. It could be getting laid or getting tortured by some scientist, you wouldn't know, and meanwhile you heard its groany yeep.

Then I went in and it was just Danny Smith. He was working in the hallway, taking nails from the painted panels and pulling the panels off the struts, yanking them free. It was the nails screaming against the plywood.

He dropped the hammer at his side, the crowbar actually, and stepped back.

"Oh, Jack. Christ you scared me."

"Sorry."

"I thought you were the architect—" He got that whole lemon-biting smile. "The architect is owed big-time."

He'd gotten most of the panels off. They were in three stacks leaning against the wall, and there were numbers on the back in architect's snotbag writing.

You could hear George Sides's voice braying out through the place, but first I walked down the hall to look around. The whole office was trashed. People had gone through it like locusts. There were computer monitors on desks with the cables hanging down and the actual CPU boxes gone. Drawers were pulled all the way out, and mail littered the floor, pillaged mail, all these torn padded envelopes that must have had CDs or videos in them, books, all the free shit journalists scam. There was even a fashion office, with a wheeled steel garment rack and just a couple of pathetic dresses hanging off it but a whole lot of stripped hangers and torn cleaner's bags.

George was on the phone. He had his stocking feet up on the desk, he looked like hell. His face was red and his hair was hanging down. He hadn't shaved and he was in the same fancy clothes. But his white suit looked gray.

He got a shock seeing me but he recovered in a hurry. He winked and made emphatic gestures that I should sit down.

The chair by the desk was piled with magazines, all his old-fogy publications, *Wooden Boat* and *Tatler* and British magazines and that day's *Financial Times*. But George came around the desk and tilted the chair, spilling all that onto the floor.

"Well, that would be a true haircut on equity," he said, lifting the phone cord over the corner of the desk. "You're talking about a goddamn crewcut."

I sat down. His bright black shoes were on the desk. He'd set them there, side by side, the ones he'd worn when I first met him.

"No. No, those are personal assets. The genius of the arrangement, the twelve-and-a-half-percent notes are not secured against the name. *Larkspur* is owned free and clear. They're secured against certain capital improvements, some of which the holders are prepared to liquidate," he said, and other stuff people say when they don't want to say the word "money."

"Yes. Yes," he said. "Of course. But guess what, the first thing we do? We sue the architects."

Someone had stacked the wooden blinds against the wall, ready to be taken away, and I stared out the window at the East River and the tarpaper and brick crush of the Lower East Side. Here and there an old white building pushed up, gleaming, and those grandfather feelings started in me. There is my own little Africa, my old Kentucky Yiddish home. I could start to cry in a second thinking about that, why we thought we'd be welcome. But that's not your problem, that's adjectives, I thought, and I tried to turn the corner.

George hung up the phone. He whooped and clapped his hands.

"Looks like we could be getting a godzilla capital injection from the Japanese," he said.

"The Japanese want *Larkspur*?"

"Oh hell yes, Jack. They love American magazines. Our mags make them stand up on two legs. That's the fourth wall of publishing. See, they don't have any ideas of their own, the Japanese lack imagination, they no gottee the software, so they have to sneak-raid all our ideas."

He did a bombing run with his hand then got up nervously and moved around the room in his stocking feet.

"I'm going away, George, so I need my money," I said.

"You're going away?"

"Yes."

He didn't ask where, he went back around his desk and stared out the window, hoping the phone would ring again. He hummed to himself as if he had been thinking it over.

"Well gosh I hate to be disobliging but I'm afraid this is not a very good time and moment and place for that. I don't even need to tell you."

"It's not a real good day for me either," I said.

He sighed a lot, and meanwhile Danny was pulling out more panels. I heard the yowl of nails against plywood, and just in the silence between nails George sagged. He sat on his desk and pushed back his hair, then idly he picked up his shoes.

It was strange. He'd stuffed tissues in them, and he felt at the tissues and turned the shoes delicately in the air to examine the soles.

"Hell, I've gone and murdered a genius pair of shoes," he said. "Leather this fine you should never wear more than eight hours straight and I was up all night with these, trying to save our child—"

He frowned and put the shoes down, but on his back counter, as if he were afraid I was going to take them hostage.

"See, Jack, leather wicks moisture, and you wouldn't know it but the human body loses as much as a pint a day of moisture through the feet."

"I didn't know it."

"It does. A good shoe needs a few days to recover."

"George, I just need my money. I'm busted and you owe me."

He spanked his pockets and tried to smile.

"Well look here, Pedro, I'm tapped out."

I was supposed to smile but I didn't. I thought, George, you're a smacked ass.

"Listen, I was going to tell you about all this but frankly I had to save a lot of people from the worst-case scenario," he said. "It's like taking someone into the kitchen. You don't want to see what goes on in the kitchen because you'd never eat in a restaurant again, Pedro, same with journalism. There are things you should never see. 'We never change quotes,' they say. Christ, of course we change quotes. We *always* change quotes."

287

He barked with laughter, and I couldn't help it, I smiled.

"We agreed on thirty-five hundred," I said.

He sighed heavily and looked away.

"Jack. Jack—" Trying out different faces. "The article needs a lot of work. It's a cure-might-be-worse-than-the-disease situation."

"I'm no journalist," I said.

"You're not sore?"

I shook my head, and he brightened. He was so fucking grateful that I wasn't upset. He got up and began taking boxes from under his desk. He had all this loot hidden there, promotional stuff he'd squirreled away and held out to me now, cuff links of frogs with little jewel eyes and French bow ties and a silver nose-hair clipper and Frank Sinatra CDs. Also a four-foot mahogany carpenter's level with brass sights. I didn't want any of it except a pair of desert boots. He had size 12 desert boots.

"Desert boots," George kept saying with a laugh, making the word into a little quotation about the seventies. "In sand color. With crepe soles. Desert boots. Ha!"

I put them on right there, I got out of those stupid suede shoes and sat on the desk, feeding the laces through the holes. George laughed, watching me. He was just waiting for me to go.

"You should hear them Japans on the phone, Jack, they can't even say the name right. Rox-poo."

"Now, George, I need money," I said. "You've got some dough, I know it."

"Jack I told you, I'm going to pay you as soon as I get my keel back in the water."

I shook my head.

"Jack," he said. He tried to sound hard. "Jack—" He was rehearsing a whole new voice with me, a tone, but it wasn't in him, it made me laugh.

I stretched out on my back on the desk. My energy left me and I just lay there.

"Jack, I'm in no mood for fun," he said.

"Me either," I said.

He walked back to the desk, he grabbed the phone.

"Listen, let's get Burry on the phone," he said, trying to sound chirpy again. "That girl could talk anybody off the ledge. Hey! Was she something last night. She was great. Poignant. Spectacular. What's her number?"

I felt like I might cry and I dropped my arm across my face. Then there was a long silence where I didn't know if George was in the room.

"Jack, I'm going to have to ask you to leave. I have to make some very important and it goes without saying confidential calls. Calls that could result in your actually being paid."

But I didn't say anything, and he left the room. He came back a minute later with Danny Smith, and Danny looked at me and murmured something and the two of them went back out. I felt calm, I felt different. I liked how hard the desk was under my back, I liked the clicking of the radiators. I lifted my arm from my eyes and you could see the high ceiling under the roof, heavy wing nuts attached to pylons, the fussy old architecture of the showy building.

I heard George talking quietly on the phone a room or two over. Then he came back in. Something had changed, I could feel it.

"This is all I've got," he said. "Seventeen of these. It's a generous kill fee by any standard, Jack. Fair by any standard."

I sat up, and he had a thin stack of hundred-dollar bills, new ones, like an expensive chocolate bar, and he counted them with his thumb, flicking the corners back rapidly and pausing to touch his thumb to his tongue. He'd learned to do that somewhere. I mean, he was clever about money, he handled it like a banker.

He placed the bills on the blotter, square with the corner, and I mashed them in half and put them in my pocket.

"Thanks," I said, sliding off the desk.

"Now, Jack, this extinguishes all obligations," he said.

In the light I saw where his face was heavier, almost sunken, here and there deeper touches of red and pink, almost like a burn.

"O.K.," I said.

But I had to sign something on his stationery, with George Sides printed at the top, and a declaration he wrote down, and after that he walked me out, staying a half step behind me as if he feared I was going to run back in. Just like a banker even though he was in his socks. Then when we got to the front door he had to undo it for me.

He held the door and looked down. His mouth was shut for once, and suddenly his face got twitchy.

"I guess James Doyle just talked to Burry. He told me what went on."

"Oh, right," I said.

George looked at me, and none of his bright bullshit, just sad. "Jackie, good luck," he said, and touched me on the back.

27

There's a whole other story that took place at the end of these events I can't go into. It's a family story. It involves my family. I went down to Phoenix like I said I would, and after I got there my dad had a heart attack. Actually at the time he had it I was taking a side trip to California, seeing if I could live there. The second day in L.A. I called my mom and just her voice—she almost didn't have to say anything. So I went back to Arizona. In a way it was my good fortune, because I was there instead of not being there when your father is maybe heading out.

I left New York right after Morgan's opening. I would have left sooner, but I wanted to stick around for his show. For a couple of reasons. I wanted to see that girl Mona again. Also Morgan said he would sell/give me a camera. I'd had this whole epiphany, I thought maybe I could have a go as a photographer, taking pictures. You didn't analyze or interpret, you recorded something plainly. You didn't have to lie to everyone in sight.

It was a big show. The gallery was packed and you had to keep going outside into the fall air to cool off. All these sylph-type women hung around Morgan, downtown girls with black see-through dresses and torn tights and heavy lace-up boots, heavy vampire makeup. But Morgan was definitely with Mona. I still thought they had a shitty relationship but she was holding his elbow a lot, so fuck her. She wore a little gray fuzzy sweater that came up over her white belly and a skirt with colored panels in it, and she had tits, just as I thought.

I was scared to say boo to her. I smiled at her a couple times is all, and she smiled back with those giant teeth. "Hello, Jack," she said. "How are you?" But not normal, like she knew everything about me. She flicked her hair back and stood there with this whole devilish goofy look on her face.

"I'm fine." I was too tongue-tied to say anything back.

After that I looked at the actual show. At an art opening only losers look at the actual show. Instead of the movie of Early Quinlan lying down on the floor that I had run in my head that night at Burry's, that the press was going to come in to see and that would forever change the political landscape, Morgan used a Woody Allen movie in the little TVs. So he still had the contrast.

He gave me a beat-up Nikon for a hundred dollars, and the next day I took a bus to Paramus, New Jersey, from the Port Authority and started hitching with the camera out. I was already taking pictures. Just of things on the road. People, cars, sometimes animals, dead things, or shit people threw out of their cars on the side of the road. Already I could see where I was wrong about it being straightforward. It wasn't straightforward. It was your whole worldview every time you took a picture. So any second someone was going to get on your case about it, tell you what the right thing to do is.

I made it to Phoenix in three days, which is good time. I.e., no matter what, I have a face people trust.

That first night I had supper with my parents, and Ralph Lopez called at nine o'clock. He was showing people my apartment, to sublet, and somebody already wanted it.

I talked to Ralph a lot, and he gave me the smut. He called

292

the governor's race right a week before: Quinlan by two points. I think he was getting inside numbers.

Also, Ralph was big for Dummer. He'd made that whole conversion. He told me a story about being on the subway and a banker guy was wearing a Bagwell button and Ralph was wearing his Dummer button and Ralph tilted over the guy to look at the subway map. Ralph is the last guy that would ever need to look at a subway map, but he mashed his button into the guy's face. Ralph's an asshole, and I like him. He's even an asshole to me, but we have a connection. Losing together feels ten times deeper than winning.

Every day I walked to the hospital from my parents' house or my brother's and every night I walked back. From my parents' you passed this old trailer park. The trailer homes had been there so long they were permanent. The owners had put in concrete skirts around the bottoms, concrete borders in scalloped or floral patterns, I guess so people going by wouldn't see the wheels, so they looked like real houses with foundations. My grandfather Hezzie used to sell borders like that, so I know a little about it.

It was a cheap trailer park with outdoor fluorescent lights that buzzed overhead in rusty metal fixtures, and a lot of it was overgrown, going back to nature. You'd see purple-green lizards squirting out on the broad purply-yellow leaves of the tropical plants, scurrying around after one another and enjoying all their appetites without any apprehension or guilt or social norms. I'd just stand there and watch them after I'd been with my dad, I'd zone out watching them go to town with the pleasure principle, even if that's a moral my dad would completely disagree with. None of them was thinking, I wish I could slip away into the fifteenth century, or 1950. They were doing fine here and now.

They had my dad slunched down on a bed and filled with tubes, that whole stereotype, and they were going to do surgery. The odds look very good, etcetera.

My brother was honchoing the whole fucking deal. Everyone was real optimistic about when he came back he was going to start swimming. That's nuts. My father is never going to swim. He doesn't do that kind of thing. I thought maybe I could get him to walk some, though, if he did come back. But I didn't say very much. I'd just stand there and now and then straighten his hair. My brother was always saying, Keep things upbeat. I'm not even going to talk about that.

Election night I watched in my father's house just like old times, only now it was just me. My mom slipped into the bedroom at eight o'clock after a dinner of iceberg lettuce and halved cherry tomatoes and that bottled ersatz dressing. She was real quiet. My brother said she was depressed. I sat on the floor in front of the TV, and I'd gone through a six-pack and was on to my dad's Canadian Club, from which he had sipped parsimoniously over the last hundred years, when they said Early Quinlan had won. Governor. And on the national coverage they had a clip of him handsome as ever thanking the voters.

I stayed up late, I was waiting for Dummer to come down. He'd lost big but he wasn't coming down till it was official. I guess he's some kind of jerk, a senator from a midwestern state, a neo-liberal, whatever a neo-liberal is.

Then he came down and squeezed through the crowd at the podium to get to the microphone. Everyone was embracing him and acting like he'd done well. But he was stricken. I could tell. I felt so all alone in America. My heart traveled out to meet Dummer's somewhere in the echoing American prairie, I prayed for a happy ending to his story.

I've been in the room a lot of times when they come down. Even when I was little, in the Twenty-fifth Congressional District, my father would hold me up on his shoulders as everyone jostled forward to see. I think about that a lot now.

Politics begins with a family. Yes, and there is a family, naked of power. Who does he come out with? Where is his kid? Who does he hug, who does he yank to his side? He's stuck in that lonely moment, hammered by flashbulbs, not making promises, not thinking about tomorrow. Not thinking about all the shit that has gone right and wrong.

Dummer started speaking and I muted it. I lay on my back on the deep carpet. The ceiling fan was going over my head, the wooden fan my dad put in as the height of modern comfort in 1985. I blinked my eyes to make it stop.

.